CHARITY ISLAND

By Dennis Collins

For Johnny

ENJOY

[signature]

Also by Dennis Collins

Turn Left at September
The Unreal McCoy
The First Domino
Nightmare
Fool's Gold

ISBN 978-0-692-76295-0

Cover photo by Dennis Collins
Interior design by Susan Leonard

Printed in the United States of America

Acknowledgments

I must begin with Diana Collins whose command of grammar and punctuation saved me a lot of heartaches, Susan Leonard for her magic with graphic design and understanding of the publishing world. She helps me present a more professional product, and Jennifer Hartley who inspires character traits in my oddball cast and has done a fantastic job of promoting my work. A special thanks to Dave and Sue Bouck for generously opening the doors of the Wooded Island Grill for my characters to roam freely. And finally, the Huron Area Writers Group for keeping me energized. And last but not least Tom Carriveau, skipper of the North Star and Charity Island Dinner Cruises for making my visits to the island pleasant.

Chapter 1

She has a beautiful and peaceful appearance. Even her name radiates comfort and safety. But today all of that is lost. This beautiful little island nestled in the deep blue waters where Saginaw Bay meets Lake Huron has surrendered her innocence. Today the soft and sandy shore of peaceful Charity Island is the resting place for the body of a young lady. The vultures are already beginning to circle. A lone man walks along the beach looking for anything new that last night's powerful wind storm may have washed up on the beach. He freezes when he spots the body, unsure whether to approach or to run. A few very hesitant steps toward the body, maybe ten or twelve feet away and then, gripped by panic he runs for the house.

Rick Todd had been hired for the summer to watch over the facilities on the island. Nobody actually lives here but there is an old lighthouse and keeper's quarters that serve as a tourist attraction and Rick's job is to keep vandals away. There is no electricity on the island except what is supplied by the solitary wind turbine, a few solar panels, and the army surplus diesel generator. It isn't much of a job but it keeps Rick out of trouble. If he had stayed on the mainland there is no doubt that there would have been a DUI in his future. He is much better off here all alone. He hurries to the house where his cell phone lay connected to the solar charger.

"Charity Island Dinner Cruises. This is Heather. May I book your adventure?"

"Hi, Mrs. Hill? This is Rick. I need somebody out here right away. There's a dead body on the beach just to the west of the lighthouse."

"A what? Are you sure? Oh geeze, I gotta get off this line and call Russ. I'll get back to you as soon as I can." The line went dead.

Cell phone in hand Rick walked back to the beach and called 911. The body was less than three hundred yards from the house and there were already birds landing on the sand nearby. In spite of his fear and apprehension he hurried to the site in order to shoo the scavengers from the area. To his relief, it looked like they had not yet begun to feast on the carrion. The woman was not dressed for the surroundings. It was more like a formal dinner party. She wore a full length evening gown covered in deep blue sequins. It was the kind of thing you'd wear to a black tie affair. He hoped he could keep the birds away. He sang, whistled, waved his arms around, and ran back and forth on the beach never coming within twenty feet of the body. All he wanted to do was keep the birds at a distance.

After what seemed like hours the faint hum in the distance grew into the steady growl of a powerful outboard motor. The pitch of the motor changed as the boat navigated its way around the limestone breakwall that protected the harbor channel. Eventually the bow of the Sheriff's Department rescue craft rounded the corner. Rick could see four people on board. He stood up and waved his sweatshirt above his head to hail them. The birds squawked and scattered.

Instead of entering the channel, the sheriff's deputy carefully navigated between the sparsely positioned boulders that stood above the water while paying close attention to spot any danger that might be lurking just below the surface. The bow of the boat softly nestled into the sand about fifteen feet west of the body. The deputy was silent as he stepped from the boat. He quickly approached the body and widely circled it twice, hands on his hips the whole time. By then, the other three men had joined him, two in uniform and the third wearing jeans and a striped shirt.

"Thanks for not touching anything," said the deputy.

"I couldn't bring myself to get near her," replied Rick

"I can see that," said the deputy pointing out that there were no fresh footprints in the sand that surrounded the woman's body.

The man in civilian clothes approached. "You ready for me?"

"Yeah, go ahead. I've got to collect a statement anyway," said the deputy.

The Medical Examiner returned to the boat to retrieve his gear.

In his younger days Dr. Sidney Benson had dreamed of being a neurosurgeon but a series of events led him to become a pathologist. It wasn't the most glamorous job but at least he was a doctor and it paid fairly well. Early in his career he decided that family practice was not for him. It was too full of ridiculous hours, unpredictable, and incredibly demanding. He applied for a position with the health department just as an opening occurred in the Medical examiner's office and it offered a very nice salary. He jumped at the chance.

Even after five years in the business he still struggled for respect. Back when he first started working for the county, while attending a cocktail party on his day off, he got called to an accident scene. He wasn't supposed to be on call that night but the officers on site couldn't reach the chief Medical Examiner. He felt as if he had been perfectly sober, having only two widely spaced cocktails at the party but he showed up smelling of whiskey and one of the deputies called his office and reported him. Rumors within the health department as well as the sheriff's office quickly spread, earning him the unfair but irrevocable reputation as a drunk. Even now, some law enforcement officers scrutinized him heavily whenever he showed up.

But today he was mostly with some trusted friends, a couple of sheriff's deputies he'd known for a long time and one that he'd only met when he reported to the rescue boat. The new guy seemed to wince when he heard the doctor's name during introductions.

Doctor Benson walked up to the body and checked for signs of life. It looked like she had been dead for ten or maybe twelve hours. Thankfully the birds hadn't got to her eyes yet. As with most unexplained deaths, there were more questions than answers. There were a few suspicious marks on the woman's neck that might indicate something other than drowning as a cause of death. He spent what seemed like an excessive amount of time examining her neck. And after closely studying the surrounding area he could see a faint outline showing that the keel of a boat may have run upon the sand and she may have been dragged onto the beach. A lot of that sort of evidence had been erased by the overnight waves. There were also a couple of depressions in the wet sand that looked like footprints and they were on both sides of the body. One of them was definitely a footprint because he could still see the outline of the toes. The doctor spent a lot of time taking pictures and measurements. Sand under the area where the arch of the foot would have been was slightly discolored so the doctor shoveled a sample into a plastic bag. Technically, that would have been one of the deputy's jobs but Dr. Sid considered all possible forensic evidence his domain.

Still wary of anyone who might seek to embellish his reputation, he didn't share his thoughts with the others but he was particularly bothered by the fact that the victim's hair showed no signs of having been wet. He called the caretaker over and asked, "How much rain did you get out here last night?"

Rick answered, "I'm not sure if it rained at all, I don't think it did. It was mostly wind. The lake kicked up pretty good and I was inside the whole time playing video games. Didn't notice any rain, I think all of that passed way north of here. Things started getting nasty right around midnight and didn't begin quieting down around three o'clock this morning, that's when I went to bed."

"It looks like this is about the only beach-like area along the shoreline," said the doctor. "Mostly I see the water coming right up to the tree line. That seem right to you?"

"Yeah, probably. There are a couple of places where there's a little beach but they're pretty well scattered around the island," said Rick.

The Medical Examiner nodded and went back to the body, looked closely at her hands, wrists, and ankles then made a couple of notes. When he was finished, two of the deputies put on latex gloves and helped him put the woman in a body bag and carry her to the rescue boat. It was just past noon.

Another boat came into view as they were getting ready to leave. This one was much larger and capable of carrying many passengers. "That's the owner," said Rick as he pointed to the boat. "His name is Russ Hill. He's the guy you'll want to talk to. He owns this place."

The boat, larger and with a deeper draft, rounded the breakwall and disappeared into the channel. "He can't get in here, too rocky. He'll be tying up at the main dock. It'll take him a few minutes to get over here," said Rick.

Eventually, an older but fit looking man who carried himself like a matador swaggered up to the group. "What the hell's going on here?" he demanded.

"We've been called to investigate an unexplained death," said the deputy. "Standard procedure."

Russ Hill, pointing to the deputy's shoulder patch shot back, "You guys are Huron County. We're in Arenac."

The deputy nodded. "They gave us the call. You the owner here?"

"That's me but I thought Arenac County had to investigate any crimes out here."

"Mr. Hill, there's no evidence at this point that a crime has been committed. And the assignment of the investigation will be decided at a higher level. We cross jurisdictions all the time. We were just more available than Arenac at the moment. This is nothing new. My bet is that it will wind up being assigned to us because we're collecting all of the evidence."

"Where's the body? The dead person?" asked Hill.

The deputy pointed to the rescue boat.

Hill turned to Rick. "Anybody we know?"

"I didn't get a real close look Mr. Hill," answered the caretaker "But I saw her face when they were picking her up. Never seen her before."

Hill looked at the deputy, "You gonna keep us in the loop? Let us know what's going on?"

"I'm sure that there will be more to this investigation and I'm sure that your input will be needed," said the deputy. He turned and waved his men back to the boat.

Chapter 2

Dr. Sid Benson could usually be counted on for lively conversation and irreverent humor when he was traveling with his Sheriff's buddies but today he seemed a little subdued. There was something about this body that just didn't seem quite right and it haunted him. He had taken extra care to collect anything that might contain trace evidence, had labeled everything, and had noted the location of each detail on the sketch he made of the scene. He knew that his investigation up to this point had been thorough and could withstand any scrutiny. Even after five years he wasn't taking any chances. It seemed that anything with his signature on it warranted a second opinion. But he'd been flawless and had proved it time and again. His record was unblemished since that one incident and he intended to keep it that way. He was a good doctor and he knew it. At times he was suspected of taunting his superiors with phony rumors just so that he could embarrass them when the truth came out. Sid had that kind of sense of humor.

But this body bothered him. First of all, the location where it was found was in about the only clear section of beach. It was like it was planted there with the intent of being discovered. It certainly hadn't simply washed up on shore. The deputies, especially the one who had negotiated the tricky approach to the island had agreed. Landing a boat, any boat, in that area required an almost intimate knowledge of the shoreline. Charity Island was famous for its natural barrier reefs and only those familiar with its very few clear approaches to the coast would even attempt such a landing.

Dr. Sid planned on doing the autopsy on the body as soon as he could get clearance. The thought came to him that the jurisdiction technically belonged to a different county. He decided that he'd lobby for the action. He wanted this case.

The Sheriff's boat finally docked at Caseville where an ambulance was waiting. The body was transferred from the boat and whisked away to the Huron County Medical Center where it would await further action.

The doctor had met the deputies at the dock and had driven his own car into Caseville from his home on the beach just nine miles to the east. He declined the offer from the deputies for dinner at The Wooded Island Sports Grill and hurried home to download the photos he had taken.

Seated at his desk with a tall glass of ice water next to his monitor, Sid removed the card from his camera and loaded it into his computer.

As he studied the photographs he made several notes in the event that he was designated as the Medical Examiner in charge of this case

Toggling from photo to photo, he kept coming back to pictures of the neck area. Examining each photo several times he was convinced that nothing had escaped his lens. But the feeling that something was amiss still hovered in his mind. What could it be?

Sid went to bed that night still wondering. His dreams were wild and meaningless. He was lost in a run down section of a run down city where derelicts roamed the streets and danger lurked in dark corners everywhere. It was a rough night and he awoke feeling more weary than he had when his head first hit the pillow. Sid had experienced nights like this before, always when he was in search of an illusive answer to an unasked question.

There was plenty of food in his refrigerator but Sid decided to have his breakfast in town, stopping at a restaurant on his way into the office. He picked up a copy of the local newspaper to bring himself up to date on the latest spaghetti fundraisers around town. To his surprise there was already a story about the body found on Charity Island. Russ Hill had wasted no time in getting his dinner cruise business in front of the public. He must have contacted a reporter as soon as Sid and the deputies had left the island. The report was predictably sketchy only saying that the body of a woman was found on the shore near the lighthouse and that police were investigating. It only casually mentioned that the Huron County Sheriff's Department was the first to respond. Perhaps somebody who reads the article might help identify the body. For now, it was just Jane Doe.

His breakfast arrived and so Sid devoured his waffles, folded the newspaper and left it on the corner of the table, a gift to the next diner, paid his tab and left.

Chapter 3

Jennifer was waiting when Sid walked into his office. She was busy organizing a drawer in one of the filing cabinets. "Get a little seasick on your boat ride yesterday?" was the question that hit him.

He stopped part way into the room to try and figure out his indiscretion. "Did we have a date or something yesterday?" he asked.

She looked at him with a knowing smile. "It's just that you said you'd call when you got back. I didn't hear my phone ring. No big deal."

Sid laughed. "Right. I screwed up. Am I in trouble?"

"Only if I have to have dinner alone tonight," smiled Jennifer.

"It looks like it's going to be an interesting case," said Sid. "Might even be a homicide. But it's technically not our jurisdiction. I'm just hoping we get it."

"Shazam," replied Jennifer. "Arenac County washed their hands of it last night. It's all yours big boy. Go get it."

Sid threw his briefcase on the desk popped the lid to retrieve his notebook. "I'll be over at the Medical Center looking at a couple more things. Be back in an hour or so."

He checked in at the Medical Center and immediately filled out a request for access to the body. The hospital in Huron County isn't equipped for autopsies so the body would be transferred to a larger hospital in a county just south of Bad Axe within a day or two. That's where the autopsy would be performed but Sid wanted a quick look while the body was still here. When he finally had the cadaver in front of him he noted that the staff had removed all clothing inventoried it and secured it in an evidence container. There was no jewelry of any kind on the itemized register. He went immediately to the neck area and ran his fingers up and down the front of her neck. It was definitely there. An Adam's Apple.

While not conclusive, its presence indicated that it was entirely likely that the body in front of him had been born a male. He moved his attention to the genital area where he thought he could see indications of not too distant surgery. A full autopsy would be needed to confirm what he already knew. The woman was a transgender.

A check of the property container revealed designer underwear and an evening gown bearing the label of a Las Vegas design house. Nothing else. No hosiery and no shoes. Sid closed the lid and replaced the padlock.

"I'd like to have an autopsy scheduled as soon as possible," Sid told the clerk.

The man hammered on his computer keyboard then announced. "You're on their list. Let you know when they've got an opening." He never looked at the doctor.

Sid knew the drill. He nodded and left.

Jennifer was gone to lunch when he got back to his office but a quick text message located her just walking into The Gathering Place, a popular eatery just beyond the city limits at the north end of town. She agreed to wait for him before ordering.

"It's gonna be crazy," said the doctor. "The victim looks like a recent convert."

A puzzled look crossed Jennifer's face. "To what? Catholicism? Judaism? Islam?"

"Womanhood," replied Sid. "There's some pretty strong indications of a recent gender reassignment."

"You sure?"

Sid frowned. "Can't be a hundred percent until I do the autopsy but there are some pretty convincing signs."

Jennifer asked, "Have you talked to the sheriff's department yet? They're the ones who are going to lead the investigation."

"Yeah, I know," answered Sid. "I was planning on making a personal visit to see if I could convince them to lengthen my leash a little more and let me be an active investigator. They need me on this one but I'll have to convince them of that."

"It would be a lot easier if it was vampires or something simple like that. When word gets out, this one's gonna taint you and everybody involved. You know how homophobic this part of the country is. You and everybody else will be toxic. I'll keep my fingers crossed for you." Jennifer buried her nose in the menu.

After lunch they said their goodbyes in the parking lot sharing a brief embrace and a quick kiss and while Jennifer headed back to the health department complex, Sid pointed his Ford pickup truck in the direction of the Municipal Building. On the boat trip back from the island yesterday he had voiced enough concerns to have the investigating officer label the case a suspicious death and list the investigation as a possible homicide.

Sid sat across the desk from Deputy Richard Ross, the man who led yesterday's operation and who would head up the investigation. "You're probably not gonna like what I have to tell you," said Sid. "But I think our victim is a male to female transsexual."

"A what?" said the deputy. "You mean a shemale? A he-she?"

Sid was silent for a moment. "I can't be absolutely positive until I can do some medical things like DNA tests, which could take months, and an autopsy. I'll give you a firm gender identity as soon as I can."

"I apologize for my unprofessional response," said Deputy Ross. "I wouldn't want to see any of my impulsive comments popping up in any of your reports."

"I'm not in the business of ruining reputations," said the doctor with just a little dig. "I'm here to talk about the investigation. You're going to need a lot of help from me and I'm hoping for some elbow room so that I can work."

The deputy slowly swung his knees back and forth in his swivel chair. "Like what? I can only go so far. I have my limits too, ya know, besides we don't even know if she had any connections to this side of the Bay. She could have just as easily come from Tawas or Standish, or even Bay City for that matter."

"I understand that we've been given the investigation so none of that really means anything," answered Sid.

"So tell me why you're so important to the investigation," said Deputy Ross.

"If it's what I think it is," said the doctor. "Your investigation will be digging pretty deep into the gay community and they're not famous for cooperating with authorities. You're gonna need somebody that they can trust. That's where being a doctor comes in handy."

Ross sighed, "Gay community? Do we even have one of those?"

"You can bet on it," answered Sid "but in these parts I'd guess that it's pretty low profile and probably a lot bigger than you think."

"Any idea how to get inside? Gain their confidence?" asked the deputy.

"I'm thinking that my status as a doctor could open some doors," answered Sid. "Most homosexuals seem to be pretty health conscious and I might be seen as a resource if I showed some understanding and compassion."

"Above my pay grade," answered Deputy Ross. "I'll talk to the Sheriff and see if we can set up a meeting with the prosecutor's office. If you're going to act like a cop, we're going to need a lot of blessing."

Chapter 4

"So let me get this straight," said Jennifer. "You're going to try to infiltrate gay society in order to solve this murder, which you have not even determined is a murder yet." She picked at her salad waiting for the chicken Florentine to arrive.

"Well, sort of," answered Sid. "I'm kind of the best shot at gaining their confidence. You know, with the doctor angle"

"So that's why it has to be you? Because you're a doctor? Only now you're suddenly a cop?"

"It's really kind of complicated," explained Sid. "I'm not going to be a cop per se. I won't have any arrest powers and I probably won't be armed. I'll be a civilian investigator, meaning that my only responsibility is to gather information and report it to law enforcement. Sort of like I do now only I'll cover a little more territory. I don't intend to reveal my association with the Sheriff's Department if I don't absolutely have to. At this point we haven't even got a clue of who she was. The Sheriff's Department has no missing person's reports and the statewide request hasn't turned up any either. It's going to take a little while before we get the fingerprint reports. The prosecutor is even talking about going to a private forensic lab for the DNA results. Before we can do much, we need to at least know who the victim is."

"So now that you're the second coming of James Bond, what's your first move?" asked Jennifer. "Hanging out in gay bars? Where you gonna find one? I've never heard of one around here. If you're planning to get cozy with these guys, you're going to have to find them first."

Sid grinned across the table, the flames from the candles sending shadows dancing across his face. "I know where to start."

The following day around noon Sidney surveyed the hospital cafeteria until he spotted the guy named Jack who always sat alone at a corner table during his lunch break. Jack was sipping a spoonful of beef-barley soup when Sid startled him by setting his tray down directly opposite Jack. "Mind if I join you?" he asked.

Jack looked startled but smiled. "You can sit wherever you like. I hope I can be good company," he said.

Sid unfolded his napkin. "You just looked so lonely sitting all by yourself, I was hoping I could brighten your day." His grin was broad and genuine.

"You're a doctor, right?" asked Jack. "I've seen you around here before."

"Yep, pathologist. I work in the lab mostly."

Jack nodded and went back to his soup. "That's probably where I've seen you. I'm an orderly and I work all over the place."

"So why do you always have lunch all by yourself?" asked Sid.

Jack looked down at the table. "Dunno, just kind of a loner I guess. I don't exactly fit in."

Sid studied him for a minute. "Gay?"

Jack stared at Sid for a moment and without raising his voice said, "I don't even know you. How dare you ask a question like that?"

Sid shrugged and casually said, "I didn't mean to embarrass you. I was just curious." He extended his hand across the table and Jack shook it.

Neither man got up to leave but there were a few uncomfortable moments of silence until Jack said, "So you do what? Analyze blood and urine and stuff?"

"Actually I'm with the county coroner's office, chief medical examiner," answered Sid.

"Ew, dead bodies." Jack seemed to shrink away.

Sid was amused that his line of worked caused more of an emotional reaction than his question about sexual orientation. "It ain't so bad," said Sid. "At least the patients don't complain and they're all done bleeding by the time I see them."

The conversation seemed to relax the earlier tension.

Jack broke the ice. In a quiet voice he asked "So why did you ask if I was gay? Are you?"

"No, I'm not but I'm one of those doctors who's kind of on the fence about homosexuality. My interest is pretty much on a professional level. Is it a choice or are you born that way? Thinking about collecting some data and opinions. You know, doing a study."

Which do you think it is? asked Jack.

"At this point, I have no idea," answered Sid. "It's just something I'm curious about. That's all."

"So what have you come up with so far?" asked Jack. He seemed sincerely interested.

Sid answered "Well, I haven't found anybody to talk to. This area must be homophobic or something. No gay bars, no bookstores, nothing. Makes a guy wonder."

"Sure seems that way," said Jack. "I've never seen any genuinely gay friendly places in the neighborhood. Saginaw is about the closest spot."

"But there must surely be gays and lesbians around here. They're everywhere on the earth," proclaimed Sid.

"Oh, they're around. Only place they can ever get together comfortably and without hiding anything is at private homes. Naturally they have their favorite bars and restaurants but they don't act any different than the other customers. The straight clientele is generally unaware and management tolerates them. They just mostly keep to themselves and don't talk about it. This is farm country and farmers don't generally have anything to do with gays, at least not out in the open. There are a few gay farmers but they stay in the closet, with the door tightly closed.

Sid nodded and finished eating his lunch. He picked up his napkin, wiped his hands and asked. "Can I count on you to help me out with my little project?"

"I don't know that I can be of any help to you but I suppose," said Jack.

Chapter 5

"You dumped her where?" shouted an angry Sammy Hubert. "And you two left the body on the beach? On an island? Man, that's way too dramatic. It was just yesterday and it's already all over the newspapers. Even the television stations are picking it up."

"It was dark and there was a storm moving in fast. We were planning to go all the way to Caseville but the weather got too bad" said Paul. "Wasn't nothing else we couldda done. If it wasn't for Henry practically growin' up on that island we probably would have capsized. We damn near drowned as it was."

"He's tellin' you like it is," echoed Henry. "We didn't have nothing to tie to the body to weigh it down so throwin' her overboard was out of the question. We didn't want to leave it out there just drifting around. Leaving it on a deserted island seemed like the best idea. The water was gettin' really rough. We had to do something right away. You told us not to hide the body. How was we to know that there was somebody on that island?"

"Well, there's nothing we can do about it now," said Sammy, his voice clearly irritated but more calm. "Are you sure that you didn't leave a trail of any kind?"

"Pretty sure," said Henry. "I cut my foot but I'm sure I didn't get any blood on her body."

Sammy stiffened. "How did you cut your foot? Was it before you dumped her off?"

"It was while I was pulling the boat back out into the surf," answered Henry. "Stepped on a sharp rock but my foot never got near her."

"Who was she, anyway?" asked Paul. "Somebody important? A celebrity or something? She sure was dressed nice."

"You don't need to know any of that," said Sammy. "All that matters is that she crossed me. The only thing I wanted you guys to do was to get rid of the body and you didn't even do that right."

Sammy Hubert had spent years building his drug business. Born and raised in Bay City, Michigan, He moved to San Diego in his early twenties where he got his start as a street level dealer. His record was clean and his knack for staying off the police radar had helped his reputation with the guys in charge. He kept moving up in the ranks until he reached the point where he had earned the right to his own territory. It was no small accomplishment and one could only reach that status by having the vision to stay ahead of market trends, beating the competition to the punch; or eliminating them. Sammy had done both.

The Mexican, (no one knew his real name,) had told Sammy that he could choose his own turf anywhere in the United States. The farther away, the better. Sammy chose Bay City, Michigan. It was big enough to get lost in but close enough to a couple of other good-size cities to guarantee a sizable clientele. Besides, he knew the territory.

Sammy had grown up in Bay City and had a few trusted friends from his street gang days. Back then he was considered to be the toughest guy in the neighborhood in spite of being neither Latino nor Black. In the old days he pretty much ran the gang. When he left for California five years ago, he said he'd be back. And he was.

In the two years since his return, Sammy had built an organization that numbered in the dozens and was still growing. One of Sammy's requirements was that anybody who worked for him had to have a clean record. When you hired people into the drug running business you didn't necessarily have a labor pool of honest, hardworking candidates to choose from and so you were taking a big risk with every addition to your staff. The bad ones were one of the hazards of doing business and Sammy knew that a few would wind up working for him. When a new employee got out of line, a sound beating and bloody departure was usually the best answer. It not only got rid of a liability but the word would spread on the street that you weren't one to be taken lightly. If you were cheated or betrayed by someone who had been around for a while, the penalty would be measurably more severe and would usually result in a lifelong disability. If a person who had worked their way into the inner circle ever crossed you, there was only one penalty and it wasn't subject to appeal.

Always on the lookout for a new twist, Sammy didn't waste any time putting the tranny on his payroll. Her connection with the gay community as well as the curious would help expand his market area. Outcasts were the most likely prospects for Meth use.

From the very beginning Trish was one of the best sales associates. Like Sammy, she didn't use drugs of any kind. She had an instant following because of her uniqueness and she was also one of the hardest working people on the street. Her clientele grew rapidly until she had three other street dealers working for her. Trish recruited her own subordinates and they were always people with whom she had a history. And they were either gay or lesbian. Sammy couldn't help but be impressed and kept a close eye on her progress. Sammy didn't rise to his level by trusting people and so he paid special attention to her every move. Eventually, he decided to bring her in a little closer. Her rapid rise, though impressive, brought with it just the kind of temptation that could make her begin to think of independence and that was something that Sammy couldn't allow. For months Trish ran her part of the business at the side of Sammy, never making a misstep and continuing to expand. This past spring Sammy had allowed her to expand to an even larger territory with twice the responsibility and she had responded without missing a beat, handling the added burden as if it were nothing.

Then, within the last month or so Sammy began to hear rumors. Trish had been hanging out at a trendy place down near Lansing and that particular club was also a known favorite of a rival from the Grand Rapids area on the west side of the state. It didn't look good and too many people had heard and shared the stories. It seemed prudent to begin watching her movements and contacts a little closer. At first he relied solely on information that came through an unproven source. The informant identified a man named Winston Bly as the close associate of a major drug distributor and the guy who had been seen hanging around Trish. Sammy had never heard of this Bly character and, if Trish was in the process of changing sides he couldn't take the time for a thorough investigation. He had to act right away.

That's when Sammy called on his two enforcers to start shadowing her. They went by the intimidating street names of Slim and Lefty. Sammy had grown up with Slim and an unbreakable mutual trust existed between them. Lefty was a guy out of Detroit that Slim had brought in. They were on the payroll as part of a group of four or five guys that none of the dealers or street level people knew about. This elite circle took care of any dirty business and insulated Sammy from the less trusted employees. They were just one step above Trish's level.

It took less than a week for the two killers to build a case on Trish. Her meetings with the Grand Rapids guy were obviously not spontaneous and their conversations had the look of business discussions rather than romance. Slim told Sammy that he had never heard of Winston Bly either, even though he was familiar with most players in the drug world. If Bly has remained anonymous, he must be good at what he does.

Trish received a phone call within a week inviting her to an exclusive black tie affair. The invitation came with a hint of big things to come. The event was to be strictly formal and in a secret location. The invitees would include upper level politicians and some well known celebrities. Sammy would send his personal chauffeur and a bodyguard to pick her up. It sounded like he might have something very special in store for her. And indeed he did.

Chapter 6

"We have a possible," said Deputy Ross.

Sid stared into the phone. "Possible what?

"Identity on the body," said Ross "Name's Patricia Scott, a transgender from Cleveland. Had the final surgery around Thanksgiving last fall. A brother reported losing contact with her and apparently they're pretty close, talk almost every day. Says he hasn't heard from her in a week so he notified the police. The Cleveland Police Department saw our unidentified body wire and contacted the office. No warrants or anything on her. She was issued a background clearance approval for a handgun purchase just before Christmas last year. That means that they've got fingerprints on file. I've asked them for everything they've got."

"Sounds great," answered Sid "but we're not even a hundred percent sure that our victim was ever a man."

"I thought you said it was a transsexual," said Ross. "You changing your story all of a sudden?"

"No," Sid replied. "It's just that I'm only going on the presence of an Adam's apple, which is nothing more than thyroid cartilage that could be enlarged because of a medical issue and then there are some surgical scars. I mean what if I get into the autopsy and find ovaries?"

"Well, we'll know as soon as the fingerprint copies get here" said Ross. "Is the autopsy scheduled yet?"

"Yep," answered Sid. "I'm headed down to Lapeer in the morning to take care of it. I should be all done by noon and have the full report written within a few days."

Sid hung up the phone and returned to his notes. He had been trying to put together a list of known gay people in the area but now it looked like the object of his attention may not have any local ties. It was a pretty anemic list anyway. So far there were only two names, a former high school classmate and well known lesbian and Jack, the hospital orderly.

The intercom crackled and Jennifer's voice announced, "The Journal is here to see you Doctor Benson."

Sid let out a sigh. "I suppose I can't avoid it. Send him in."

There had been newspaper interviews in the past on the rare occasions when an unexplained death had occurred so Sid was not surprised. After all, any good reporter would try to sniff out a story wherever one might be found.

"Hello Doctor Benson, my name is Cliff and I'm a reporter with the *Huron County Journal.*" The handshake was firm and confident and the man looked like something out of central casting, tall, handsome, and very well dressed. A bit too sophisticated looking for a small town newspaper.

Sid pointed to the chair across the desk. "Have a seat. What do you need to know?"

The reporter placed a small voice recorder on the desk between them. "I understand that you have a body that was found in an unusual place, under unusual circumstances, and dressed in unusual clothes. There's also a rumor that it's an unusual body," said Cliff.

Sid looked at the reporter and wondered who had leaked the information. "You're right about the clothes as they relate to the location where the body was discovered but the rest of the details will become clearer as the investigation develops."

"The word is that the dead woman had undergone a sex change operation. Is that true?" asked the reporter.

"We have no evidence to support any such thing," said Sid. "Where did you hear that?"

Cliff just smiled. "Can't reveal my sources, y'know. I also hear that you'll be taking an active roll in the investigation. Would you care to comment on that?"

Sid felt that the questioning was taking on the feel of an interrogation and that this was no ordinary reporter. He was digging too hard. "I've been requested to render my medical opinions, if that's what you mean."

"Medical opinions regarding the original gender of the victim?" asked Cliff.

"Among other things," answered Sid.

"Like what other things?" persisted Cliff.

Sid paused for a deliberately awkward amount of time before responding. "Doctors are frequently asked their opinions on any number of conditions. I have no idea what they will ask me."

"But will you be playing a bigger roll in the investigation?" asked the reporter.

Sid smiled. "You just never know."

The reporter stood, indicating that he had enough details to build into a story, offered his hand and Hollywood smile once again and said "Thank you for your time." He turned around and let himself out of the office.

"Well, did you survive?" Jennifer stood smiling in the doorway.

"I guess we'll know when the story comes out," answered Sid. "I kinda threw him a bone. Let's see if he chews on it."

Chapter 7

Medical Examiner to join Sheriff's investigation of mysterious death of possible transgender. The headline in today's Journal prompted Sid to shut off his cell phone as he drove down to the Lapeer Regional medical center. The article suggested that Sid had been granted police powers and had been added to the inquiry as a special forensics investigator. In a sense the statement was true but the journalistic embellishment made it sound like he was the new Sherlock Holmes. It might not have been so bad if it hadn't been a front page story.

The autopsy went fairly quickly with the cause of death having apparently been strangulation. It would now become an official homicide investigation. As suspected, the victim had undergone a gender reassignment. All of Sid's fears had now been fulfilled. He was in the middle of a very sensitive and stigmatizing investigation. Everybody involved would be somehow soiled in the eyes of an intolerant and unforgiving segment of society. It was unfair and illogical but that wouldn't stop the jokes in the local bars or the sideways glances from the self anointed aristocracy. Small towns tended to be like that.

Sid left the hospital, stopped at a Taco Bell and carried his lunch out to his car. He slid the seat all the way back, unwrapped his burrito, and turned on his cell phone. To his surprise there were only a half dozen messages waiting for him and three of them were from Jennifer, all berating his cowardice for shutting down his phone. There was one from the Sheriff's department and so he dialed that one up next. It was Deputy Richard Ross. "Congratulations buddy, you've made the big time. Now, would you mind telling me what this is all about? Where did this reporter get his information about the body and who told him about the sex change thing?"

Sid closed the message and went on to the next. It was the Huron County Health Department informing him that any future interviews would need their approval before releasing. Sure thing, he thought and opened the final message. It was another message from the Sheriff's department but this one was from the Sheriff himself. "Doctor Benson: My office has received fingerprint information from the FBI background check people and apparently it matches the fingerprints of the victim of a possible drowning that you are currently investigating. I will pass this information along to Deputy Ross, our investigating officer and you can coordinate with him."

Sid guessed that the Sheriff had not yet read this morning's Journal. He texted Jennifer that she was just jealous of his celebrity and slid his seat back under the steering wheel. The ride back to Bad Axe was constantly interrupted by message received signals, which Sid ignored. He arrived at his office to find Jennifer, hands on hips waiting in his doorway.

"Y'know," she began. "I'm learning to hate you. You don't give me a hint of warning and I spend my entire day on the phone trying to make excuses for your inexcusable behavior. Maybe you thought you were playing with that reporter but the rest of the County officials didn't think it was funny and they've been hounding me since I walked in the door. And all this time you're down in Lapeer playing doctor and your phone is shut off."

"Hey, listen," said Sid. "Reporters make stuff up all the time. They want everybody to believe that they know things that nobody else does. They know that most people would rather let the story die than keep it in front of the public by challenging it. Fringe truth is just a form of job security. And I always shut my phone off when I'm in a hospital."

Jennifer stalked back to her desk. "Just what did you tell him anyway? He made you sound like the chief of detectives."

"I haven't read the full story," confessed Sid. "But the only place I gave him room to make things up was when he asked me how big of a role I'd be taking in the investigation. My answer was actually honest because I really don't know and I was intentionally ambiguous. I guess I just sort of let his question hang."

"Yeah, right," said Jennifer. "Well, he took your bait and ran with it like an angry barracuda with a hook in its mouth and now my boss, your boss, the sheriff's department, and maybe even the mayor wants to know what's going on and they're all demanding answers from me."

"Would dinner at a nice restaurant help?" asked Sid.

"No," answered Jennifer. "But cocktails might. As long as they're doubles."

"You're on. Right after work," said Sid

He disappeared into his office, sat down at his desk and dialed Deputy Ross's number.

"Okay," said Ross. "Just what did you tell this guy?"

"Actually the interview was pretty vanilla, about as innocent as it could get," said Sid. "But that Cliff guy from the *Journal* kept trying to get me to reveal everything I know. He was persistent and kept making assumptions, so if he got a little carried away, I'm not surprised."

"He really didn't come up with anything new but the way he told the story made it sound like we were on to some international intrigue," said the deputy. "The boss didn't see it until about an hour ago and he doesn't like it at all."

"So am I in or out?" asked Sid.

"Nothing has changed as far as I'm concerned. You can still sniff around and see if you can come up with anyone who might help the investigation but if there are any interviews, our department will do all the interrogating. You can observe but you won't be allowed to ask questions. That's our job."

"I get it," answered Sid. "I don't have anything so far, but then I haven't really talked to anyone."

Chapter 8

Patrick Scott lived a tortured life. Somehow it seemed that his internal wiring had been short circuited almost from birth. He was never interested in boy things like sports or playing war. His curiosity leaned more toward cooking and making nice things. His mannerisms weren't very masculine either. From a very young age his dancing looked very girlish and his parents thought it was cute. He didn't enjoy playing with the other boys, preferring to hang around with the neighborhood girls.

Along about the fifth grade his father became concerned. Classmates were teasing him almost constantly, calling him a fairy. Patrick was totally asexual at that age but he knew that he wasn't like the other boys, nor did he want to be. He was content to remain genderless in a world that demanded that he choose sides.

His father arranged an appointment with a private counselor who specialized in that kind of behavior. It only took a few sessions for Patrick's father to have his worst fears confirmed. Patrick identified himself as a female and that would likely never change. At first the father was unwilling to accept the reality of it but he loved his son and vowed to never abandon him.

Patrick's older brother took on the roll of protector, defending his delicate brother against bullies. The entire family rallied around the baby brother with the strange preferences. They would not abandon him. By the time Patrick reached high school the peer pressure became unbearable. His counselor eventually recommended a school where arbitrary sexual preferences were treated sympathetically and so Patrick was sent off to California to complete his education.

It didn't take long for Patrick to see that many of his fellow students weren't products of supportive families. Unlike Patrick, who was sent there out of love, several of his classmates were only there to hide them and keep them from embarrassing their families. They were misfits and had been told as much.

Patrick appeared happy and well adjusted but the demons tortured his mind every night. He felt cursed to be a female with all the hardware of a man. His walk was quite feminine and he knew it. His features were fragile and even his voice had a light, girly quality. These were all involuntary statements of his condition. He was drifting closer and closer to a female identity and he knew that nothing could stop it.

California is also a stronghold of the drug culture and it seemed like everyone in that school was using some sort of recreational drug. Patrick started out with marijuana simply because he wanted to fit in. But soon thanks to his curiosity along with encouragement from others, he was experimenting with more exotic drugs. But he never really felt comfortable taking chemicals that would eventually harm his body and his use gradually tapered off until it disappeared.

It's unusual for a young person to start using drugs and then back away without becoming addicted the way Patrick had and this characteristic had been noticed by some of the dealers who then wanted to recruit him. It took a lot of talking but eventually Patrick became one of the main suppliers on campus. His apparent innocence kept him above suspicion and he was never discovered by the school or by the authorities.

As he grew older and his teenage hormones tortured his daily functions, he began to think about undergoing a sex change operation and there were counselors on the school staff with plenty of information and contacts on the subject. One of them arranged a meeting for Patrick with a male to female transgender who had gone through the entire process five years prior and had been able to make the necessary adjustments. Her name was Hanna.

Hanna was a serious woman with a successful career. She had not neglected any details or taken any shortcuts in her transformation. Patrick was truly impressed and, although he paid very close attention, he could not detect any remnants of masculinity in this confident and attractive woman. Her tasteful wardrobe and flawlessly styled hair bore testimony to the fact that she didn't undervalue herself.

The interview proved valuable to Patrick because Hanna had experienced so many of the same feelings of despair that Patrick suffered and she was able to echo his feelings quite intimately. She assured Patrick that his mannerisms and his slender build and delicate features were absolutely perfect for the metamorphosis. The postoperative woman that emerged would be movie star beautiful. Patrick was indeed ahead of the game. But most of all she stressed the feeling of relief that he would experience when the process was complete. He would, for the first time in his life feel like he had a legitimate place in the world.

But she didn't sugar coat the sacrifices that he'd need to make in order to complete the transition. It wasn't like he'd be walking into a hospital as a man and walk out as a woman. The process would be long, arduous, and sometimes frustrating. It would begin with psychological counseling to determine if his gender dysphoria was genuine. Then there would be hormone treatments and more counseling. It would take months and possibly even longer depending on how effective the hormones were and how much reconstructive surgery would be required.

She warned that during the process there would be those who would seek to exploit the coming female. The porn industry would be interested and persistent but they needed to be strongly discouraged. The experience in and of itself would be highly stressful and skeletons in the closet would only make things worse.

For the first time in months Patrick had no trouble going to sleep in spite of the challenges that he knew lay ahead.

He contacted his parents, told them his thoughts and asked for their support. Patrick's father had a successful business as a manufacturer's rep for several industrial suppliers and told him that he'd contribute as much as he could to make his child feel whole. Things were falling into place.

Chapter 9

Sammy Hubert frowned as he read the newspaper. There was a medical examiner involved in the police inquiry that had taken on the identity as a homicide investigation. He knew that the death would be ruled a homicide and that it would be written up as a featured story in the news. He wanted it that way. He wanted that bastard over in Grand Rapids to see what happened to people who even looked like they were crossing him.

But he wanted the case to be handled exclusively by the cops because they wouldn't have the time or the resources to be as thorough as a dedicated coroner. Doctors are smart people and they know how to think outside the box. That makes them dangerous. A lot of cops could probably do the same thing but they live in a world ruled by a bureaucracy that prevents them from being that effective.

He began to look for weak links in his organization, things that might make him vulnerable. Humans always seemed to represent the highest risk. Slim, his main enforcer was as solid as they come and would never make a traceable error. The same went for his assistant, Lefty who had Slim's endorsement. Paul and Henry, the two guys that he had charged with getting rid of the body had already made some dangerous mistakes. If they were somehow identified and connected with the body, they might very well crack under pressure. He would watch them.

It had been a few days and Henry was still very likely afraid to admit that his cell phone was missing. The most reasonable explanation was that he had lost it while battling the rough water of Saginaw Bay while frantically rowing back out to the thirty foot cruiser anchored less than a quarter mile off of Charity Island. He remembered having it when they launched the ten foot dinghy and loaded the lifeless body on board but after that all memory was lost in the struggle to keep from capsizing as they made their way to the island, dumped the body and rowed back to the cruiser. The only vivid memory of that one hour period was when he stepped on a sharp rock while pushing the boat back into the surf after arranging the body on the beach. He recalled that it hurt like hell and that he ripped his t-shirt off of his back to wrap around his foot. A lot of what happened during that stressful hour was lost in the confusion. He didn't even remember peeling off the latex gloves although he was sure that he had them on while he was handling the body. With the boat bouncing the way it was, that would have been the most likely time for the cell phone to be pulled loose from the clip on his belt and it probably fell overboard. Jack and Henry had returned to their regular duties of making meth and cutting heroin and neither had mentioned it even during their terrifying interview with Sammy. That's the way Sammy wanted his hired help to be, always aware that his wrath was something to avoid.

Sammy closed the newspaper and turned his attention to the internet where he did a deep search on Doctor Sidney Benson. The doctor had been with the health department for a little over seven years and with the Medical Examiner's office for five. He took over as chief Medical Examiner almost two years ago. It seems that his approval for that office took an unusually long time because of some questions about his performance in his early years. Sammy mulled that over for a moment. More bad news. This guy obviously doesn't want to make a mistake and probably has something to prove.

Sammy knew that his longevity was the result of his keen attention to detail and so he decided it was best if he kept Dr. Benson under very close scrutiny. He called Slim. "Hey, How about you and Lefty stopping by my place this afternoon. I've got something I'd like you to look into for me."

"Whatever you say," said Slim. "I'll have to get ahold of Lefty. Four o'clock sound okay?"

"Four o'clock," said Sammy. He hung up the phone.

"I want you to shadow this Doctor Benson," said Sammy. "He's the county Medical Examiner. The Sheriff's department has brought him onboard their investigation. The newspaper made it sound like he's a full member of the team but you can't always believe what it says in the papers. See how involved he is and let me know."

Slim cleared his throat. "Should we be prepared to take him out?"

"I'm hoping it won't come to that," said Sammy. "I only wanted one killing and that one was only supposed to send a message, not bring the roof down on us. Too much attention is bad for business. I want this whole affair to die a slow and silent death."

Chapter 10

Jennifer was waiting with a smile on her face when Sid walked into the office this morning. "There's a message on your answering machine from the Sheriff's Department. Deputy Ross wants you to call as soon as you get in. Says it's important. I hope he tells you that you're fired."

"Gee thanks," said Sid as he entered his office. He threw is briefcase in the corner and plopped down behind his desk. He dialed the Sheriff's number.

"You drive by the lake on your way to work today?" the deputy's voice asked.

"Of course I did, I live on the lake, remember?" answered Sid.

"What was the water like?" asked Ross

"Like a mirror," said Sid

"Good, then you won't get seasick. I want you to meet one of our guys at the boat launch in Caseville around one o'clock. We need to pick up some more possible evidence on Charity Island," said the deputy.

"What is it?" asked Sid.

Deputy Ross said "A cell phone. The kid who takes care of the place... what's his name? Rick, yeah Rick. He found it on the beach near where the body was. Says he's got it in a bag of rice."

"So why do you need two guys to pick up a cell phone?" asked Sid. "Besides, that's not my kind of evidence. That's your stuff."

"Can't send one guy out in a boat alone and we don't have anybody else so you're nominated."

Sid thought it over for a minute. "How big is the boat?"

"I don't know," answered Deputy Ross. "Eighteen feet... twenty maybe. It's the same one we took out there the other day."

"Okay," answered Sid. I'll be taking my secretary along. Any problem with that?"

"Whatever," answered the deputy before abruptly hanging up.

Sid yelled out the door to the outer office. "Hey Jennifer. I hope you didn't just get a new expensive hairdo. We're going for a boat ride right after lunch and lunch will be on the County."

Jennifer appeared in the doorway. "A cruise, you say? The Caribbean or Europe? I'll need to know what to pack."

After a quick lunch at the Riverside Roadhouse, Sid and Jennifer made their way down to the harbor where they found a Sheriff's cruiser with the trunk open and a deputy gathering lifejackets and a fire extinguisher in his arms. "Hey guys. Looks like I'll be your ship's captain for the day. I've been to the Island quite a few times and this afternoon we'll be going around to the north side and through the channel to the main dock. It's just a short walk up to the house from there."

"I want a tour of the house while we're there," said Jennifer. "I hear it's pretty nautical. Maybe I'll discover some neat decorating ideas."

"I'll see if I can get us invited inside," said Sid.

Sid locked the doors on his five year old Ford pickup and walked with Jennifer down to the boat ramp. He didn't notice the Toyota with two men inside parked in the next row. When Sid was out of sight, one of the men got out of the car and placed something on the underside of the pickup truck just forward of the rear bumper. There was a slight clicking sound as the magnet attached itself to the frame.

Back in the Toyota Slim said. "I don't want to waste the battery so we'll wait here until they come back and then I'll turn it on with the remote. These trackers run a pretty long time on a charge, thirty days or more but I don't want to take a chance on losing him.

The trip to the island was smooth and swift. Jennifer took advantage of the sunshine, spending the entire time lounging on the afterdeck reading a week old copy of the local newspaper. Sid spent his time sitting in the first mate's chair and chatting with the deputy. In a little over a half hour they were making the big sweeping turn around the reef and into the harbor channel. There wasn't much to see at the harbor other than a picnic pavilion and a few old abandoned docks.

"The place is pretty much owned by the government," commented the deputy as he tied up the boat. "I'd guess at least seventy five percent. They've declared it a wildlife refuge. Pretty privileged wildlife too because outside of migratory wildfowl, the only critters on this island are chipmunks, foxes, and raccoons. There aren't even any squirrels out here."

"Really?" asked Jennifer. "How about deer?"

"Nope," said the deputy. "Just chipmunks, foxes, and coons."

"That's what you say," responded Sid. "But I've been looking at these woods here and there's over two hundred acres of uninterrupted wilderness. There's gotta be some Bigfoots in here somewhere. Gotta be."

Jennifer threw a lifejacket at him.

When they got up to the house, both Sid and Jennifer were surprised to see a neat cottage standing next to the old lighthouse. The caretaker explained that the original house had fallen into decay and had been replaced just a few years ago with a new building on the original foundation. The power was supplied by solar panels and a small wind turbine. A generator was used to complement nature's renewable energy during periods of high demand.

The wraparound covered porch was complete with high end white enameled wicker furniture and the deck on the porch had a seagoing look to it. Inside it would remind people of what life was like in the early nineteen hundreds. A huge dining room with a long oak table serves gourmet meals to the dozen or so tourists who enjoy the weekend dinner cruises that give them a summer alternative to the hectic vacation pace of the resort towns along the coast of Saginaw Bay. Just stepping inside is like stepping back in time.

"I could live here," said Jennifer. "The solitude and privacy are right up my alley, not to mention the tanning opportunities. I don't need people. I'm sure I could make friends with the animals in the forest if I needed someone to talk to."

"I doubt it," said Sid. "There aren't any squirrels here."

Rick, the caretaker and the deputy stepped into the house as Sid and Jennifer were admiring it. "Well, this is what we came for," said the deputy holding up a quart size Ziplock bag.

"All I see is rice," said Jennifer.

The deputy smiled. "There's a cell phone in here somewhere. I suppose it's time to head back."

They thanked Rick for his time and Sid added that he should remain vigilant and to call if anything else, no matter how innocent looking caught his attention.

Before going back to the boat, Jennifer excused herself and retreated to the bathroom where she changed into shorts and a tank top for the sunny ride home. "You may have a dress code in the office but I'm declaring this a satellite location," said Jennifer.

Chapter 11

Slim was anything but slim. In his younger days he had been a competitive body builder and although his torso had thickened over the years, he still had a very intimidating physique. Muscles bulged everywhere but he had learned not to be too pushy. He wanted respect and maybe some reasoned fear but not to create terror.

This morning Slim sat in Sammy's office. "He went somewhere in a boat. My guess would be back out to Charity Island. The only reason I can think of to visit out there would be to have another look around, see if he missed something."

"Or," said Sammy. "Somebody on the island may have discovered something new and asked them to come out and have a look. I can't imagine what it could be but a couple of our guys were on that island and under a lot of stress at the time. It's possible that one of them might have left some sort of trail without realizing it. I'd sure like to know what took them out there."

"He hasn't done anything or gone anywhere since he's been back," said Slim. "I put a GPS tracker on his car and the only places he's been are his office, home last night and back to his office this morning. Lefty's keeping an eye on him right now. He'll let us know if he starts to move."

"Let me explain something," said Sammy. "I've never been arrested or even suspected of being in the narcotics business. You've probably heard of Griselda Blanco and Pablo Escobar, right?"

Slim nodded.

"Well those two brought a lot of attention to themselves by committing outrageous murders, unnecessary murders that were headline stories on the international news and an embarrassment to the local police. They could have sent the same message to the right people by keeping everything in the family. But they chose flamboyance over practicality. The same with Bonnie and Clyde, Dillinger, and even Jesse James. I won't make those kinds of mistakes.

The real successful bosses are names that you never hear but they control at least as much and probably a lot more than any of the names you're familiar with. That's because they've always been below the barbed wire. And that's where I am and where I intend to stay. You and Lefty are clean as well and that's why you're so valuable to me. I need you and you need me. That's why I want this murder noise to go away. The right people have the message and they're the only ones that matter. Hell, they don't even know my name but they're certainly aware of the cost of doing business in my territory. They probably won't seek revenge because we didn't kill one of theirs. It was our own and that's the way I planned it.

We have to make sure that this doctor doesn't sniff around too much. Let him go as long as he doesn't get too close. But if he starts warming up, we'll have to remove him. But it will have to be an accident or something that can be pinned on someone else. We can't allow an amateur to trip us up. I'm planning some big moves, bigger than you can imagine. They'll be profitable and peaceful. But this doctor bothers me."

Slim had been staring at the floor. Now he elevated his gaze to meet Sammy. "I think we should take out those two guys who dumped the body. They don't know much but they know you, they know me, and they know we're involved. We can make them disappear and nobody will even notice."

Sammy mulled it over. "You're probably right. Both of those guys are pretty nameless. One of them grew up around Tawas City but moved away over twenty years ago and he's only been back about four years. All of his old friends are gone. The other one has no ties to this area at all. Both of them are pretty much vagrants. Give me a couple days to think about it and then tell me how you plan to do it. I trust you but it never hurts to be careful."

"I've been thinking about this for quite some time and have a few ideas," said Slim. "I'd also like to get a better handle on this Winston Bly fellow. It bothers me a lot that I've never heard of him and I've always felt like I had my ear to the ground. Not many things happen that I don't know about. I'd like to get a better picture of just who he really is. I'll get back to you if I find anything out. We'll be ready if anything pops up."

"I've always valued your thoroughness," said Sammy.

Chapter 12

Winston Bly grew up in Grand Rapids, Michigan. Born to an unwed mother, given up at birth, and spent his early years in one abusive foster home after another, he was a product of the streets. He learned to survive and was totally on his own by the time he was twelve. Blessed with a very high IQ, he was able to educate himself through perseverance and hanging around libraries instead of street corners. His life was far from peaceful tough. Living in abandoned buildings was a risky way to grow up. Survival skills were learned the hard way and Winston was constantly on the lookout for ways to escape. He could see people living comfortable and secure lives and he knew that the pathway for joining that part of the world didn't flow through street crime. Odd jobs carried him into his teens but he needed something far more substantial. He eventually found a place to call home when he offered to shovel the snow from the sidewalk in front of a small neighborhood grocery and beer store. The owner, an old German man allowed him to set up living quarters in a small shack behind the store in exchange for odd maintenance jobs around the property. The former storage shed that Winston called home had electricity, running water, a small wood-burning stove, and a padlock for the door. Winston had everything he needed. Over the years Winston proved himself to be loyal and honest, leading to his hiring by the store owner as a clerk and cashier. When the old German's partner moved on to his own business in the suburbs, Winston became the new partner and shared in the ownership of the store. Eventually, the old man died leaving full ownership to Winston. It didn't make him rich but it proved that hard work and honesty pays off. He was his own man on his own terms and he could pay his bills.

The area was pretty well drug infested and Winston, though constantly exposed and sometimes pressured, never succumbed to the temptation. He never took the easy way out. He was well known to all of the street dealers and their suppliers but it was also known that his opposition to drugs would forever stay on the streets and never involve law enforcement. Winston was the type of crusader who looked on drugs as a disease rather than something criminal. The Grand Rapids drug crowd didn't exactly embrace Winston but they knew that the cops were well aware of his position so they made sure that he was unmolested and could move freely among them. Winston actually grew up with the drug industry's top man and had been close friends with him as a teenager. Although Winston made it a habit to always try talking the street dealers into changing their ways and becoming productive citizens, it never really caused a division between him and the main guy. The man in charge of the streets saw it as a way of weeding out potential problems before they came to a stage of violent removal. He viewed Winston as his screening service. Many of the street dealers frequented the store making it a focus of the local police force. The cops knew that neither Winston nor his business were involved in drug dealing but, just the same surveillance teams often parked on his corner.

His customer base knew that Winston was clean and the store was on the level and so business remained untainted. A few outsiders, however assumed that the innocent little neighborhood beer and grocery store was a big part of western Michigan's drug trade. Some of them spread rumors suggesting that Winston was behind the drug business in Grand Rapids. But others identified Winston as the key to leaving the drug life behind them and they were vocal as well. Your vision of Winston pretty much depended on who you talked to.

One day he was introduced to a pretty young lady who told him that she had started dealing way back in high school and had only continued selling drugs because she needed the big paychecks to settle some serious medical bills. She didn't go into detail about her past but she was looking for someone to intercede on her behalf to see if she could peacefully extract herself from this sordid business. She didn't want to cause any trouble for anyone, she only wanted to get on with her own life. Her current problem was that she was constantly being moved higher in the organization and meeting higher level suppliers and distributors. Her knowledge was becoming a liability and she would have to do a lot of convincing if she wanted to reach an amicable separation.

Winston didn't know any of the other drug lords in Michigan but he was the kind of guy who was always willing to try. The woman gave Winston some contact information for her boss known only as Sammy. She didn't reveal any sensitive information, she only used Sammy's "vanilla" email that he used for every day use.

At one of their meetings his new friend Patricia "Trish" Scott was almost frantic. The boss had invited her to attend a big formal party and had promised some exciting news. Trish didn't want any more big promotions, she just wanted out. Her medical bills were all paid off and now she felt it was time to rejoin the normal and sane world. She was whole now and wanted to begin enjoying life for the very first time.

"Wait until you meet him face to face and then tell him that I'd like to speak with him. I'll contact him after I hear from you. In the meantime I'll talk to some people that I know around town and see if I can get an introduction to this Sammy," said Winston.

"Thanks," said Trish. "I feel better already."

Chapter 13

Sid and Jennifer were looking at another dull day at the office. Sid had just finished the final draft of the autopsy report when a FedEx truck pulled up at the building and the driver opened the door and handed Sid a cardboard envelope. The return address was the Michigan State Police Forensics Laboratory. Sid had almost forgotten the sample of suspicious looking sand that he had sent them after their first trip to Charity Island and he certainly hadn't expected a response so quickly.

He sat down at his desk and began to read. The report confirmed that the sample contained traces of human blood and that the technicians at the lab had been able to piece together enough to establish a DNA signature and it did not match the sample of the victim's blood. At this point no matches had been found through NCIC checks.

"Well," said Sid. "I have a clue and I'm sure that the Sheriff's department will be thrilled to hear it. I never even thought to mention it when we were out there."

"I'll betcha you'll be in trouble for not telling them about it earlier," said Jennifer. "They aren't crazy about being upstaged, ya know."

"I guess we'll see," said Sid. He dialed Deputy Ross's number.

The deputy picked up the phone. "Ross."

"Hey, this is Sid, you busy?"

"Whatcha got?" asked the deputy.

Sid told him about the report from the State Police Lab and profusely apologized for his forgetfulness and accidentally leaving him out of the loop.

"No harm on that one," said Deputy Ross. "Right now everything we have is just between you and me. Drop the report off in my office and I'll add it to the file. But if you screw up like that in the future, I may not be so friendly."

"Anything else going on?" asked Sid

"Well, I've been in contact with the victim's family and they're understandably broken up. Unless you have something new, we have no legal grounds to hold the body any longer. They want us to release it to a funeral home in Cleveland."

"I have no objections," answered Sid.

"Oh, and the family wants to talk to you and me. They're headed up this way tomorrow. Saved me a trip down to see them. You'll have to make yourself available, it's part of the investigation. Be here at one o'clock."

"Absolutely," answered Sid. "I'd love to be able to piece this thing together. Right now we know absolutely nothing about Patricia Scott except that she's dead."

"I haven't exactly been sitting on my hands," replied Deputy Ross. "Been doing a little background work here, trying to get a picture of just who we're dealing with. Here it is. Born Patrick Scott in Cleveland, Ohio September twenty-forth, nineteen ninety six. After local elementary schools, attended a private academy in California that specializes in students with gender identity issues. Graduated last June, top of her class and seemingly well adjusted. Never in any trouble and no behavior problems. Turned nineteen in September and had her final surgery in late November. Got nothing since. No boyfriends or anything on record."

"It might give us a starting point but nothing else," said Sid. "I'd feel better if she had a few skeletons or better yet, enemies in her past. At least we'd have somebody to suspect."

"You're beginning to sound like my boss," said the deputy. "But it's the best I can do for now. Hopefully tomorrow will shed a little more light on things. Most homicide investigations start out like this. It will grow. You'll see."

"Can I bring my secretary along?"

"What's with you and her?" asked the deputy. "You never seem to want to go anywhere without her. Can't say I blame you though. According to my water rescue guy, the deputy that took you guys out to the island yesterday, she's got great legs."

"All I know about her legs is that they keep her butt up off the ground. Tell your deputy to keep his attention on handling the boat. Safety first, ya know. And is that a yes? I can bring her along? She's the one who owns the voice recorder."

"Sure you can bring her if you think she'd be of value to the investigation," said Deputy Ross. "Besides, I'd like to see those legs."

"Get your mind out of the gutter," said Sid. "Besides, she's spoken for."

Jennifer was leaning against the doorway to Sid's office. "I hope you're not referring to me. I can do my own talking."

Sid hung up the phone. "You probably won't feel too much like talking when we meet these folks tomorrow. They're the family of the deceased and they're looking for answers."

"Do I have to go?" asked Jennifer.

"You always have the option to wimp out if you're a coward," answered Sid.

Jennifer stuck her tongue out at Sid, wheeled around and retreated to her desk.

Chapter 14

Slim's cell phone rang, it was Sammy.

"I want you to go ahead and dig up some background on this Winston guy. It bothers me that I've never heard of him. I thought I knew who all of the distributors and their buyers were. If he's somebody really big, we've got some research to do. I don't need some weird dude coming after me if he had something going with her."

"Yeah," said Slim. "Like I told you the other day, I been wondering about him too. I don't think he could be too important though because he was the one talking directly to her."

"But remember," said Sammy. "That's how I hired you. Didn't want any middle men in our dealings. Just you and me. Couldda been the same kind of deal with them."

"I'll get on it," said Slim. "I got people. Should be able to get a clear picture in a few days, week at most."

After ringing off with Sammy, Slim contacted a friend in Battle Creek, a town not far from Grand Rapids to see if he knew anything about Winston. The friend said that he knew just about everybody in the Grand Rapids organization and that he knew a guy named Winston but he was pretty sure that he wasn't part of the drug gang although he sort of mingled with the top man. He'd get to work on it.

Two days later Slim received a call from his friend on the west side of the state. He'd done some checking and had found only one man named Winston who was known to the Grand Rapids drug society. According to his source, Winston was a neighborhood grocery store owner and not connected to the mob business in any way. He was known to be a stand up guy though and so he was pretty much left alone. The big boss in Grand Rapids has a standing 'hands off' order on this Winston character. Winston didn't hang out very much around Grand Rapids but he definitely enjoyed the good life and was known to frequent a place called Rum Runners a classy night club in the Lansing area. Word on the street was that he was actually anti drug and was constantly trying to get people away from the influence. That was all that Slim's friend could come up with.

As far as Slim was concerned it was enough though because Winston's Lansing hangout was the same place he'd seen Trish in conversation with the mystery man. Slim got the address to Winston's grocery store and contacted Lefty. They needed to see Winston to be sure.

The following morning two men pulled up in front of the neighborhood grocery store and wandered inside. The place was clean and well stocked. A brightly lit cooler took up one entire wall displaying dairy products alongside of soft drinks and eventually a worldwide selection of bottled and canned beer. A young man pushed a cart full of canned goods down an aisle as he replenished the stock. All in all, the store had a welcoming appearance and was a rare survivor among neighborhood grocery stores. The place even had a well stocked meat counter and a respectable produce section. Slim walked directly to the checkout counter and asked for a package of Marlboros. The man who rang up the sale was the Winston that Slim had seen at the Rum Runners in Lansing.

He paid for his purchase with a smile on his face and left. Jumping in the car next to Lefty, he said. "We got something to tell Sammy and he ain't gonna like it."

Slim didn't waste any time giving Sammy a call. He asked if they could come directly to Sammy's office to relay some important information.

"Good news or bad news," asked Sammy.

"I'll let you decide," answered Slim.

"Get here as soon as you can," said Sammy.

The light in Sammy's office was dim. Sammy liked it dim. "What have you got?" asked Sammy.

"Looks complicated," said Slim. "There's no doubt we got the right guy but he doesn't seem to be part of any organization. He's just a local businessman who happens to be an old friend of the top guy. He's a total civilian."

Sammy's face formed into a concerned mask. "Then what was he doing talking to Trish?"

"That's the confusing part," said Slim. "My understanding is that this Winston guy is like a street preacher, always bending people's ears on the evils of drugs and trying to convert them. When we were checking on Trish and saw them sitting together in the nightclub, they didn't look like lovers. They always seemed to be in deep conversation and they always parted with a handshake instead of a hug. Looked like a business meeting. Did Trish ever give you the impression that she wanted out?"

Sammy rocked back and forth in the big leather chair. "I'd have to think about that but it doesn't seem like it. She always did her job and did it well. If she was thinking of quitting, I certainly never knew it. But, there was one thing. When I called her to set her up for you guys, she didn't seem too excited about the prospect of another promotion. At the time, I just figured that I had caught her by surprise. If all of this is true, I've made a huge mistake."

"That means that we'll have to take out those two flun-kies, Paul and Henry. They're the only ones that can tie us to the killing," said Slim.

"You're right," said Sammy. "They couldn't even get rid of the body properly. Instead of taking it to a landfill, they decided to load it onto a boat and take it up to Oscoda or some place like that. Didn't even bother to check the weather forecast and got caught in a wind storm and wound up leaving her on the beach of a touristy island all dressed up like a prom queen and it got statewide attention. Scatterbrained guys like those two are too dangerous to keep around. Move ahead whenever you're ready.

And another thing, we're gonna have to keep track of this Winston too. If Trish had any serious ideas about moving on, no telling what she might have told him and he might see himself as her protector. Trish was the only dealer in the whole organization with enough inside information to do some damage."

"Oh, we'll make sure Winston's cool," said Slim. "But according to my sources, he's pretty much trusted to mind his own business when it comes to the organization."

"I don't want to take any chances," said Sammy.

"Got it," said Slim. "We'll be thorough."

Chapter 15

Sid and Jennifer arrived at the Sheriff's office about a half hour before the scheduled meeting with the murder victim's family, Trish's parents and brother.

"I've only spoken to the brother," said Deputy Ross, "and he seemed really broken up. Says that he'll do everything he can to help us find the killer."

"We certainly don't seem to have much to work with at this point," answered Sid. "All I know of is that blood sample from the beach and so far that hasn't matched up with anything and the cell phone which may or may not be connected to anything."

"That's about it," said Ross. "Aside from the fact that the getaway car seems to be about a ten foot fiberglass dinghy. And we're only guessing at that. The State Police lab has the cell phone and we'll know more as soon as they have a chance to have a look at the sim card."

Jennifer spoke up. "Did the brother indicate that he has anything to offer?"

Deputy Ross seemed surprised by Jennifer's insight. "We didn't discuss it on the phone but I did request that he bring anything that he might have, like a list of Trish's friends both before and after the transformation and a list of any enemies she might have made, especially because of the transformation."

"What do you mean by enemies because of the transformation?" asked Sid.

Deputy Ross responded. "When the Sheriff found out we were dealing with a transgender victim he decided to do a little research and discovered that a number of people who have re-identified their gender have been victims of hate crimes and many are murdered every year."

"Just because they had a sex change?" asked Sid.

"Oh yeah," answered the deputy. "No other reason. Lots more of that kind of stuff going on than I ever dreamed. The boss wants it looked at as a hate crime until we can prove different."

The intercom on the deputy's desk jumped to life. "A Mr. Scott to see you," said the voice.

Deputy Ross raised his eyebrows at the announcement, looked at Sid and said, "I thought the whole family would be here." He pressed the respond key and said, "Send him in."

A slim, neat, well dressed young man who looked to be in his mid twenties walked timidly through the doorway. The three people in the room rose to meet him, introducing themselves and each expressing their condolences. The deputy motioned to one of the three chairs arranged in a semicircle in front of his desk. After everyone was seated, Deputy Ross said. "I was expecting your parents to be with you. I hope they weren't feeling unwelcome."

"No, nothing like that," said the young man. "They're finalizing the funeral plans. It's going to be mostly a memorial service because my sister's body is being cremated this afternoon. I can tell you everything there is to know." He handed a spiral notebook to the deputy. "These are all of her friends dating back to when we were kids. I've got them chronologically and geographically arranged. She went to high school out in California, you know and so the friends that she made out west are identified that way. There's not a whole lot to report after she settled in Bay City except for a few characters who I never met and I only know their first names."

"Did she have a job?" asked the deputy.

"As far as I know, she was still looking," said the brother. "She hadn't been to any business or vocational school. She was planning to look at her options and try to get on the job training somewhere. She claimed that there were certain lines of work where her sex change could work to her advantage but she never elaborated."

"Do you know if she was dating or seeing anyone?" asked the deputy.

"I don't really think so," replied her brother. "There was one guy somewhere in the Grand Rapids area who she had met and she claimed that he was going to try to help her get some sort of career started but I don't think they had anything going romantically. She never told me his last name. The only thing I know about him is that his name is Winston and the he supposedly started out living on the streets and worked his way up to become a successful business owner. I put his name in that notebook that I gave you. It's Winston."

Sid interrupted. "It's my understanding that you and your sister were very close. Did you talk often?"

"Almost every single day," said her brother. "I've always been the big brother who watched over her and she depended on me for advice and support. Sometimes, especially when she was first starting her procedure she just needed to talk to somebody she could trust. I would never let her down. Never." He buried his face in his hands and cried.

Deputy Ross ended the interview because it appeared to be too taxing on the young man. "I can see that this is very hard for you and you've been through enough. I suggest you just leave that notebook with us and we'll contact you with any questions we might have. I'm sure that more thoughts will come to you with the passing of time."

The deputy turned toward Sid. "Do you have any questions, Doctor Benson?"

Sid responded. "I have a couple of things to ask if you're feeling up to it."

The young man looked up and nodded.

"Was your sister pleased with the result of her operation? The reason I'm asking is that a change like that is a huge decision and pretty much irreversible. People sometimes question their decisions after the fact. Did your sister mention anything like that?"

"Oh no," answered the young man. "She told me several times that the change made her feel free for the first time in her life. I know that, in her heart, she knew it was the right decision. She was born with a female soul and she knew it."

"Okay, thanks," said Sid. "I was just curious about the possibility of depression."

"I think we're done here for now," said Deputy Ross. "We'll call if we need anything more and you do the same if any new thought, no matter how insignificant it may seem, pops into your head."

They said their goodbyes and then it was just the deputy, Sid, and Jennifer in the office.

"What was the deal with your question?" asked the deputy.

"Well," said Sid. "I've been reading up on these kinds of situations and sometimes there's sort of a buyer's remorse in sex changes and the person begins to question their judgment and then self worth. That can lead to severe depression and when that happens, people tend to surround themselves with losers. Everything in their life changes and usually for the worse. Sometimes they become suicidal. I was just trying to get a feel for the victim's mindset."

Chapter 16

Slim and Lefty had their work cut out for them. Not only did they need to investigate the Winston connection, they needed to take out two guys who could be the source of great concern. Slim suggested they get the killings out of the way first. Having dealt with Paul and Henry in the past, they didn't have to build any trust so setting them up should be easy. Slim decided that it would be best if the bodies were never found. As far as he knew, neither man had any ties to anyone in the area so they wouldn't likely be missed. Slim would continue to pay the rent on the apartment that Paul and Henry shared so that it would further blur the trail. Sammy could move one of his other flunkies into the place and they could make up a story about being a cousin or something. Nosey neighbors are easy to fool.

Lefty began by contacting an old friend, one that owed him. The man he chose had needed help covering up a domestic murder a few years back and so Lefty figured him for a very safe choice. The man had a secluded hunting cabin that sat in the middle of two hundred and forty acres in Kalkaska County a couple of hours north of Bay City. Slim asked the man to meet him at a Bay City bar and bring the key to the cabin with him.

Later that day Slim and Lefty made a trip up to the cabin to get it ready. They took two vehicles, the Toyota and a one ton pickup truck that would be left parked next to the cabin. The chore of getting things ready inside was easy. The main room had four daybeds up against the walls and a lone table stood in the middle. They moved the table to one side of the room and laid a large plastic tarp in the center of the floor. It took up almost the whole room. Then they laid a rolled up carpet on the floor. It was stuffed with rags that made it look like a body all wrapped up.

Lefty, who had been a heavy equipment operator in his younger days took the truck into the implement rental shop in town and returned with a flatbed trailer carrying a small backhoe. Before they left for the day, Lefty had found a small clearing deep in the woods, just off of one of the access trails and had moved a couple of small trees and opened a medium size excavation that was seven feet deep. It was easy digging in the sandy soil.

The following morning, Lefty picked up a new trac phone at a drugstore and tried to call the two flunkies. He started with the one named Henry but all of his calls went directly to voicemail. After noon Lefty began dialing the one called Paul. Paul answered on the third ring.

"Hello, this is Lefty. You know who I am?"

"Yeah, I remember you," answered Paul.

"I want both of you guys to meet me and my friend on Center Street in front of the library at nine o'clock tomorrow morning. Got it?" said Lefty.

"Sure, what's up?" asked Paul.

"Just be there. It's important and you'll be paid well," answered Lefty. And he hung up.

Slim dug out two Smith and Wesson model thirty-nine, nine millimeter semi-auto pistols from the gun safe and fitted both of them with Hush Puppy suppressors. These were the same weapons used by the Navy Seals in covert operations. "Seems a shame but we'll be destroying over two thousand dollars worth of state of the art ordnance after this gig. Sammy's paying for it but it still seems like a waste."

Lefty commented. "Not as much as forty years of our lives in prison though."

Slim and Lefty pulled up to the curb the following morning at eight fifty-five. There were two men standing on the sidewalk waiting for them. "Where did you guys park?" asked Lefty.

Paul pointed to an old Ford pickup truck that seemed to be about equal parts of sheet metal and rust in the public parking lot across the street.

Lefty gestured to the rear door of the Toyota Camry. One of the men opened it and they both climbed in. Slim said over his shoulder. "Get your seatbelts on, we don't want nobody hurt."

The men did as they were told as Slim set his course for the northbound expressway.

"Where we headed?" asked Henry.

"Got a little job for you up north," said Slim. "It's a lot like the last one only this one has to be neater. We'll let you know what to do when we get there."

The group rode in silence until they were north of Bay City and then Slim asked. "Hey Henry, has your phone been shut off or what? I tried to reach you about a dozen times yesterday."

Henry squirmed in his seat. "I lost the damned thing."

Lefty turned to look at him. "Whatta ya mean? When did you lose it? Was it on your last job?"

"Not exactly," answered Henry. "It was after we dumped the body."

"How long after?" demanded Lefty.

"I'm not exactly sure," said Henry. "I know I had it when we put her in the dinghy but I didn't notice that it was missing until we were back on the cruiser. I'm pretty sure it slipped off of my belt when we were fighting those big waves on our way back to the cruiser. It's at the bottom of the lake, I'm sure of it."

Slim and Lefty looked at one another but neither man commented.

They arrived at the cabin shortly before noon and Slim pointed to the pickup truck parked next to the cabin. "You guys will be driving that baby back home. Sammy will pick it up at your place."

"Okay," said Henry. "Show us what ya got and let's get this thing over with."

The light inside the cabin was dim. It took a few seconds for everyone's eyes to adjust. Lefty went in first followed by the two hired hands with Slim bringing up the rear. The men all were drawn to the object that was rolled up in the carpet. It was laying on a plastic tarp up against the leg of a table leaving no room to walk around it. They approached it from the same side, Slim and Lefty lagging slightly behind.

"Just wrap him up in that plastic and put him in the back of that truck outside and I'll tell you what to do from there," said Slim.

As Paul and Henry bent over to pick up the load with their backs to the other men, Slim and Lefty both drew their weapons and fired almost simultaneously, once each, point-blank headshots. Even the potent nine millimeter handguns emitted barely a pop with their efficient silencing devices. The two men collapsed on the tarp and Lefty immediately emptied their pockets, collecting their keys and cash. The bodies made a neat package when the tarp was wrapped around them. Slim and Lefty loaded them into the end loader bucket on the backhoe and drove back into the woods where they had dug the grave. It didn't take long to cover the evidence. Lefty even returned the two white pines to their original location on the sandy loam. When he was done, the site looked undisturbed to all but the most inquisitive eyes.

Lefty loaded the backhoe on the trailer, dropped it off at the rental yard and headed back to Bay City. Slim had about a twenty minute head start and waited at Sammy's office for Lefty to catch up. By four o'clock that afternoon the pickup truck had been returned to the garage at Sammy's office and Sammy had been fully briefed on the day's activities. Next they moved Henry's rusty Ford pickup truck away from the library and dropped it off on a lonely street in Saginaw known for its gang activity. Anything of any value, including the license plate will be gone from the truck by morning and in a week or so the cops will put a sticker on the back window and call a junk yard. The only thing left to do was get rid of the murder weapons. Slim took them back to his modest little house, removed the magazines and then thoroughly wiped them down. He called a trusted friend who had access to a blacksmith's forge and extracted a promise that by morning both pistols would be hammered into iron slabs. After dropping the guns off, he stopped at a nice Bay City restaurant for dinner and then drove home. Later that evening he walked to a bar over on Midland Street and returned the key to the cabin to its owner. He toasted himself for a good days work.

Chapter 17

Sid and Jennifer sat in the daily morning meeting with Deputy Ross in the Sheriff Department's conference room.

"We have traced the cell phone that was found on the island," said Deputy Ross. "It belongs to a Bay City man named Henry Mason. His record is pretty clean except for a couple of minor traffic violations. I've asked the city police department for their help in locating him. So far there's been no response at his residence of record and they've put out a watch for his vehicle. They'll let me know what they come up with."

"It was one of those basic flip phones," added Sid. "Their batteries hold their charge for quite a while if they're not being used and I understand that it was pretty well charged up from what I read in the report. This Henry guy might have been one of the guests from the last dinner cruise."

Deputy Ross shook his head. "No Henry Mason on the manifest. He wasn't on the company boat. I'd say that this phone is our first real clue."

"How about his employer?" asked Sid. "Got a line on where he works?"

"Nothing," said Deputy Ross. "He might be working some kind of day labor or just picking up odd jobs on his own or maybe he robs gas stations but we got nothing on any kind of regular job."

"So what do we do now?" asked Sid.

The deputy held up his hands. "The lab is still working on the cell phone to see if they can extract any information out of the memory or maybe some DNA but it's not too promising seeing as how it got all wet. But if we can get anything, we've got that blood sample to compare it with."

"I've been thinking about that blood sample," said Sid. "Whoever left it must have cut their foot on a rock or something. I've gone over the pictures that I took at the scene and they don't show anything that looks like it could have caused any kind of injury but the photos don't show a very wide area."

"Yeah," said Deputy Ross. "It might be a good idea to take another trip out there only this time I want to go along too. The winds have been dead calm ever since the first time we were out there and we weren't treating it as a crime scene at the time. The next dinner cruise is scheduled for the day after tomorrow. There hasn't been anyone out there lately and unless that caretaker has been trampling around, nothing should have been disturbed. A closer look could be in order. Tomorrow morning okay with you?"

Jennifer spoke up for the first time. "Fine with me. I could use the work on my suntan."

The deputy laughed. "I'll call the caretaker and let him know that we'll be out there. Oh, and we'd better pack a lunch."

"You guys don't have to worry, I'll take care of that," said Jennifer.

On the ride back to the health department offices Jennifer asked, "I wonder if all police investigations go like this. It seems like there's almost nothing to go on. To be honest, I don't see any way of ever figuring this one out."

"I've only been close to a couple of other homicide probes," said Sid, "and they started out with a lot more evidence. It was still a struggle to put together a case that would hold up in court. This one looks like a real challenge but I enjoy the adventure. I honestly think we'll find something. If we could identify the source of injury that caused that guys bloody foot, it would be a help. At least it might give us a little clearer picture of what happened on the beach that night."

"I sure hope you're right," said Jennifer. "But if you're not, at least maybe I'll learn something new."

The next morning Jennifer was waiting for Sid and the deputies near the boat launch. She had a large cooler sitting next to her car with a small bag of charcoal leaning up against it. "I saw a couple of barbecue grills near the lighthouse the last time we were there. I'm planning a great picnic lunch. Even brought some iced tea."

Sid smiled, picked up the cooler and headed toward the Sheriff's boat.

Chapter 18

Sammy's office had the appearance of a successful import-export executive in its respectable neighborhood. He had purposely rented space in Hampton Township near Bay City. It was a quiet community a couple of miles from the big city and had a police force of under a dozen officers. It was a good place to be anonymous. None of the dirty street business was ever conducted out of this office. Its existence served to lend a sense of legitimacy to Sammy's impressive income. He sometimes held high level meetings here but none of the lower tier dealers even knew the place existed.

Today he sat alone in his office and pondered his dilemma. Up until a week ago he was proud of his organization. Back then he had never even considered killing anyone although he knew that it might someday become necessary. It really bothered him though that it was his own compulsive conclusion based on flimsy evidence that led to a possibly avoidable murder. It was a decision made in a moment of needless panic. It was a judgment based on rumors from questionable sources. It was regrettable, indeed but irreversible. And it had led to two more murders. Sammy never wanted things to be this complicated but although he longed to stop the bloodletting, he dare not relax his vigilance. Now was a time more than ever to observe things with clear eyes and to make smart and decisive choices. No time to get lost in false remorse.

Sammy hoped that this was the end of the murder chapter in his life. It bothered him morally and it could be very bad for business. Killing people had never been part of Sammy's plan. It was one of the main reasons that he left the west coast. Murder seemed to come too easy out there. He had always considered himself to be way too smart for that kind of thing. Murder is a sure way to bring attention to a business and attention was the last thing that Sammy wanted. Killing Trish bothered Sammy on more than just one level. He had genuinely liked her. He'd gotten so used to her perfume and pleasant smile that it was hard for him to accept the fact that she had been born a man. But in a deeper sense she was very unlike other drug dealers and distributors. She seemed to have a sincere regard for the clientele. She occasionally helped some of the younger, more vulnerable customers find counseling and rehabilitation. Sammy had read her as a girl with a conscience who suddenly found herself in an unconscionable occupation. She was an attractive puzzle and a good person.

But it had happened, it was over and she was dead. Sammy's thoughts of her had to be buried just like the remains of the two unfortunate victims who had bungled the job of getting rid of her lifeless body. It was time to move on but with a vigilant eye and a clear head. Sammy whispered. "Where do we go from here?"

He looked at the current state of affairs. There were two people who would need special attention, the Medical Examiner and the character named Winston. Slim and Lefty were already alerted to the situation and were keeping tabs on both men. Sammy didn't consider either man to be an imminent threat but he had an uneasy feeling about them and wanted them both watched closely just to be sure.

The doctor had a GPS device attached to his pickup truck that Slim could monitor the medical examiner's movements from his cell phone and Lefty had his buddy from the west side of the state gathering intelligence on Winston. Sammy was comfortable with the arrangements but still uneasy with the entire situation. It never should have come to this. He hoped that he was through with killing but knew that he had to remain realistic and to accept the fact that he had to be prepared to do it again. He understood this. It was the business he chose and it's not always pleasant.

Things were still moving along briskly out on the street. It was as if nothing happened. Sammy's distributors never asked about Trish and why she suddenly disappeared and the two street dealers who were moved into the lab never questioned their sudden promotion. Things like this were just accepted in the drug trade. The organization had a long list of vetted candidates to fill any openings.

The ringing telephone interrupted Sammy's reverie. It was Slim.

"I thought you'd like to know that the doctor and his secretary are on a boat headed for Charity Island again and this time there are two sheriff's deputies with them."

"They must think that there's something worth looking at out there," said Sammy. "I sure wish I knew what it was."

"I followed the GPS signal down here to the pier," said Slim, "and I got here just in time to see them leaving the dock. Then I noticed that there was a ferry boat tied up here advertising Charity Island dinner cruises. I wandered over there and checked it out. The captain says that they have a dinner cruise scheduled for tomorrow so I signed up. None of us have been over there so I figured I'd go see what I can see."

"Good idea," said Sammy. "Can you blend in?"

"Got that going already," said Slim. "Told the guy I heard that it was a hotspot for perch and I was a fisherman, wanted to get a close up look at the waters around the island and maybe pick his brain to help me avoid the boulders and reefs when I take my own boat out there."

"Good," answered Sammy. "Keep it simple and forget-table. I want to know what you find out as soon as possible."

Chapter 19

The ride to the island was over smooth water and under a blazing sun this morning. Sid pulled off his shirt and slathered sunscreen over his shoulders while the two Sheriff's Deputies sweltered in their uniforms. "At least we don't have to wear body armor on this trip," said Deputy Ross.

The patrol boat slipped quietly into the channel and pulled up to the pier. Sid was surprised to see Rick, the caretaker waiting for them at the dock. "Right on time," said Rick. "You said you'd be here around nine and it's five minutes to nine right now."

Jennifer was the first one off the boat with the bag of charcoal under her arm. Sid and Deputy Ross were close behind carrying the cooler. The other deputy secured the mooring lines and joined them.

The caretaker led them over to the four-seater cart, loaded the picnic gear in the small truck bed and motioned for them to jump in and head for the lighthouse. "I'll walk" he said. "Need the exercise."

"Nonsense," said Jennifer. "Me and the good doctor will follow up on foot. Besides, I want to look for squirrels."

Rick turned around and said, "But there aren't any squ…" He stopped mid sentence when he saw the doctor smiling and Jennifer giggling."

Deputy Ross called a brief meeting when they got to the lighthouse. "We'll be looking things over more closely this time. This island is not considered the crime scene but right now, it's the closest thing we've got." He turned to the caretaker. "Mr. Todd. Have you been back down to the beach since you found that cell phone?"

"No sir," answered Rick. "I was thinking about scrounging around down there today but when you called yesterday and said you didn't want it disturbed, I figured I'd better wait for you guys."

"Good," answered the deputy. "You can come along with us today in case we have any questions."

"What are looking for?" asked Rick. "Maybe I can help."

"I have no idea what we're looking for," said the deputy. "How about you?" he turned to Sid."

"Rocks," answered Sid. "I want to look at rocks."

"Well, you'll find plenty of those around here," said Rick.

They headed for the beach, Sid and Jennifer leading the way. Sid went immediately to the spot where he had taken the sample of blood-soaked sand. The disturbed area was still visible on the sandy beach. He backed up toward the lake until his heels were being licked by the tiny waves that rippled up on the shore. He could see at least a half dozen softball size rocks between where he stood and the place he had seen the suspicious looking dark spot on the sand. Sid snapped about ten pictures of the rocks from different angles. Then he dropped to his knees and carefully examined each rock without touching them. Most were limestone but a few of them were darker in color and seemed to have some sort of pattern in them. He focused on those. Finally he produced a pair of latex gloves and a clear plastic bag from his back pocket and carefully deposited three of the rocks in the bag.

The two sheriff's deputies spent their time carefully examining the sand around the area taking pictures in ever widening circles. Not far from the four day old impression left from the boat keel, Deputy Ross bent over and picked something up from the sawgrass that dotted the beach in small clumps.

"Whatcha got?" yelled his partner.

Deputy Ross held it up. "Ballpoint pen." He turned the pen sideways and read out loud, "American Marina, Tawas, Michigan. Don't know if it means anything or how long it's been here but it might have fingerprints or DNA on it. We'll check it out." He dropped it in an evidence bag.

Jennifer said she was tired of watching grown men crawl around on the beach and headed back up to the lighthouse to get the grill started.

There was a large picnic pavilion near the lightkeeper's house and an empty grill sat next to it. Jennifer scrubbed the grill surface with a sandstone rock and then wiped it with a cloth. After the coal was lit and burned down to a red glowing ash she sprayed a little cooking oil on the rack and loaded it up with big hamburgers. Jennifer busied herself washing the top of the picnic table and then set out the potato chips, condiments, and poppyseed rolls.

Turning toward the beach, she put her fingers to her lips and let out a loud, shrill whistle. "Come and get it," she yelled.

The men trudged up to the table and they all smiled at Jennifer before sitting down and filling their plates with burgers and deli counter potato salad. There were a couple of six-packs of chilled iced tea on the table, one unsweetened and the other was sweet tea.

After everyone had stuffed themselves, Jennifer cleared the table and packed the leftovers back in the cooler.

"Think it was a profitable trip?" asked Sid.

"I guess we'll see when we get everything checked out," said Deputy Ross. "I see that you picked up a few things too. Thinking of becoming a rock collector?"

"You laugh," said Sid. "But one of these rocks just might

contain some DNA that matches that blood sample that I found in the sand."

"You sayin' you can get blood from a rock?" laughed Deputy Ross.

"Chert," said the young caretaker.

They all looked at Rick. "What?" said Sid.

"Chert, it's a kind of rock left over from the ice age," said Rick. "It's all over this island. From what I understand, it's some sort of flint. That's what you put in that plastic bag. The Indians used to make stone tools and arrowheads out of it."

"You saying there's Indians on this island?" said Jennifer.

"Not any more," said Rick. "Not for hundreds of years. But at one time they lived here and that chert was the reason. They made axes, knives, and all kinds of things out of it. They were originally the Sauk tribe. Probably over a thousand years, they were here and then the Chippewa tribe came along and fought with them, pretty much drove 'em all out and now their descendants all live in Oklahoma."

"How do you know all this?" asked Deputy Ross.

Rick pointed toward the keeper's house. "Books. That place is full of 'em. They sell them to the guests that come out here. The whole history of the island is in them, even the part where Abraham Lincoln issued an executive order to acquire the island for the federal government just fifteen days before he was assassinated."

"I wonder why he would want this island?" said Sid.

"The lighthouse." Said Rick. "Strategic navigation aid. It was during the Civil War."

"But it's privately owned now, right?" asked Deputy Ross

"Oh yeah," said Rick. "When they went to the electric powered lights back in nineteen thirty-nine, they realized that they could save about five miles of underwater cable by putting up a new lighthouse at Gravely Shoal a little ways northwest of here. You can see it from the beach." "You must have been reading all those books in the Lighthouse," said Jennifer.

"Not much else to do out here," said Rick. "Especially on crummy days.

"Getting back to these rocks," Sid held up the bag. "A couple of them are broken and I'm guessing that you could get a nasty cut if you stepped on one. One of them looks like it could have some human tissue on it so I want to have a closer look at it. Thankfully the birds haven't picked it clean"

"Thankfully, you didn't mention that until we were all done eating," said Jennifer.

Chapter 20

Slim parked at the far end of the parking lot where he could use his high powered binoculars without being noticed. He had a clear line of sight to Dr. Benson's pickup truck and could have a close look at anything the medical examiner brought back from the island with him.

When the boat returned to the dock, Slim watched as the two sheriff's deputies carried the cooler over to the secretary's car and deposited it under the hatchback. The doctor carried nothing but a clear plastic bag that appeared to have a couple of rocks in it. Slim remembered that one of Sammy's flunkies said that he had cut his foot on something when they were depositing the body on the beach. The rocks just might be significant. Sammy was right about not wanting a doctor investigating the murder.

Slim made some notes about what he had seen and then started his vehicle. He'd see what more he could learn tomorrow when he was going to pretend to be a tourist on a dinner cruise. By the time he pulled out of the parking lot, the deputies had left and both the doctor and his secretary were long gone. He fired up his cell phone and opened the application to track the doctor's movements. He saw that the pickup truck was headed toward Bad Axe and the Health Department office and so he continued south to Sammy's office. When he got there he was surprised to see Lefty sitting across the desk from the boss.

Slim pulled up another chair and joined them. "Didn't see too much today but that doctor might have found something that interested him. He had a bag with some rocks in it when they got back from the island." He turned to Lefty.

"Remember that Henry character telling us that he cut his foot when he was on the island? Could be that's what the rocks were all about. We don't know for sure."

Lefty nodded. "Guy's doing a lot of snooping around. Making me nervous. Any ideas?"

"I'm going to the Island tomorrow and I'll look around," said Slim. "See if I can shake anything loose. I'll talk to a few people. Someone's gotta know something."

"I've been listening real hard too," said Lefty. "A friend of mine over on the west side of the state says he knows a lot about this Winston guy. I guess they have coffee together and talk almost every morning. He says that Winston has mentioned a woman who wanted his help. I told him to get me all the information he can. This could be trouble."

"I thought that Winston was a straight up guy," said Sammy. "Thought everybody trusted him."

"That's what they tell me," answered Lefty. "But when it comes to women, well… Let's just say I want to know more about what kind of relationship that these two had."

"Can you do it without running up a red flag?" asked Sammy.

Lefty nodded. "My connection is a real professional. Used to be a private investigator until he realized where the real money is. As a matter of fact he still has his license. Comes in handy at income tax time."

"Just be careful," said Sammy. "Both of you. I don't need anyone noticing that someone is interested in what is going on. Right now, I don't believe that the cops know anything about Winston and I want it to stay that way. As far as that doctor goes, I think he's grabbing at straws. He's looking for anything he can find and it hasn't been much so far. I just hope he doesn't stumble onto something he can sink his teeth into. He still makes me feel a little uneasy, especially since I found out he's a pathologist. They're just like detectives ya know."

"I'll see if I can find out what he picked up on the island today," said Slim. "The trip out there is an all day thing and the guy at the dock says that there's plenty of time for guests to wander around and explore. I intend to do a lot of exploring. It's supposed to be in the eighties and sunny tomorrow. I'll look like a tourist, shorts, deck shoes, and a ball cap. I should blend right in."

"One other thing," said Sammy. "Those two guys that you took up north, are they gone forever? They're not going to be found by some pheasant hunter this fall, are they?"

"They're about seven feet down and way off the beaten path," said Slim. "They won't be coming back to haunt anybody."

Chapter 21

Sid got to work early this morning, examined the rocks that he picked up on the beach and was able to recover some samples of what looked like human tissue. He packaged everything along with the rocks and prepared to send them off to the State Police Laboratory for a closer look.

Jennifer arrived just as Sid was taping up the box. "Oh you shouldn't have," she said. "Looks too big to be a ring though."

"Not for you," Sid said. "But you can get these on a UPS truck today and take my place at the deputy's meeting. I've got a conference over at the hospital today so I'll be back sometime later this afternoon."

It was all Sid could do to stay awake through the boring discussion about appropriations and budgets. He really knew very little about those functions but it was his turn to represent the health department office at the meeting. He was just thankful that someone else taking notes and would hand out copies later. When the lunch break finally signaled the end of the meeting, he made a beeline for the cafeteria and a cup of hot coffee to prop his eyes open. He had a slice of pizza and a big piece of apple pie on his tray along with his coffee. He turned around and saw the orderly, Jack once again sitting alone in the corner. Jack looked up and motioned for Sid to join him.

"The pizza's usually crummy," said Jack.

"Yeah, I've heard," said Sid. "But this one looks like it just came out of the oven, hasn't dried out yet. I decided to take a chance. If it doesn't work, the apple pie is always good. So what's up?"

Jack leaned forward and spoke very softly. "That autopsy that you did earlier this week, was that a woman?"

Sid nodded.

"The word around here is that she was a transsexual. That right?"

Sid cleared his throat. "Where'd you hear that? I thought that the new privacy policies pretty much stopped all the rumors around here."

"Only for living people," said Jack. "Your right to privacy dies with your body is the way I understand it."

"Does it make a difference what she was?" asked Sid.

"Well, maybe," said Jack. I have a friend who had been pretty close to a transgender woman and now that woman has dropped out of sight. Her name was Trish."

Hearing the name stunned Sid. "She wasn't from around here. How would your friend know her?"

"It's her isn't it?" Jack sat back and finished his coke. "Trish was sort of a regular around here, was friends with most of the gay people in the area. The friend that I mentioned had a sex change about ten years ago, before she moved here. Only a few people know it though."

"Can I talk to her?" asked Sid. "Would she be willing to talk to the Sheriff's Department? They're investigating this as a homicide."

"Why weren't you honest with me up front?" said Jack. "You led me to believe that you really cared about the plight of gay people. Do you think we're all happy with who we are? You were looking into a crime all along. Do you care about us at all?"

Sid considered his words carefully. "Jack, the last time we talked you didn't even admit that you were gay. All I said was that I wanted to know more about the condition. How was I to know that you wanted help or support? I'd be more than happy to work with you but I have to tell you that I'm not the most qualified to answer all or even most of your questions. I'm still willing to help and I'm sure that there are some things that I can do. But you never asked."

"I suppose you're right," said Jack. "But I can't help feeling betrayed."

"Be careful," said Sid. "You'll never be able to help yourself if you're going to play the victim game. Even if you really are sometimes treated unfairly, it's just an excuse. You can't control what others do but you can influence your own destiny through your actions."

Jack sighed. "Well then, maybe we can help one another. I can introduce you to the young lady who knew the deceased."

"Really?" said Sid. "How soon can you make that happen?"

"Within the hour," said Jack. "She owns a flower shop not too far from here and I can call her and see if she has time for you."

"I'd be grateful if you'd do that for me," said Sid.

Jack produced an old cellular flip phone and entered a number. After a short conversation he turned back to the cafeteria table, scribbled an address on a napkin and slid it in front of Sid. "She's waiting for you," he said.

Sid was out the door almost immediately, leaving his untouched slice of apple pie as a reward for Jack. He searched through the numerous strip malls at the north end of town until he found the one that was home to Marsha's Flowers.

There were no customers in the shop when Sid walked through the door. Two pretty women were just putting the finishing touches on an elaborate display. One of them turned to Sid, smiled and asked. "Are you Doctor Benson?"

Sid looked down and realized that he still had his hospital ID card dangling from the lanyard around his neck. "That would be me," he answered.

"I'm Marsha, we can talk in the office. Linda can watch the showroom. This way," she said as she led the way around the counter.

Marsha certainly didn't look or act as if she had ever been anything but a beautiful woman. None of her movements even hinted of masculine posture. She motioned to the empty chair in front of the big desk and said, "Can I get you anything to drink? We have coffee, water, and soft drinks. Sorry, no Martinis." She grinned.

"I'm fine," answered Sid. "I'm sure that you know why I'm here, right?"

"I think so," said Marsha. "It's about Trish. Is it true that she passed away?"

"I'm afraid so," said Sid. "I'm part of the team investigating her death. It was a homicide."

"Oh, how horrible," said Marsha. "I hope I can be of some help but honestly, I didn't know her all that well. I was just trying to help her adjust to her new identity. I assume you know about me, right?"

"Well, I know just a little bit about you but I didn't know her at all," said Sid. "So you're already way ahead of me. Can you just tell me what she was like? What kind of person she was?"

"First of all," said Marsha, "you have to understand where she came from. She was a boy all the way up until high school and that's how she was treated. It must have been very difficult because she was just about the most feminine creature I've ever met, petite and delicate. She had spent the first part of her life in a conflicted state, feeling one way but all expectations were pulling her another. I know this because I went through a similar period in my life. Once she made the commitment, and it's an extremely weighty one, to have her body altered to match her being, she told me that she began having some hope; some identity.

Fortunately she had family support and they helped her by providing her with the right environment in high school and furnishing her with the best counseling and then supporting her decision. Not all of us were blessed with that kind of approval.

When she first came to me, she was on the timid side, not sure of herself at all. It took a lot of encouragement to keep her smiling. She continued to mingle with gay people because she felt some sort of obligation to support their dilemma. But eventually it dawned on her that, for the first time in her life she had a single identity. She was a woman, one hundred percent female. No lingering remnants of masculinity. It takes time for those things to sink in. She wasn't sure about ever becoming an advocate either. For now she just needed to adjust to life as a woman. The other stuff could come later.

I only wish that she hadn't got herself involved with those drug dealers."

Sid sat straight up. "Drugs? She wasn't on drugs. I've got the toxicology report sitting on my desk."

"Oh, she wasn't taking drugs," said Marsha. "She was selling them."

Chapter 22

Sid asked for a special meeting with the Sheriff's deputy that afternoon and then called Jennifer to see if she was willing to meet him down at the County Building. His pulse was racing as he walked in the door.

"So what's so important?" asked Deputy Ross.

"I've just been informed that the homicide victim was a drug dealer," said Sid.

The room was silent for a minute and then the deputy spoke. "Where did this come from? Is it a credible source? And where do you get off freelancing on this investigation?"

"I wasn't intending to go around you. It was a spontaneous thing and I wanted to get to it before the opportunity evaporated. One of my connections in the gay world set up an impromptu interview and I ran with it. I probably should have called you but I was only looking for some insight on the victim's personality. I never expected any information like this to come out."

"Start at the beginning and run it by me," said the deputy.

Sid relayed the events of the day beginning with his encounter with the orderly in the hospital cafeteria. He tried to remember every single detail right down to the slice of pie that he left for Jack and the name of the second employee at Marsha's Flowers. Jennifer took notes on her laptop as Sid recounted his day.

"Why haven't you told me about this guy at the hospital?" asked Deputy Ross.

"Well, he hasn't been part of the investigation," said Sid. "He was just my connection to other gay people in the area and he hadn't hooked me up with anyone until today."

"They're all part of the investigation," said the deputy, "make sure you keep me in the loop with all of your contacts, even if you don't think they're important. I'll make those decisions."

"You got it," said Sid.

"Now tell me more about this flower lady," said Deputy Ross.

"The subject never came up but I had the impression that none of the locals are aware of her male to female transition. You certainly can't tell by looking or by talking to her. I'd tread lightly in that area if you're going to interview her," said Sid.

"Good point," said the deputy. "The last thing we need is for the Sheriff's department to get accused of some sort of bias. Do you think you can persuade her to drop in and talk to us? Right now she represents the one and only lead that we have for getting to know what the victim's life was all about. I mean, all we've got so far is a family who she hasn't lived with for over four years, some high school classmates who were never close, and a guy named Winston who lives clear across the state who we haven't even positively identified yet. "

"I'll see what I can do," said Sid. "She didn't seem like a petty person. She was completely straight forward when I talked to her. She was also quite fond of the victim so I would think that there's a good chance she'd be willing to help."

Sid flipped open his wallet and dug out the business card from Martha's Flowers. He stepped out into the hallway to make the call. While Sid was out of the room Deputy Ross broke the silence. "Well Jennifer, what did you think about your trip to the island?"

"It was fun," she answered. "Rick, the caretaker out there was telling me that they're expecting to get swamped with conservation department people any day now, the Federal Government variety. Seems that they've discovered some sort of pelican's nest on a different island just about a half mile away and I guess that species has never been known to nest in this part of the world before. Biologists and conservationists will be all over the place doing studies and taking pictures. You can bet that they'll leave a mess behind. Charity Island is the only place that they can bring in a big boat so they'll be using it as a base and ferrying back and forth in small boats. It's a good thing that we combed that beach before they got there. It's gonna get crazy out there."

"I didn't know anything about that," said the deputy. "But then it's not technically our jurisdiction. I'll have to see who I need to contact. I don't need a bunch of environmentalists screwing up our crime scene."

Sid stepped back in the room. "My call went to her voicemail. It's after business hours and I don't have her personal phone number. I left a message for her to call. I gave her your name and number too. Can it wait until tomorrow or should I try to look it up?"

"Not that big a rush," said the deputy. "Leave me the number of that flower shop in case she's willing to talk."

When they got out to the parking lot, Jennifer asked Sid, "Next time you visit one of these transsexuals, how about taking me along?"

"It was such a spur of the moment thing that I never even thought of it," said Sid. "Wasn't trying to keep you out or anything. As a matter of fact, I wouldn't have expected you to be too excited about coming along."

"It's just that I've never met anyone who's had a sex change before. Just curious I guess," said Jennifer.

Sid laughed and shrugged. "I'm afraid you'd have been horribly disappointed. She looked and acted like any other thirty something woman you've ever met."

Jennifer smiled. "You're a man, what do you know? Bet I could tell."

Chapter 23

Slim stepped aboard the ferry boat carrying a small cooler that held a six pack of Budweiser, a deli submarine sandwich, a small bag of chips, and a Snickers bar. In his navy blue shorts, Sperry Topsiders, and blue polo shirt he looked like any other tourist. The ensemble was completed by a ball cap with a Detroit Tigers Old English D on the front and a camera hanging from a lanyard around his neck. He settled into one of the seats along the starboard gunwale near the pilot house. The ferry had begun its life way up north many years ago shuttling passengers back and forth from the mainland to legendary Mackinac Island. Bigger and more modern boats had made the old girl obsolete and now she served a much smaller market. The light breeze made barely a ripple on the water. This looked to be a smooth trip.

When they got close to the island, Slim pulled the camera out of its case and began filming the approaching coast line. It seemed like a normal tourist thing but it also served to record the contour of the island and its approaches to the beach. The ferry boat wouldn't come anywhere near the beaches though. The reefs and barely submerged boulders guarded those access points. It was a lot the way he remembered it from his youth. He and a few buddies used to bring girls over to this place back when they were teenagers. There were no dinner cruises back then, just a falling down and deserted lighthouse keeper's dwelling. It was a perfect place to get friendly without being disturbed. The big boat rounded the limestone breakwall and entered a narrow and winding channel that ended at a substantial looking dock. The captain made the approach look easy. They gently bumped the pilings as the crew jumped off and secured the mooring lines.

It was about a ten minute walk to the lighthouse the captain kept the small crowd entertained by pointing out the various flowers and wild plants that grew along the path. He also talked about the unique limestone composition that made up the bedrock of the island. The walk was both pleasant and educational.

As they approached the lighthouse keeper's residence Slim noticed a young man pushing a wheelbarrow filled with bags of topsoil for the flowerbeds. He nodded and waved. The young man smiled back. It was obvious that this guy was a full time resident of the island and would very likely be the person who found the body. Slim made a mental note of how the young man was dressed and what he looked like. He'd want to catch him alone later and see what he could get out of him.

Once they were at the destination with over two hours until the meal would be served, the group began to separate into pairs and a few solo explorers who scattered around the scene. Some climbed the lighthouse stairs and some wanted to see the inside of the house while others wandered into the small gift shop. Slim waited for the man with the wheelbarrow to stop near an old well pump and watering trough.

He approached the young man. "Workin' pretty hard out here in the sun, ain't ya? Could you stand a cold beer? He stuck out his hand. They call me Slim."

The caretaker looked up and shook hands. "I'm Rick and, man, I'd love one but I'm not allowed to drink alcohol as long as we have guests on the island."

"Right," said Slim. "I should have known. I didn't see you on the boat. Are you here all the time?"

"Almost," said Rick. "I kind of watch over things out here all summer. I get over to the mainland every couple of weeks or so but mostly I just hang out here."

"Must be lonely," said Slim. "I'd say that nothing ever happens in a place like this."

"Yeah, usually, but it's been kind of crazy lately," said Rick "I actually found a dead body a few days ago, right there on the beach." Rick pointed over his left shoulder.

Slim acted surprised. "You found it? What? A fisherman fell overboard or something?"

Rick chuckled. "You wouldn't believe it. A beautiful young woman and she was all dressed up like she was going to a wedding or something. Freaky."

"Wow," said Slim. "What happened? How'd she get there?"

"No idea," said Rick. "But the cops have been out here like three times. They're saying she was murdered."

"I think I might have seen something in the papers about it," said Rick. "Do they have any idea who did it?"

"If they do, they're not saying," said Rick. "They've pretty much gone over every inch of the beach. They've taken a million pictures, a shovel full of sand, a few rocks, and a ball point pen. Oh yeah, and that cell phone that I found the day after they picked up the body."

Slim maintained an emotionless expression. "Well, at least they've got some clues. Was the cell phone all wet?"

"I've seen worse," said Rick. "It didn't look too bad. I'm guessing they could have saved the SIM card. It was in this general area where I found the body but I can't say for sure who dropped it."

"Interesting," said Slim. "I guess it's not all that boring then. Have a good day."

Rick waved goodbye and went back to the wheelbarrow. Slim turned and walked down to the area of the beach that Rick kept pointing to while they were talking. He didn't have to search too hard. There were footprints in the sand all over the area that the deputies had been searching. Slim's main area of focus was the spot where an impression in the sand suggested that a small boat had landed. The site was mostly sand with a variety of different types of rocks widely scattered from the edge of the water to the scrawny plants that grew about five feet inland. It looked like a dicey spot to bring in a boat of any size. No wonder they wanted to get in and out so quickly, especially with an approaching wind storm. Slim didn't want to look too obvious so he didn't linger at the beach. He walked about a hundred feet down the shore and when he was out of sight of the others, he pulled out his cell phone and called Sammy. After a brief conversation he found a path that led to the lighthouse. When he got back up to the lighthouse he sat down under the picnic pavilion and opened a can of beer. The ferryboat captain was at the next table working on some sort of ledger. "Hot out there," said Slim. "I went for just a short walk on the beach and I got roasted." He smiled and tipped his beer can toward the captain. "I just heard about the excitement you had here a few days back. Did the cops search the woods or anything?"

The captain put down his pencil. "This is the first time I've been out here since it happened but when I talked to the owner and he said that they concentrated on the beach. With all this sand, there would have been footprints headed toward the woods if anybody would have gone that way. I'm sure they're not done. It's my understanding that they'll be back with a State Police Crime Scene Investigation Team."

"From what I've seen of the beach, there's not much left to pick through," said Slim.

"Well," said the captain, "I'm not a cop but I know that they can be pretty thorough. You can bet they'll be back and the State Cops don't like being shut out. They'll find something. I know they will."

Chapter 24

Slim and Sammy sat across from one another while Slim related the events of the day. Sammy agreed that taking the cruise to the island was a good idea.

"The cell phone is a serious concern," said Sammy. "The only number that he had for me was one of those untraceable trac phones. I usually keep them less than a week and then ditch them. I burned the one that Henry had the number for a couple of days ago. We had an agreement that my name wouldn't be anywhere in the address book on his phone. Finding that phone shouldn't lead the cops to us but it still makes me nervous because it could give them a name to work with. Besides, he may have a dozen other numbers stored in that phone that could somehow be connected to me or to others in the organization. "

"I'm pretty sure he never had my number," said Slim. "But there are other things to worry about besides cell phones. The skipper of the ferry boat says that they're expecting a State Police investigating team to visit the island any day now. He figures that they'll dig up things that the sheriff's guys missed."

"What's your feeling?" asked Sammy. "They gonna find anything?"

"Well, I tried not to look too obvious when I was checking out the scene," said Slim. "The area is pretty sparse, mostly sand. It would be pretty easy to spot anything laying there but on the other hand, with the wind blowing the way it was a lot of stuff could be buried under the sand. According to your guys, they were only on the island long enough to drop off the body. There was a storm coming up and they were in a tiny rowboat, it was just like a ten foot dink or something. The beach looked pretty clean to me."

"Okay, what about our other problem?" asked Sammy. "The guy they call Winston. Anything new on him?"

"I haven't talked to Lefty yet," said Slim. "We try to keep these conversations off of the phones. I'm going to meet with him tonight and see what's up."

"Good," said Sammy. "I'll want you to be here first thing tomorrow morning. I'll have to get things going in Bay City out on the street but that should all be set up before eight o'clock. I expect to be here by eight thirty. I'll see you then."

Chapter 25

Deputy Ross announced at the morning meeting that the Sheriff had requested assistance from the State Police in the investigation and that a representative would be there within the hour for a thorough briefing.

"Why would he think we need help?" asked Sid. "I thought we were doing just fine on our own."

"My guess is that it's something political," said the deputy. "I protested too but the boss said that it was his decision and something about a spirit of cooperation."

"Will I still be part of it?" asked Jennifer.

"I don't see why not," said Deputy Ross. "You've kept impeccable records of everything that has happened up to this point and the state is only sending one sergeant, at least for now. I'm sure he won't be interested in taking notes."

"Is it going to be a local guy? Someone you know?" asked Sid.

"Nope. He's coming from Lansing."

A soft knock on the door announced the arrival of State Police Detective Sergeant Duffield. He was a giant of a man with soft eyes and a Santa Claus smile. He certainly didn't look like a cop. "I'm the bastard from the home office," he said with a laugh. He placed his briefcase on a table, shook hands with everyone, and took a seat without waiting for an invitation. He began. "I want you to know right away that I'm not here to second guess you or to undermine any of the work that you've been doing. I have the utmost respect for your professionalism. I've familiarized myself with all of you through the reports and meeting minutes that the sheriff sent. I believe that you've done a thorough job. About the only thing I'm sure that I can help you with is resources and we've got a lot of them. After I hear everything that you folks have to say, I'll bring you up to speed on the results of the testing we've done on the materials that you've provided. Some of it may impress you."

Deputy Ross made all the formal introductions and then gave a very in depth report on every phase of the investigation, even including the flower shop owner and the gay orderly from the hospital. Duffield interrupted a few times to have points clarified. The extensive narrative took them up to their lunch break and Sid invited them all to the Peppermill restaurant for a meal on the Health Department.

Small talk during the meal revealed that Sergeant Duffield was born in Detroit and spent summers at his grandparents lakefront cottage near Caseville. He talked about his fond memories of diving off the raft that was anchored out front and dragging the twelve foot aluminum boat into the water and then rowing out a hundred yards or so from the beach and catching buckets full of Perch. "I guess they're mostly gone now," he said.

"Not really, they're just harder to find," said Jennifer.

When they returned to the office, Sergeant Duffield was all business. "I have a report for you folks as well and I'm hoping that you'll be satisfied with what we've come up with so far, even if it makes a lot more work for you."

"Okay, let's hear it," said the deputy.

The detective pulled a thick report from his briefcase. "I'll let you have this after I make my presentation and you can make copies for your team. Let's talk about the cell phone that was found on the beach. It's a trac phone and we've established that it was sold to a Henry Mason from Tawas City, directly across the Bay from Caseville. First of all there were absolutely no telephone numbers stored in the memory and most, almost all of the calls made from this phone were pretty useless to this investigation. They were to pizzerias and places like mail order clothing stores. The most common number dialed was to a marina where the subject kept a thirty-four foot cabin cruiser. As a matter of fact, the very last call made from this phone was to that marina the day before you discovered the body. We have a team of investigators at that marina with a warrant this morning conducting interviews and going over the boat. I'll have more on that after we hear from them. We'll also have twenty four hour surveillance on the boat in case anybody shows up.

Another very interesting thing is that there were three unanswered calls made to this phone from another trac phone over the next two days. We haven't been able to establish who owns that particular phone but we have acquired its current use record. Here's where it gets interesting. Someone used that phone just yesterday to contact a third anonymous trac phone in the Bay City area and based on the tower that the signal bounced off of, it looks like that call may have been placed from Charity Island."

"So let me get this straight," said Sid. "Somebody was trying to reach the phone that was picked up on the beach starting on the day it was found and for another day or so beyond that. And whoever was trying to reach it likely made a call to someone else yesterday from Charity Island?"

"You got it," said Duffield. "We're still trying to identify the owners of the other two trac phones but so far all we know is that they were purchased at different Walmart stores. Not holding my breath on that one."

"You've already told us a lot of things we didn't know," said Deputy Ross. "This is the first we've heard about the cabin cruiser. I'm really curious about that. I wonder if it has a dinghy?"

"We wondered the same thing," said Duffield. "It's on the list of things to check and labeled special attention. There ought to be plenty of DNA on that boat as well. Might be a more important clue than the cell phone. I'll make sure that you guys get the full report, including pictures.

I've been working with the two guys who are checking things out at the marina for almost five years. They were handpicked by me when I got the authorization to put together a deep investigating team. I have a pretty much free hand to run things as I see fit. Our record has been pretty good, excellent as a matter of fact.

Tomorrow, the guys will be here with me and we're planning to make a trip over to the island. I'd be pleased if all of you folks would be willing to accompany us."

"Put me down as a yes," said Jennifer. I'm getting used to that island life. Even thinking about a grass skirt."

Chapter 26

The investigating team met at the Caseville marina early the next morning. Sergeant Duffield waved a handful of papers and announced, "I'll be providing the entertainment on this trip and I'm sure you'll all find it interesting."

With three State Police officers, one Deputy Sheriff, a medical examiner and his secretary aboard, the twenty foot runabout was full but not overcrowded as they cast off the lines and slowly maneuvered up the no wake channel. Once they were in the bay and the boat comfortably on plane, Duffield unfolded the papers and said, "Preliminary results from yesterday's visit to the marina in Tawas. Search of the cabin yielded a bloodstained tee shirt. There was a considerable amount of sand on the tee shirt as well. The shirt has been sent to the lab for processing. There were two different sets of fingerprints found all over the boat. One belonged to Henry Mason and the other set has been submitted to be cross checked with the data base for possible identification. A forensic team has been requested to survey the boat for DNA samples.

The interview with the caretaker of the marina revealed that Henry Mason is a former employee. His position was reduced due to downsizing about two years ago but he still serves as a fill-in during the busy seasons doing launches in the spring and haul-out and winterizing in the fall. Henry's boat had been a storage seizure because of three years of unpaid fees. Mr. Mason was able to purchase it by paying the winter fees. He receives free dockage in lieu of wages for his part time work. The boat left the harbor sometime in the afternoon last Monday and returned after a severe windstorm at some point during the pre-dawn hours of Tuesday. Mason was raised on the lakeshore and his dad was a commercial fishing charter skipper. He is considered an expert seaman who knows the local waters very well and is frequently known to leave port in less than ideal weather conditions."

"The tee shirt certainly sounds interesting," said Deputy Ross. "Hopefully the blood sample will match up with the traces that Doctor Benson found in the beach sand."

"And the tissue that came off of that rock that I picked up on the beach," said Sid.

"Can we get a copy of your report?" asked Jennifer.

"Give me your email," said Duffield. "I'll make sure that you have everything as soon as we get it."

When their boat had wound its way through the entrance channel to the island there was almost no place left to dock. All of the spaces were filled with other boats. They tied up to the corner of a pier and climbed to the dock.

"I thought that it was rare for visitors to arrive in their own boats," said the deputy. "This isn't a public dock, it belongs to the guy who owns the lighthouse and the ferryboat."

"I just hope it's not newspaper people," said Sid.

There was a good size group of men and women gathered in the picnic pavilion who seemed to be conducting some kind of meeting. When they saw men in police uniforms headed their way, the talking stopped and they waited until the new visitors were standing in front of them. "Can we help you, officers?" asked the man who seemed to be in charge.

"I was about to ask you the same question," said Duffield.

"I'm Fred Sanders and we're here on authority of the United States Government," said the man.

Duffield put his hands on his hips. "In what capacity?"

The man pulled a document from his back pocket. "The U.S. Fish and Wildlife Service. We're here to do research on the White Pelican discovery. Our mission will take precedent over whatever you're doing here, it's highly important." The man had a smile on his face.

Sergeant Duffield's demeanor abruptly changed. "Be informed that your birds are not more important that our homicide investigation and if you get in our way, you will be arrested and charged with interfering with a law enforcement felony investigation. And that is not negotiable."

"But we have federal authorization," protested the man.

"I didn't stutter," said Duffield. "If you give us any trouble at all, you'll be calling your attorney from a jail cell. Oh, and you'll be taken to the mainland aboard an open boat with your hands handcuffed behind your back. This lake can be pretty unpredictable. It can kick up in a heartbeat." He motioned for the others in his team to follow as he turned toward the beach. "Lead the way," he said to Sid.

Walking toward the shoreline, Duffield pulled out his cell phone and hit the number for State Police headquarters in Lansing. "Hello. Can you put me through to Lieutenant Elam please?"

Sid pointed out the spot where the body had been located and the other related details. Duffield raised questions regarding where the cell phone was found and asked Deputy Ross to show where he picked up the ballpoint pen. They were still examining the scene when Fred Sanders from the federal wildlife service came strolling up the beach holding a cell phone in his outstretched hand. "My boss wants to talk to you," he said.

Duffield sighed, took the phone from him and put it up to his ear. He listened for a few minutes and then recited the Michigan State Police Headquarters telephone number. "Ask them for Lieutenant Elam of the special investigations division and he'll tell you just how to go about filing your complaint. As of now this is my jurisdiction and any more interference from your damned birdwatchers could result in multiple arrests. You can either wait for us to complete our work here or the entire island will be quarantined. You can fight that in court if you wish but by the time you get done with it, your pelicans or penguins or whatever you're studying will be vacationing in Brazil. It would be most beneficial for all involved parties if your people would refrain from interfering with law enforcement officers engaged in a felony investigation." He handed the phone back to the Fish and Wildlife researcher, pointed his finger directly in his face and said, "You won't get another warning."

Neither of the other state policemen nor the deputy paid any attention to the confrontation. They were concentrating on the beach area, one of them with a metal detector. It didn't take long for the metal detector to begin squealing. The policeman produced a small trowel and began probing gently at the sand.

"That's exactly where the body was found," said Sid. "Actually it's right under the spot."

The officer held the metal detector in one hand while dropping to his knees with the trowel in the other. Soon a small gold colored object was uncovered less than a half inch below the surface. It was a woman's vanity makeup case. He picked it up by the edges and deposited it in an evidence bag. "Might be significant," he said. "The lab can have a closer look."

Jennifer had a small digital camera and spent the whole time shooting pictures of the team as they scoured the beach. She had driven a wooden stake into the sand on the spot where the impression of the keel of a boat had been found on the first day of the investigation. It served as the reference point to identify the position of anything that might be discovered. Sid obliged her by pointing to the exact spots where the cell phone and ballpoint pen had been found along with the rock that may have caused the suspected foot injury. She was careful to include her baseline wooden stake in the background of each photo. She finally had to acknowledge that diligent police work had produced several significant clues well beyond what was discovered on the first day.

The team spent another two hours covering every inch of the beach within a fifty foot radius that included a good portion of knee deep Saginaw Bay. Finally Duffield called the group together for a meeting. "It looks like we've covered the area quite thoroughly and have come up with something that could be meaningful. It's entirely feasible that the compact that we found belonged to the deceased and was covered with sand as the result of the very active wind and surf that night. Hopefully we'll know more after we've had a chance to dig into it. We might as well load up and go home. And I don't want anybody saying goodbye to those birdwatchers."

Chapter 27

"I don't like it one bit," said Sammy. "How many trips do they have to make out to that damned island? And you say there was three state cops with them this time? It's gotta be that doctor driving this thing. Regular cops aren't that persistent. I'm afraid we're gonna have to do something about him."

Slim looked at his notebook. "One of the state cops was carrying a metal detector and another one had a shoulder bag. They had that stuff with them when they got on the boat and everything looked the same when they got back to the harbor. Doesn't look like they found anything new."

"What do you think we should do?" asked Sammy. "This guy is sniffing around way too much for my liking."

"We've covered our tracks pretty well," said Slim. "I can't think of anything we've left for them to follow. There's nothing on the girl's body to connect any of us, I wore latex gloves the whole time, don't know about Lefty. And as far as Henry and Paul goes, they're buried deep enough that there won't be any animals digging them up. The truck that belonged to Henry never had our scent on it and there just isn't anything else."

"What about the boat?" asked Sammy. "They had to have some kind of boat to get the body over to that island."

"Don't have a clue about that," said Slim. "It could have come from anywhere. We don't even know where their starting point was. I'd say that it's insignificant."

"How much longer are you going to be able to track that doctor with your GPS set up?" asked Sammy.

"It's got a thirty day lithium-ion battery in it so it should be good for close to another month." said Slim. "Those things usually last a lot longer than advertised. We should know all we need to know long before the battery dies."

"I want you to keep a close eye on this guy," said Sammy. "I'm getting a real strong feeling that we're going to have to take him out."

"You gonna want it quiet or messy?" asked Slim.

"If the need arises, we'll make the decision at that point," said Sammy. "Until then I just want him watched."

"Got it," said Slim.

"What about our other problem? This Winston over in Grand Rapids," said Sammy.

"Lefty's working on that. Trying to set up a meeting and talk to him. Want to see how much he knows and just how deep he's involved. Right now, I'm thinking he might need closer attention than that doctor. He had personal contact with Trish before we got to her. I want to know what they were talking about. Who knows, she may have spilled a lot of important stuff. We have to make sure there's no leaks."

Sammy folded his hands on the desk. "Up until now, I never felt the need to ask this but just how did it go when you carried out the Trish thing?"

Slim reached for the water bottle sitting on the corner of Sammy's desk. "Well, there's no such thing as an easy hit but we did our best to keep it simple. I was driving and I opened the door to the back seat and Lefty slid in beside her. I could tell she was nervous when we picked her up. She asked why, if it was a formal affair why neither one of us was wearing a tux. I said that we weren't invited to the party, that it was going to be a lot of well known, important people and we didn't fit in. Nobody said another word until we got off the main road and onto the little two lane gravel road where Henry and Paul were sitting in the pickup truck. They flashed their lights to let us know they were waiting. As soon as the car began slowing down, Lefty just reached over and grabbed her by the throat. She was unconscious before she ever knew what was happening. Once we were stopped, I came around and opened the door and Lefty dragged her out of the car without ever letting go of her neck. He wanted to be absolutely positive she was dead before wrapping her up and throwing her in the back of the truck. Lefty made sure that there was no pulse before he ever let go. It took longer than I expected but we wanted it to be done with. There was a little blue purse that matched her dress and we wrapped that up with the body. That's about it."

"No screaming or kicking?" asked Sammy.

"Nothing," said Slim. "She never knew what happened. Lefty closed off her arteries instantly and she was out cold in a couple of seconds. She didn't suffer if that's what you're worried about."

"That's good," said Sammy.

Chapter 28

State Police Sergeant Duffield sat down at the morning meeting in Deputy Ross's office and opened his notebook. "I'll be getting out of your hair soon and letting you get on with your investigation. I'll stay in touch and keep you up to date on lab findings and other stuff through email." He pointed his notebook toward Jennifer. "But I do have some good stuff to get you going before I leave. That compact that we found yesterday, I sent that back to Lansing with the officers who were with us on the island. The lab opened it up and found a slip of paper inside with a name and phone number on it. It's a Grand Rapids area code. He handed a note to the deputy.

"We know the name," said Ross. "Winston Bly, we were thinking about running him down and have a little chat but decided to soft pedal it until we knew more about him."

"There's more," said Duffield. "The evidence team that was assigned to check out the boat found a small blue purse that's the same color as the dress that the deceased was wearing. They were able to extract some usable DNA from a hankie that was inside the purse and they have that in the lab to see if it matches hers. Funny thing though, her fingerprints were nowhere to be found on the boat. If she was on board, she was likely dead before she got there. Our people aren't finished looking and so there's no telling what we might find next. But for now, that's it." He got up and shook hands, thanking everybody in the room for their professionalism. "I'd better get out of here, they're expecting me back in Lansing before lunch."

After the Sergeant left, Deputy Ross turned to Sid. "After working with you these past few days, I can see you're serious about this and would really like to contribute. Think you could handle an interview?"

"What do you have in mind?" asked Sid.

"Well, I thought that you and me could do a quick interview with the lady from the flower shop this afternoon, and if I'm satisfied with the way you handle it and if we're both comfortable, maybe you and your secretary can take a ride over to Grand Rapids and find out what Winston's connection is to this whole mess. It might look less threatening to him if a civilian showed up. Sound okay?"

Sid looked at Jennifer and she suddenly came alive. "Do I get to sit in on today's interview too? You know, to see how they're done."

Ross looked at Sid. "Why are you grinning? Do you have a problem with it?"

"No sir," said Sid. "The more experience the better."

"Okay then. You can go back to your office and catch up on your regular stuff as best you can and I'll try to set something up for this afternoon. I'll call you as soon as I get something firmed up. I'm shooting for about two o'clock, okay?"

"Got it," said Sid.

"Well, it looks like you're going to get your wish," said Sid as they pulled out of the sheriff's department parking lot.

"Hey. I was just sitting there. The deputy brought up the interview. It's part of the job," said Jennifer.

"I just hope that you behave yourself and don't ask any embarrassing questions," said Sid.

"Me? I'm the consummate professional," answered Jennifer.

Once they got back to the medical examiner's office, they barely talked to one another. Jennifer busied herself with the fifty-some fresh emails in her inbox while Sid opened the envelopes and scanned the twenty or so letters in the mail basket. Fortunately there was nothing too pressing in either accumulation of memos and letters. Jennifer was able to forward a few files, enough to satisfy any nervous client and to answer a couple of inquiries with standard form letters. They were quickly caught up and even had time for a quick stop at the drive-through.

"Are you excited?" asked Sid.

"About what? answered Jennifer.

"You're finally going to get a chance to see your very first transgender and probably even talk to her," said Sid.

Jennifer stuck the straw into her milkshake. "It's no big deal."

Sid's cell phone rang. It was Deputy Ross. Sid listened for a few seconds and then said, "See you there." He turned to Jennifer. "Two o'clock. Sheriff's office."

Chapter 29

Slim and Lefty were enjoying the scenic drive across the state, headed for Battle Creek and a meeting with Lefty's connection. The man they were going to meet was an upper level drug supplier and had insisted that they have a face to face meeting on his turf before he would go any farther. Given the business they were in, it wasn't an unusual request.

"Does this friend of yours actually know Winston, or what?" asked Slim.

"I know that they've talked to one another in the past," said Lefty. "But I don't know if they're friends or anything like that. My buddy seems to know a lot about him so I'd say they were at least acquainted. Actually, Winston is a friend of my buddy's boss, the number one man. I guess they grew up together."

They pulled up in front of what looked like a typical working man's bar that sat on a corner in an industrial neighborhood directly across the street from a small factory. The door stood wide open and there was no screen door. When they entered the place, it was obvious that they had just missed a lunchtime crush. The bartender was working at clearing all the beer bottles and shot glasses from the bar while a woman pushed a small cart from table to table collecting empty plates, soup bowls, and silverware. Neither one looked up when Slim and Lefty walked through the door.

A man was sitting alone in a corner booth wearing a sport coat and tie with a hat perched high on his head. He motioned for them to join him. It took a few seconds for Lefty's eyes to adjust to the dim light and recognize his friend. He tapped Slim on the shoulder and pointed. The men strolled over to the booth and sat down across from the guy who was just finishing a hamburger. Lefty made the introductions identifying his acquaintance as Rudy and ordered a round of beers from the bartender who had finally noticed them.

After the drinks had been delivered Rudy said, "Welcome to my office. So what's your interest in Winston?"

Lefty answered. "We have a client in the Bay City area who would like to know a little more about Winston. Seems that he's been in contact with some of our client's employees and we'd like to know the nature of their relationship."

"I don't imagine that you're willing to reveal the identity of your client, are you?" said Rudy.

Slim took over. "Due to the sensitivity of his business, he prefers to remain anonymous. I'm sure you understand."

Rudy tapped his fingers on the table. "Understand. I've got the same sort of situation. So are you looking for information or an introduction?"

"If the information is good enough, I'd rather do it that way. I don't need to meet him unless I can't get a handle on where he stands," said Slim. "So far you're the only one who knows that we're interested. The less people involved the better."

"Rudy nodded. "Okay, let's have your questions."

Lefty looked at his notes. "What's Winston's connection with the Grand Rapid's organization?"

"None, he's not part of it in any way. He just happens to know the big man from way back when they were kids on the street together. Word is, he saved the boss from a group of street thugs who were trying to kill him a long time ago. It's a deep friendship, nothing more."

"He wouldn't be doing any public relations work or anything like that?" asked Slim.

"Winston stays clear of anything to do with promoting the organization," said Rudy. "He's even been known to discourage people from joining them. The boss says that if Winston can chase them off, he wouldn't want them around anyway."

"How well do you know him? Ever go partying with him? We've heard that likes to hang out at some fancy club over in Lansing," said Slim. "Know anything about that?"

"We have a few drinks together once in a while but we ain't what you'd call close friends. Winston makes really good money with his store but he doesn't like the neighborhood to think he's a party animal," said Rudy. "He prefers they only see his hard working side. He gets out of town when he wants to kick up his heels. He's not wild by any stretch of the imagination and has plenty of self control, never embarrasses himself. He wants to have that serious businessman image. I knew he always goes somewhere else to enjoy a night on the town but until you told me, I didn't know it was Lansing."

"How about women?" asked Slim. "He have a girlfriend?"

"He talked about one the last time I saw him," said Rudy. "Said she was a real knockout but a little on the young side. I guess he was helping her out with some kind of crazy situation, sort of counseling her if you know what I mean. From the way he talked, he was hoping to be able to help her get past whatever her problem was and then see if she was interested in lighting things up."

"Did he ever give you her name?" asked Slim.

Rudy turned his head back and forth trying to remember, then snapped his fingers. "Trish, her name is Trish."

Chapter 30

Deputy Ross had one more call to make before he expected the lady from the flower shop to arrive. He took the note that Sergeant Duffield had given him and dialed Winston Bly's number.

"Hello?" Winston answered on the third ring.

"Hello, this is Deputy Richard Ross from the Huron County Sheriff's Department. Do you have a moment to talk?"

"Whatever you need," said Winston.

"We're investigating a situation that was transferred to us from another county and I was hoping to be able to send one of our representatives over to interview you. Are you willing to help us?"

There was a pause. Then Winston answered. "What's it about? Was it this county?"

"No, we didn't get the referral from Kent County but I'm afraid I can't discuss details without a signed confidentiality consent agreement. I can tell you that the interviewer will be a civilian in a private, unmarked vehicle and is willing to meet at a location of your choosing."

"Can you tell me if it's a criminal investigation?" asked Winston.

"The investigation involves a crime but at this point I can't disclose any more. Can we count on you?"

"Well, I suppose," said Winston. "Can we meet at a restaurant? Some place public?"

"It's you're choice," said Ross. Just give me an address and time, preferably around lunch hour and my people will be there."

"All right. Let's make it at the Golden Wok on Beltline Ave. I don't have the address. Noon okay?"

"We'll get the address and see you there," said Ross. "There will be a reservation in the name of Doctor Sydney Benson. Ask for his table."

Sid and Jennifer arrived at the Sheriff's office about twenty minutes ahead of schedule.

"Just what are you hoping to learn from Marsha?" asked Sid.

"Well," said the deputy, "considering the fact that they've both undergone the same, unusual operation, I figure that they likely felt some sort of common bond and could very well have shared thoughts that they wouldn't talk about with anyone else, even family."

"Maybe," said Jennifer. Both men looked at her. She continued. "Their bodies might be female but their DNA would still be male and men don't discuss intimate things like that."

"It's possible," said Sid. "But this is a unique situation and there's a lot more than just the physical aspect. There would be things like merging into the social scene, the hesitancy to assimilate, self confidence. All sorts of cultural challenges. They'd have plenty to talk about. A lot would depend on how well Marsha has adjusted."

"We'll know soon enough," said Deputy Ross. "She should be walking through the doorway any minute now."

A gentle knock on the door announced Marsha's arrival. "Come in," said the deputy.

A smiling woman stepped through the door and looked around the room. "My, my. All these people. Am I that important?"

Deputy Ross stood up and offered his hand. "I think

you've met Doctor Benson and this is Jennifer Garland, his administrative assistant."

Marsha sat down. "So just what is it that you want from me?"

Deputy Ross motioned for Sid to begin the interview. "We know almost nothing about the victim. We don't know her circle of friends, her job, her hangouts, or her personality. Since you knew her better than anyone else we've talked to outside of her immediate family, we were hoping you could help us paint a picture of her."

"I'm afraid that we weren't terribly close," said Marsha. "I was concentrating on trying to help her work her way into her new life. I'll help you all I can. I'm just worried that it might not be much."

"Well, let's find out," said Sid. "Do you know who she hung out with?"

"As far as I know, she didn't have many really close friends," said Marsha. "She knew me because her transformation counselor had put us in contact. She had had lunch once with me and that hospital orderly who introduced you to me. There may have been two or three others but I don't know who they would be."

"Was the orderly a friend?" asked Sid.

"I don't really know how close they were but she was quite comfortable around him. You know, joking and teasing. I only met him that one time," said Marsha.

That's strange," said Sid. "He kind of led me to believe that you were her friend and he just sort of tagged along."

"Oh they knew each other," said Marsha. "That was obvious. I think she may have even been his drug connection. He's quite a pot smoker from what I heard."

"You mentioned that you thought she was involved in the drug trade," said Sid. "How do you happen to know that?"

"One of the few times she talked about that was when she told me that she was going to get out of that business. Said she didn't need it any more," said Marsha. "I guess it was big money and she had only become involved so that she could pay off her medical bills. These transformations don't come cheap, you know."

"Any idea who she worked for?" interjected Ross.

Marsha rubbed her forehead. "She was pretty secretive about that aspect of her life. Not something she was proud of. She did let a name slip one time though. But I'm not sure if she worked for this guy or if he was just another dealer. She called him Sammy."

"Did she say when she was going to get out of the business?" asked Sid.

It was as if a light came on inside Marsha's brain. "You know, she and I just talked about that a week or so back. She had found a man, a man who was recommended to her by a former addict. I understand that this man had acted as an intermediary between suppliers and customers who wanted to straighten out their lives but were worried about retaliation from their suppliers and had been quite successful. He had an unusual name. Was it Winthrop? No, that's not it. It was Winston."

"Did this Sammy and Winston know one another?" asked Ross.

"I seriously doubt it," said Marsha. "I think Trish told me that she was meeting Winston somewhere in Lansing and I know that she was doing her drug business mostly around Bay City and Saginaw so that's where I'd assume that Sammy is."

"We'll be contacting the Bay County Sheriff's Department to see if they have a Sammy on their radar," said Ross.

"How about a boyfriend?" asked Sid. "She ever mention anybody?"

"My goodness, no," said Marsha. "She wasn't nearly ready for anything that daring. It can take years to advance that far."

Deputy Ross fished a business card out of his wallet and handed it to Marsha. "Thank you very much. I'd like you to take my card and call me if you should happen to think of anything else. You've already helped us understand a few things much better. We'll let you know as much as we can about how our investigation is going. I'd like to keep you in the loop just in case we find something that jars a memory."

"I understand," said Marsha. "I loved Trish and will do anything I can to help."

After Marsha left, Sid turned to Jennifer and said. "Well?"

Jennifer simply shrugged.

Chapter 31

Sid picked up Jennifer at her apartment building at the north end of town. It was eight o'clock in the morning and she was waiting outside with a computer bag slung over her shoulder and a travel mug in her hand.

"Been waiting long?" asked Sid

"Less than a minute," said Jennifer. "You've got your timing down pretty good."

"Just lucky," said Sid. "You have breakfast yet?"

"My eyes aren't open enough to see what I'm eating yet," said Jennifer. "I figured I'd nag you into stopping somewhere along the way."

"If you can hold out for an hour or so, we can grab something to eat before we jump on the expressway," said Sid.

The ride across Michigan was pleasant with the sun at their backs. They rolled into Grand Rapids about twenty minutes before noon. Sid's GPS told them that they were seven minutes away from the Golden Wok.

When they walked in, the hostess said. "Sit anywhere you like."

Before she was able to disappear, Sid said. "We're supposed to have a reservation."

"Oh yeah," said he hostess. "We almost never do that. You must be Doctor somebody, right?"

"Benson," said Sid. "Doctor Sidney Benson and another guest will be joining us soon."

The hostess grabbed three menus from the reservation desk and led them to a secluded table tucked in a far away corner. "Can I get you something to drink while you're waiting?" she asked.

"Tea" said Sid. "You gotta have tea in a Chinese restaurant. It's always the best."

While Jennifer was examining the menu, a tall thirty something man wearing dark slacks, a pale blue Oxford shirt and Herringbone Tweed sport coat walked in off the street, spoke with the hostess for a moment and then headed directly for the table.

He smiled and stuck out his hand as he approached. "Doctor Benson? I'm Winston Bly. I understand that you'd like to talk."

Sid stood, introduced Jennifer and said. "Have a seat. Today's your lucky day. Lunch is on Huron County. Order whatever you like and don't worry about the price."

Winston slid into a chair. "I'm really curious why you would come all the way from Huron County just to talk to me. I've never even been to Huron County."

"I'm the Huron County Medical Examiner and Jennifer here is my secretary. We're here to investigate a crime that actually took place outside of our jurisdiction. It sort of got dumped on us."

"Okay," said Winston. "But what has it got to do with me?"

"It's come to our attention that you have had some contact with a Patricia Scott, otherwise known as Trish. Is that correct?"

"That's true. She asked me to represent her in negotiations with an employer. I do that sort of thing from time to time," said Winston. "We've only met a couple of times and there has been no action taken at this point."

"When did you see her last?" asked Sid.

Winston stared at the ceiling for a moment then said, "I don't remember the exact day but it must have been about a week ago. She was going to talk to her employer and see if she could set up a meeting between me and him. She said it might take a few days. I haven't heard anything from her yet."

"Was there anything between you two?" asked Sid. "I mean was it all business or was there a social relationship?"

"At this point all I'm doing is trying to help her resolve a difficult situation," said Winston. "She's a kind and beautiful girl and I certainly wouldn't mind getting to know her on a different level but right now our association is purely professional."

"I'd better not put this off any longer," said Sid. "Trish Scott was murdered. Her body was found on an island in Saginaw Bay six days ago. Because of some special circumstances, I've been attached to the official investigation."

Winston was clearly shaken by the revelation. He dropped the menu on the table and looked at Sid, then Jennifer. His mouth opened but he seemed unable to speak. Tears welled in his eyes and finally he said. "No. It isn't true, it can't be. She was looking forward to life with more enthusiasm than anyone I ever met. It just can't be."

"I wish it weren't true," said Sid. "But we need to find out who killed her and why. Who was this employer that she had a problem with?"

"I can't say that I know who he is," said Winston. "The only name I ever heard was Sammy. I don't even know where to find him. I got the impression that he was in the Bay City area but even that was kind of vague."

"What kind of business is he in?" asked Sid.

Winston leaned in. "Can you guarantee me any kind of immunity?"

"Not if you're an accessory to a felony," said Sid. "But if

you're uninvolved and just have information, there should be no problem."

Winston looked around to see if anyone was within hearing distance. "It's my understanding that he's some sort of drug kingpin because he seems to call all the shots. He's really low profile. As far as Trish knew, he wasn't known to the local cops and Trish was one of his distributors. She had started out as a street level dealer but showed a knack for staying invisible to the law. I guess that she had been promoted a few times and had been given her own territory and stable of dealers. She was kind of frantic because she had the feeling that the boss was going to give her another promotion. It scared her because she already knew too much about the organization and if she got any closer to the top, they'd never turn her loose. The boss invited her to attend some kind of formal affair and she figured he'd use the occasion to offer her some higher position. She planned to head him off at the pass and have him meet with me before making any new proposals. She was worried about being assassinated."

Sid and Jennifer looked at one another as the waitress arrived at the table. Jennifer said, "Can you give us a few minutes?" The waitress nodded and headed back toward the kitchen.

"How did you come to be involved in the first place?" asked Sid.

"It's kind of a long story but, as a kid I was your classic homeless teenager," said Winston. "I lived on the street and survived by my wits. I eventually found a job that came with some crude but secure living quarters. One of my street buddies came to me one day and asked for some help. He didn't explain his predicament and I didn't ask. We'd been through a lot together when we were both foraging for every-thing. You learn not to ask questions. He needed help, a place to hide out for a couple of weeks and so I let him bunk at my place. He told me that I likely saved his life by hiding him out and that he'd never forget it. He eventually became an extremely powerful man. Now, you've got to understand how street people are. He never told me his business and I've never asked. The word is that he's one of the biggest drug dealers in the state but me and him have never discussed it. He knew from the beginning that I was a straight and narrow type guy so he never burdened me with his secrets. We both like it that way. We still live in the old neighborhood. I now own the place that I was working in back then, it's a beer and liquor store that sells groceries, meat, and produce with an upstairs apartment. He has a big fancy house on the same block. We talk from time to time but just about things like sports and stuff. Every once in a great while he might ask if I've seen any strangers hanging around but he never tells me why he needs to know.

Anyway, every now and then I'll run into a kid who seems headed for trouble. You know, messing with drugs and that kind of thing. I've been able to help a few of them straighten out their lives and get away from all that crap. There have been a couple who were afraid that the mob would be coming after them but after I talked to my buddy and promised that they wouldn't create any headaches, the heat dropped off. In any case I eventually developed a rep-utation as a mediator for anyone with a substance abuse problem. Even the cops have heard about it and I seem to have their blessing. I have absolutely nothing to do with the drugs or the dealers and everybody respects that. I'm sure that having an influential friend comes into play but there has never been any sort of arrangement."

The waitress returned to the table and both Sid and Jennifer ordered lunch. Winston declined saying that the news about Trish had stolen his appetite.

"So you have never met Sammy?" asked Sid.

Winston shook his head. "I don't even know what he looks like. All I know is that he moves around a lot. Trish told me that she's never met him at the same place more than a couple of times. I don't know if he's like that with everyone though. She said that he might be open to meeting with me but only at some neutral and really public site. I guess we'll never know. These drug guys never really trust anyone and they constantly spy on one another. I'm wondering if they had a tail on Trish and saw her meeting with me. Something as innocent as seeing the two of us sitting in a bar together could be enough to tip over a paranoid mind."

"So you have been meeting her in a bar somewhere?" asked Sid.

"Yeah," said Winston. "We met a total of three times at a place called Rum Runners in Lansing. It's an upscale place with a tropical theme and caters mainly to the college crowd. I never had the feeling that we were being watched."

"If somebody was watching you, do you think that they might connect you with your friend in Grand Rapids?" asked Sid.

"I've never kept my friendship with him a secret," said Winston. "Because of my business, I know a lot of people and I'm sure that many of them are aware. The mob guys all know."

"Can we count on you to work with us on getting this situation resolved?" asked Sid.

"I want this thing solved as badly as you but I can't help you with anything to do with the drug business. It's something that I'm willfully ignorant about," answered Winston. He handed Sid his business card. "Call me if you need me and I'll make time to meet with you again." Winston got up and slowly walked out of the restaurant.

Chapter 32

Jennifer couldn't finish her order of shrimp egg foo yong and so she carried a take-out bag to Sid's truck in the parking lot. She waited until they were on the road to speak. "Well, what was your impression?"

Sid turned onto the expressway, "He seemed to be pretty straight forward, if you ask me. There was absolutely no doubt that he was surprised when I told him that Trish was dead. He sure has a weird relationship with the drug dealers and cops though. At least that should be easy to check out. I'll get with the deputy in the morning and see if he can find anything out."

Jennifer opened her laptop and brought up her file on the case. "I don't know if we learned anything helpful today other than establishing the fact that Trish and Winston have met and the location of those meetings. I guess it has to be put together with all the other stuff we've got to see if anything makes any sense. Didn't you tell me that this investigation had practically no clues to work with? No wonder you're not a cop."

Sid smiled. "We got a name that matches the one that both Trish's brother and the flower shop owner gave us too. That's got to be significant. Somewhere on some police department's database, I'll bet there's a drug dealer named Sammy. I'd start with trying to locate him."

Jennifer yawned and reclined her seat. "Time for a nap. Wake me up when you figure it all out."

Sid drove for another hour in silence and then decided that it was time for a fuel stop. A truck plaza appeared on the horizon and Sid headed for the exit. Jennifer stirred, opened her eyes and said, "Are we there yet?"

"Just stopping for a fill-up," said Sid. "And while we're here I want to check the air in the tires. One of them has had a slow leak for the past couple of months. I had it fixed but I want to see how it's holding up."

"While you're doing that, I think I'll run inside and powder my nose," said Jennifer.

Sid started the gas pump and then rummaged through the glove compartment and emerged with an air pressure gage in his hand. He began checking the tires with the left rear, then the left front, right front, and when he got to the right rear, he noticed something strange. On the frame of the truck there was a small box shaped object. It didn't look like anything that belonged there. He reached in and grabbed it to see if it would move and he could slide it from side to side. It was held in place with a magnet. He had no idea how long it had been there or if it was dangerous. He ran back to the cab and retrieved his cell phone, quickly pressing Deputy Ross's speed dial number.

"Hey, this is Sid," he yelled into the phone. "Somebody's been messing with my truck. I just found something scary. I think it might be booby trapped."

"Okay, calm down," said Ross. "Tell me what you've found."

"It's some kind of box," said Sid. "It's on the frame behind the rear tire. I think it has a magnet on it."

"I think I know what it is," said Ross, "is there anything written on it? Take a look but try not to move it."

Sid dug the flashlight out of the console in the truck and crouched by the rear wheel, cell phone up to his ear. "It says, Tracker"

"That's what I thought," said Ross, "don't disturb it. It's harmless. Somebody wants to know what you're doing all day. It's a GPS tracking unit. You're being followed."

Sid was stunned. "What? Why? Who?"

Ross chuckled. "All I can tell you is that it isn't me. Someone is very interested in your daily travels and if it's who I think it is, they will be very impressed with today's trip."

"What does that mean?" asked Sid.

"I think it means that you have aroused the interest of the killer. Don't touch that tracker, just leave it where it is and drive straight here. I'll provide you with a loaner vehicle until we figure this thing out. Where are you now?"

"I'd guess that I'm not too far west of Flint in a truck stop on I-69, probably two hours or so from your office."

"Give it about fifteen minutes before you leave and take the direct route here. You'll have an escort all the way."

By the time Jennifer walked out of the truck stop gift shop, Sid was back behind the wheel and had regained a reasonable amount of composure. Sid had never felt threatened before and this situation was quite unsettling. He did his best to appear totally calm.

Jennifer pulled the door open, jumped into the truck and squirmed into her seat belt. "What's the matter with you?" she asked.

Sid's laugh was almost involuntary. He looked at Jennifer and said, "You were gone so long, I was afraid you'd been kidnapped." He looked up and saw a Shiawassee County Sheriff's cruiser pull into the parking lot, its driver looking back and forth until he spotted the pickup truck. Sid flashed his lights and exited the driveway. In a few moments he was back on the expressway with the Sheriff's patrol car sitting comfortably in his rearview mirror.

"How were your tires?" asked Jennifer.

Sid was considerably more at peace with the presence of the law in sight. "Everything looked exactly as it should," he responded. "We should be back in town in less than a couple of hours. Not planning on any more stops."

"Are we going directly to the health center so I can pick up my car?" she asked.

"Naw," said Sid. "Deputy Ross called while you were in the gas station and he wants us to stop by the Sheriff's office first. Must want a debriefing session or something."

"Do I have to go?" asked Jennifer.

"I think you'd better," said Sid. "You're part of the team and you were present at the interview."

"That brings up another question," said Jennifer. "If you're officially working for the County Sheriff, are you being paid? More importantly, am I?"

Sid glanced at her sideways and remained silent as he drove.

Chapter 33

"I'm going to need to get your fingerprints on file," said Deputy Ross. "They'll be on that tracking device and we'll need to see who else's are on there."

"What are you talking about?" asked Jennifer.

Sid turned in his chair in the small deputy sheriff's office. "I didn't want to alarm you but when I was checking the tire pressure, I found something attached to the frame of the truck that definitely doesn't belong there."

Jennifer's face paled. "Something like what?"

"Nothing to be afraid of," said Ross. "It's only a transmitter that relays a satellite signal telling where the transmitter is. Somebody sitting in front of a computer screen can follow the little back box wherever it goes."

"You mean somebody like a stalker," shot back Jennifer. She turned to Sid. "That question about getting paid for this adventure is becoming more important by the minute."

Sid laughed and Deputy Ross held up his hand and said, "I'm actually surprised that the subject of compensation hasn't already been raised. I kind of anticipated it though and have placed it on the agenda for the next council meeting. It's not without precedent. We actually have a budget for contractors and it gets used from time to time. The city likes it because there are no benefits or commitments attached and the waivers relieve the county of liability under normal circumstances. I think you'll be able to look forward to some sort of financial recompense. I'll keep you informed."

"So what do we do about the black box?" asked Sid.

"Remember that State Police Sergeant, Duffield?" asked Ross. "He'll be here in the morning with his tech team to see what they can do with it. He claims that some of them can be hacked pretty easy. He wants to see what we've got. For now, you'll have to consider your truck impounded as part of the investigation. In the meantime you can take one of our undercover cars but I don't want you getting crazy with it. It might look like a family buggy but underneath it has all the interceptor hardware. I'd like to have you two back here by nine tomorrow morning and we'll go over the stuff you did today. We're accumulating a few more puzzle pieces every day and it's time to start putting them together to see if anything looks like a picture."

Jennifer was visibly uneasy as they drove back to the Health Department headquarters. Sid insisted they stop for a drink to give her a chance to settle down. "As soon as we get back to the office I want you to grab a flashlight and go over every inch of my car," said Jennifer. "You might not be too nervous about this but I sure don't want anyone knowing every move I make, especially since this is a homicide case."

"Good idea," said Sid. "I was every bit as jumpy as you when I first found the transmitter but I seriously doubt that anybody might bug your vehicle. There's no harm in being careful though. And if it makes you feel any better you can leave it parked right where it is and we can both use this car for the next couple of days."

"I don't know if I'm that paranoid," said Jennifer. "But if I see some stranger sitting in it when we get to the parking lot, I'll really freak out."

When they pulled in at the Health Department building, there was a County Sheriff patrol car, with both front doors open sitting next to Jennifer's car and two deputies busily scanning her car with detection wands. "Looks like they're way ahead of us," said Sid. One of the deputies recognized Sid and waved.

"How did you know which car was hers?" asked Sid.

"Not too hard," said the deputy. "We knew her name and just looked it up. We've gone over everything and it looks like it's remotely possible that something might have been planted here and then removed. There is a spot on the frame that appears to have been recently wiped clean. I'm guessing it's from when she got her last oil change. I wouldn't get too excited. It's probably nothing. Can't say for sure but you may not be the only one they're interested in."

"To be honest, I can't understand why," said Sid. "We're really pretty small players in this whole thing. I wish we would have found that thing on my truck sooner though. Now they know that we were out in Grand Rapids today and if they know about Winston they'll want to know what we were doing there."

Jennifer stood with her hands on her hips for a moment and then pointed at her car. "Do you want me to open the doors so you can have a look inside?"

"Wouldn't hurt," said the deputy. He waited for Jennifer to drag her keys out of her purse and unlock the doors. The two deputies made quick work of sweeping the interior of the car and it came up clean.

"Oh, darn. I left my doggy bag in your truck," said Jennifer. "I was looking forward to that for supper. I love Chinese food."

"We can grab a quick bite somewhere before we head home," said Sid.

Jennifer followed Sid to the Hitching Post Bar where they chatted over tacos in a secluded booth. "I don't want you to get any big ideas," said Jennifer. "But I was wondering if I could stay at your place tonight. Do you have a spare bedroom?"

"Sure. You've never been to my house, have you?" asked Sid. "We can stop by your place and you can pack a few overnight things and then you can either follow me home or ride with me. Oh, and bring a bathing suit. We can go for a swim and maybe have a moonlight bonfire. It'll get your mind off things."

"I'd almost forgotten," said Jennifer. "Your house is right on the lake, isn't it?"

"Yup," said Sid. "At heart I'm nothing but a beach bum."

Chapter 34

Slim sounded anxious when he called Sammy's number. "We need to have a face to face as soon as possible. I'll be bringing Lefty along."

"Stop by the office at noon," said Sammy. Both men hung up without any more words.

"Looks like we might need a little talk with Winston Bly," said Slim. "By all appearances, he had lunch with our Medical Examiner yesterday at a restaurant in Grand Rapids. We tracked his vehicle out there yesterday and it was parked for about an hour and a half at an address that turns out to be a Chinese restaurant just a few blocks from Winston's store."

Sammy leaned forward and shook his head. "So many mistakes. And the biggest one of all might have been killing Trish. It very well may have been unnecessary. And I have to stand tall for that one. I was impulsive, so ready to believe that she was going to betray me. I didn't investigate it nearly thoroughly enough. And then I insisted that the body be left somewhere that it would be found just to make sure that the Grand Rapids organization would get the message. And the ironic thing is that they probably never knew that she existed. Two more men have died since then and it may not end there." He stood up and walked around the desk. "Any ideas?" he asked.

Lefty spoke up. "If you're looking to avoid more problems, I'm thinking that we might be able to arrange a get together with Winston and ask him what the meeting was all about. From what I've heard, he's the kind of guy who keeps his distance from both the cops and the mob. His only connection is with the head man over in Grand Rapids and that is strictly a personal relationship and has nothing at all to do with his business. If he told that doctor how things are, then maybe we've got nothing to worry about. My guy over on the west side might be able to set something up."

"It's a place to start," said Sammy. "I sure would like to get this thing put to rest without any more killing. So far, business hasn't suffered but if the cops come sniffing around we might have to shut everything down for a while and now is not a good time for anything like that. I'm in negotiations with some people down in the southeast corner of the state to take over a sizable chunk of territory down there that has become available for reasons that will remain unstated for now. But if everything goes according to plan, you two will be moving to a much nicer neighborhood."

"Another possible problem," said Slim. "The doctor's truck hasn't left the Sheriff Department parking lot since they got back to town. That bothers me. Makes me think maybe they've discovered the tracking device."

"What would that do?" asked Sammy.

"As far as I know, it would just mean that they would probably take it off and we couldn't see where he's going any more," said Slim. "I was wearing gloves when I attached it so there's no fingerprints to worry about, but I don't want him to know that he's being followed."

"Is there anything that they can trace?" asked Sammy. "I'm sure it has some kind of a serial number that will show where it was sold."

Slim shook his head. "Bought the whole set up at a flea market over a year ago. No paperwork at all. There's no way it can point to me."

Lefty joined in. "That girl was with him. Maybe they just took her car. That way they could shack up at her place overnight without his truck being parked outside. Keep the neighbors noses out of it if you know what I mean."

Sammy was on his feet and pacing now. "We're not sure whether the cops have found that tracking thing but just to be on the safe side I'm saying that we'll have to give the doctor plenty of space right now. If the cops did find that thing, Dr. Benson's head will be on a swivel for a few days. I suggest we get something going with Winston. See what he has to say."

Lefty called Rudy, his connection on the west side of the state and told him that he'd like to set up a meeting with Winston as soon as possible. Rudy agreed to get something going immediately. "We're available any time, anywhere," said Lefty. "We'll be there as soon as you can arrange something. And move as fast as you can. It's important."

Sammy returned to his desk and plopped down in the soft leather chair. "I'm not sure how I want to handle this," he said. "I don't like the idea of any more dead bodies but on the other hand if somebody starts getting too close we may not have a choice. This Winston and the doctor are the two I worry about the most. If your meeting with Winston happens soon, I only want one of you to go out there. Slim, I'd prefer that you'd meet with him. I want Lefty close by just in case."

"I know that you're worried that the doctor might have been spooked," said Lefty. "But I can keep an eye on him without him ever knowing that he's being followed. I've been doing this stuff for a long time. He won't catch on. I guarantee it."

"I'll take you at your word," said Sammy.

"Unless they make some kind of amazing discovery," said Slim. "The only murder they're aware of is Trish. It's pretty much a lock that they'll never find out anything about those two goons that we buried up north. As it stands right now, the cops are investigating one murder and there has been nothing at all to connect any of us."

Lefty's phone chirped. He put it in speaker phone mode. "Hello."

The voice on the other end asked, "Winston wants to know if this has anything to do with some girl that died recently."

Sammy looked at Lefty and nodded.

"Yeah, we're looking for a little information," said Lefty.

There was a pause and some muffled conversation in the background. "He says he doesn't really know anything but if you still want to talk you can meet him at Rum Runners in Lansing at eight o'clock tonight."

"Tell him to sit at the bar and someone will find him," said Lefty. "Eight o'clock." Lefty ended the call and turned to Slim. "I figure that you should play dumb like you haven't a clue about what happened. Make it sound like we think it was someone from his side of the state that killed her. Sound good?"

"Try to get a good feel for what he knows," said Sammy. "See how much he knows about that Grand Rapids outfit. I'm still not entirely convinced that they weren't trying to steal her from us."

"I'll get everything that he's got," said Slim.

Chapter 35

Sid waited in the car while Jennifer ran into her apartment. He was grateful that things had been slow in the Medical Examiner's office, it gave him time to get fully involved in the homicide investigation without any pressure from the office. He took the notebook out of his shirt pocket and began documenting the day's events. Thumbing back through his notes to the very beginning, he was amazed at just how much information had been gathered to this point. And the loose ends that were still out there told him that they had barely scratched the surface.

He was startled when Jennifer returned and jerked the car door open. She surveyed the interior of the Ford Taurus. "Maybe you can work out a trade with the Sheriff's Department," she said. "This baby is a whole lot nicer than the cab of your smelly old truck."

Sid stopped at a little place called The Oak Beach Pantry and picked up some hot dogs, buns, and marshmallows. When he climbed back in the car he turned to Jennifer. "It's been a long time since I've had a weenie roast on the beach. They're no fun when I'm all by myself, ya know. I've been living in a lakefront house for five years. Got the boat, a twenty footer with all of the accessories, got a jet ski, all those toys and I rarely ever use them because it seems like I'm alone all the time."

"Kind of a shame," said Jennifer.

They pulled into Sid's driveway, a winding asphalt path that ended at the door to an oversize three car garage with a second story. The garage was attached to what appeared to be at least a four bedroom house with a deck that wound around three sides of the building. The landscaping was sparse but tastefully done. Sid pulled the garage door opener from his briefcase, opened the door and drove inside, closing the door behind him.

"Wow," said Jennifer. "It's a lot nicer than I expected. How much lake frontage have you got here and what is that extra garage door for?"

"That door opens into a motor home bay, but I don't have one. I store the boat and jet ski in there in the winter," answered Sid. "And I've got one hundred twenty five feet of beach. Plenty of room for a volleyball court."

They entered through the laundry room, continued through the spacious kitchen and the small dining area and on to the main living room with two large windows facing the lake and a sliding glass door in between them. There was a short hallway leading to a bath that was adjacent to a den, also with a lake view. The den strongly resembled a man cave complete with leather couch, a large completely stocked bar, pool table, and a fifty five inch flat screen. A stone fireplace occupied most of one wall flanked by bookshelves filled with leather bound volumes. A desk and computer stood in a corner.

"No wonder you never go anywhere," said Jennifer. "It's cool but I'll bet there's lots of house cleaning needed in a place like this."

"Actually, I almost never lift a finger," said Sid. "I have this retired, married couple who are kind of caretakers. He was the groundskeeper and general handyman for an office complex and she handled the housekeeping staff at one of the local retirement homes. They're originally from Poland and still struggle with English a little. They drop by a couple of times a week and he handles all the outdoor chores while she cleans the inside. I pay a generous wage and they love the job. It supplements their pensions nicely.

This place has four bedrooms and two full baths on the second floor and normally only one of the bedrooms gets used. There's my room and then another one that I keep ready, just in case and the other two just need linens on the beds and they can be ready too."

"It's nice," said Jennifer.

"It's lonely," said Sid.

From the spacious deck overlooking Lake Huron it was only three steps down to the limestone patio and another three to the beautiful sand beach. A fire ring surrounded by log benches sat off to the right with a stack of split red oak piled neatly behind it. The scene was completed by a rustic looking table that sat on sturdy legs anchored in the sand.

A narrow dock extended out to a boat hoist cradling a sleek looking Glastron GT205 and on the other side of the dock was a smaller hoist that secured a red, white, and black Sea-Doo Jet Ski.

"There's a couple hours of daylight left," said Jennifer. "I'm going up to the house to change and then get a little sun."

As they walked around the deck to go into the house, the highway came into clear view. Sid didn't pay any attention to the old Toyota that slowly cruised by the house. Jennifer was silent but watched the car without blinking until it was out of sight. The man driving never glanced in the direction of Sid's house but the video camera nestled in the crook of his arm recorded every detail.

Sid lowered the boat into the calm water and Jennifer climbed aboard. She instantly curled up in the plush seat across from the operator's console. Sid sat down behind the wheel and powered up the engine. As soon as he was well clear of the hoist, he brought it on plane and flicked on the stereo system. He selected some reggae music to give the ride an exotic feel.

Jennifer pointed to a distant green line that crawled across the horizon like a caterpillar. "What's that?" she asked.

Sid grinned. "That's Charity Island, your home away from home. Don't tell me you don't recognize it."

"Sure looks different from this far away," said Jennifer. "Such a peaceful looking island. It's a shame somebody had to die there. But, you know, it hasn't spoiled the serenity or the beauty of the region. I thought it was a beautiful island. Do you think we'll get another chance to visit it?"

"I wouldn't rule out anything in this investigation. As far as it being soiled by a murder, the world is not a fair place," said Sid. "I'm sure that throughout history, there are plenty of sad stories about almost every island in just about every lake and every ocean."

After a gentle cruise along the shoreline, Sid negotiated his way back into the boat hoist, raised the craft out of the water and finished covering up the boat just before the sun settled into the bay. It didn't take long before there was a crackling fire glowing in the fire pit on the beach and the first hotdog was dropped in the sand, washed off in the lake and returned to the table. Soft music played in the background and honest laughter rang out from the beach as marshmallows flared on the ends of sticks and two county employees forgot the rest of the world and discovered a new universe. The office would be different tomorrow and the man cave would be different tonight. The sunset and the simple bonfire had worked their magic as they had for countless other couples on countless other beaches on countless other summer nights. The bonfire flickered into glowing embers.

Jennifer looked into Sid's eyes and said. "Your beach doesn't have to be lonely any more."

"I know," he said. "I know."

Chapter 36

Slim looked at his watch. It was seven thirty. He liked being early, the first one there. It gave him a chance to scan his surroundings thoroughly. Slim was pretty good at spotting the enemy no matter how good they were at blending in. He had his methods. There were certain keys he looked for and his system never failed him. Rum Runners was clean tonight, almost empty. He relaxed and ordered a beer.

At exactly eight o'clock Winston entered the bar. He stopped just inside the door and surveyed the room, a habit he learned from his years of living on the streets. He walked over to the bar and found a barstool in a row of empty barstools, sat down and ordered a Bloody Mary.

Slim slowly wandered down the bar and stopped behind Winston. He offered his hand and Winston took it. "I'm Slim a friend of Trish's. You're Winston, right?"

"That's me," said Winston. "Would you like to take a booth so we can have a little privacy?"

"Yeah, that'd be fine," said Slim. He picked up his beer and followed Winston to a corner booth.

"Are you here to tell me what happened or ask what happened?" said Winston.

Slim smiled. "I was hoping you could shed some light on things. Trish was an important part of our company and as far as I can tell the cops aren't getting anywhere. We know that Trish has been talking to you and want to know what it was all about."

"What's your interest in all of this?" asked Winston.

"She was an associate and a dear friend," said Slim. "We'd like to find out what happened to her and we have an uneasy feeling about her involvement with your Grand Rapids organization."

"To begin with," said Winston. "I'm not involved with any organization in Grand Rapids or anywhere else. I'm an independent businessman. Not part of a gang. Not involved in drugs, and I only heard about Trish earlier today. I'm afraid I'd be of no use to you." He started to get up.

Slim put his hand on Winston's arm. "Please forgive me," he said softly. "I didn't mean to insinuate anything but some friends of ours have said that they've seen you and Trish together and when they checked you out, it was discovered that one of your close friends has, shall we say, a reputation. Maybe it doesn't mean anything but it made us curious. We just wanted to know how deep it went."

Winston sat back down. "If your people had done a decent job of checking me out they would have discovered that I have no questionable activities on my records anywhere. I'm not involved in drug dealing or any other illegal enterprises. My relationship with Trish was on a benevolent level. She wanted to put this dirty business in her past and I was trying to help her. She was afraid of trying to break away on her own because she felt that her knowledge of the organization made her a liability. It looks like she was right." Winston was trembling.

Slim was silent for a time and then he spoke. "I'm truly sorry about what happened to Trish but, honestly I'm as much in the dark as you are. How were you planning to help her, anyway?"

Winston tugged on the straw in his Bloody Mary. "I've told you that I'm not involved in any drug gang and that's true, but the neighborhood where my business is located has its share of drug addicts and I've had some success helping a few people beat the habit and reclaim their lives. A guy that I know is said to have a great deal of influence over the street dealers in that area and he sees to it that they don't interfere when I'm working with someone. I know that it sounds strange but our friendship is unique. I don't get involved in anything that he or his friends are doing and I've made it known that I don't want any part of it. It works out for both of us."

"So what were you going to do for Trish?" asked Slim.

"She was supposed to arrange a meeting between me and somebody named Sammy," said Winston. "My job was going to be to convince Sammy that all Trish wanted was to be able to walk away. She had never been arrested or anything so the cops didn't know anything about her. There would be no chance of her being picked up and questioned for anything or being offered any deals. She said that Sammy was a reasonable man who liked to keep a low profile and had a good relationship with everyone who worked for him. She would agree to move out of state if that's what he wanted. Both Trish and I thought we could find common ground with Sammy."

"How much did Trish tell you about Sammy? Did she ever describe him?" asked Slim.

"She told me almost nothing and never said what he looked like," answered Winston. "Only that he would be the guy who would have to okay her departure. She liked him and respected his judgment. She thought he'd be reasonable."

"One other thing," said Slim. "I understand that you had a meeting with some people from the sheriff's office in Huron County today. Is that right?"

Winston was stunned by the question. "How could you possibly know about that?" he asked.

"We just keep our ears to the ground," answered Slim. "What I want to know is if Sammy's name was part of your conversation."

"I think they may have asked if I knew him but that's all," said Winston. "I told them that I've never met him and know absolutely nothing about him."

They brought the name up?" asked Slim

Winston nodded.

"Nothing more?" asked Slim.

"Nothing more," said Winston.

Chapter 37

Deputy Ross leaned back in his chair. "Would it be a problem if we asked you to leave your truck here for another day or so? The State Police would like to bring in a couple of specialists to see if they can find anything more. Stuff like fingerprints and things."

"As far as I'm concerned you can keep it," said Jennifer. "That car that you put us in is so much nicer and more comfortable than that old truck he drives."

Sid ignored Jennifer's comment. "If you need the truck you'll just keep it anyway but thanks for politely asking. Any idea how long you'll need it?"

"That will be up to the State Police but I can't imagine it being more than two days at tops," answered Ross. "They should be here any time. We'll have a better idea once we talk to them."

Jennifer spoke up. "There's a bag on the front seat that has yesterday's egg foo yong from Grand Rapids in it. I suggest you throw it out if anybody plans on spending any time inside the truck."

"Have any luck running down anyone named Sammy down in the Bay City area?" asked Sid.

"Nothing so far," said Ross. We're checking a wide area of surrounding counties to see if the name rings any bells. We know that there is a sizable organization in the area but it was always thought to be an extension of one of the downstate groups. But this morning, Bay County informed me that they don't have any names connected to it."

"According to Winston he's never heard the name Sammy over on his side of the state either," said Sid.

"I wouldn't feel too frustrated," said Ross. "Breaks and clues seem to fall out of the skies sometimes. All we can do is keep working with what we've got and we have more than you realize. The cabin cruiser, for instance. We know who it belongs to, we know that the victim's body was on that boat and that she was likely dead by the time she got there. The boat also offers a good explanation of how she ended up on the shore of an island although it's a mystery why anybody would choose to leave her there."

"It may not be such a puzzle as to why the body was left there," said Sid. "If someone wanted the word spread about a body of a murder victim being discovered, leaving it in an exotic place like that would practically guarantee that it would be in lots of newspapers. Whoever the message was intended for would see it for sure."

"I'm figuring that sooner or later Henry Mason will show up at the marina to take his boat for a ride or at least to clean up the blood," said Deputy Ross. "That cabin cruiser just might be our ace in the hole. Henry doesn't know that we've found it and probably still feels safe when he's on it. It's being watched twenty four, seven."

"As for right now, we've got to get back over to the Health Department and take care of our real jobs," said Sid. "Call us if you need us."

Sid eased the Ford Taurus out of the county garage and turned down the street that bordered the impound yard. There was only one other car on the road, a lone Toyota cruising leisurely past the fence. The driver seemed to be concentrating on the cars in the Sheriff Department lock up. As they dropped in behind it, Jennifer reached in her purse grabbing a notebook and pencil and noted the license number on the Toyota. Sid turned left at the next corner without ever catching up to the car.

"One thing in our favor," said Jennifer, "is that whoever it is that was following us doesn't know what we're driving now. Makes me feel just a little safer."

"On the other hand," said Sid, "they must know where my truck is parked and exactly how long it'd been there. That fact can only be sending them one message. Chances are they won't try planting another tracking device on anything because they know we'd be looking for it."

To further muddy the water, when they got to their office Sid parked the Taurus in a visitor's spot instead of his reserved space at the Health Department building. "No use just handing them information," he said.

There was a full day's work waiting for them when they got back to their office. In spite of the deputy sheriff's assurances, neither of them seemed comfortable all day, frequently glancing out of the office windows. It was nearly quitting time when Jennifer poked her head into Sid's office and said, "Ya know I packed enough stuff to last me a week when I came to your place last night. If it isn't too much out of line…" Sid interrupted her. "I've been thinking about that all day. Why don't we stop by your apartment and pick up your car and you can leave it in my garage. That way nobody can find it or tamper with it. You can stay as long as you want. If you help with the dishes, of course."

Chapter 38

Sid was fresh out of the shower and in the process of shaving when his cell phone began chirping. He didn't recognize the caller's number but he did recognize the area code. "Hello?"

"Hi Sid, this is Eric McCloud, remember me?"

Sid recognized his old friend from medical school. They had started their careers at the same time and both wound up being medical examiners, a vocation that neither one could have predicted. "Hey Eric. What's going on with you these days?"

"Same old thing day after day, but I just stumbled on a case that you were involved in way back when we were first getting going."

"Got my curiosity up," said Sid.

"It was back when you were still an assistant. One of your very first cases. This young woman was killed by a hit and run driver. It was common knowledge that she had been cheating on her husband and that he had sworn to kill her. He had a violent history and was considered dangerous. Turns out the car that hit his wife had been stolen and had been totally wiped clean by the time the police found it. Based partially on the way they found the car you were able to get the death ruled a homicide."

"I remember it well," said Sid. Bill Brown, the husband came up with an alibi. A witness said that they were at an all night card game and the husband was there every minute. I don't think anybody bought it but the prosecutor felt that the case was too weak to bring to trial because Bill Brown's

lawyer said he could produce at least a half dozen eye witnesses placing his client at the card game."

Yeah, that's the one," said Eric. "About a week ago, somebody driving a stolen car at high speed nails this Bill Brown
as he's staggering home from a bar in Bay City. Car throws
him fifteen feet in the air and he lands in some heavy shrub-
bery. Turns out he gets out of it with nothing more than a
broken ankle and a concussion. He wakes up in a hospital
that has a chapel that is maintained by the local Catholic
parish. Anyway, when he opens his eyes there's this nun
praying over him. The nun is a spitting image of his deceased
wife. This totally freaks him out and for two days Brown's
a complete zombie, just lies there and stares at the ceiling.
Finally, couple of days ago he asks to talk to a cop. So Bay
City Police send an officer over to interview him and he says
that he wants to come clean about his wife's death but doesn't
want to spend half of his life in prison. The cop suggests that
he talk to someone from the prosecutor's office to see if there
are any deals that can be worked out. The district attorney's
office knows this guy because he's lived on the fringe of the
law all his life. A prosecutor asks him if he has anything at
all that might be of use to them. After wracking his brain, it's
like a light comes on in his head and he says that he might
have something.

"There's a guy," said Bill Brown, "that they call Lefty. His
real name is Greg Smith. He's a bad ass dude. I think he might
even be a mob hit man. He's the guy who was supposed to be
my alibi for when my old lady got killed. Anyway, he needed
a favor from me about a week or so back. He wanted the key
to my cabin up north and so I gave it to him, no questions
asked. He told me to forget he ever talked to me. He's a scary

guy and would never ask for anything like that without good reason. I think he wanted to hide a body up there."

"So why would this be of any interest to me?" asked Sid.

"Well I've been following your latest adventure though the communication network on our county sheriff sites and I know that you're looking for someone named Sammy. The only place I've seen that name is where this Bill Brown says that this Lefty guy referred to a Sammy, like he was somebody important.

"Wow," said Sid. "Can you send everything you've got to the Huron County Sheriff's Department care of Deputy Ross? It could be absolute dynamite."

"Will do," said Eric. "Anything we can do to help."

Sid didn't mention a word of his telephone conversation to Jennifer when they left for town.

"What do you think of me?" asked Jennifer as they headed for the sheriff's office.

"In what way?" responded Sid.

"Oh, I don't know," said Jennifer. "As a woman, as a person, as a working associate, as a life partner?"

Sid smiled. "I like the life partner best. Why? Are you thinking of a lifetime thing?"

"I wouldn't consider anything else," she said.

"Sounds pretty good to me," answered Sid

"Is that a proposal?" asked Jennifer.

"I'm hoping it will be some day," said Sid.

They were both smiling when they rolled into the county garage.

When they joined Deputy Ross in his office, he was sitting at his desk and deep into reading a report. He turned to Sid. "When did you talk to this Bay County Medical Examiner"?

"This morning just before I left the house," said Sid. "I haven't read any of it yet. My buddy said he'd fax it right over."

"Could be really important stuff," said the deputy. "The State Police should be here any minute. I'll see what they think."

"What are you guys talking about?" asked Jennifer.

"The medical examiner from Bay County is an old friend of mine, we went to med school together," said Sid. "He called me this morning to relay some information that could be related to the investigation that we're involved in. I told him to fax it to the deputy here."

"Why didn't you mention it on the drive in this morning?" asked Jennifer.

"We had more important things to discuss," said Sid.

Jennifer smiled.

Sergeant Duffield knocked on the door of the office accompanied by two State Police Patrol Officers, a tall fresh looking cop who was obviously new to the force in impeccably pressed dress blues and a woman who appeared to be in her mid thirties with corporal stripes and a few ribbons on her uniform. The lady was smiling while the other officer stood at attention in the doorway.

"Welcome," said Ross. "Come on in and pour yourselves a coffee. Hopefully we have new information and lots of work to do today."

"Well, let's see what we've got," said Duffield. He silently read the report that had come from Sid's friend, nodding and raising his eyebrows as he scanned the pages, finally commenting. "This could be something. Makes me think I'm going to have to break up my team for the day." He turned to the female officer. "Why don't you get acquainted with these folks while me and John here go out and have a look at the doctor's truck?" He stood up and led the other officer out to the impound lot.

"My name is Christine and I've been with the department for almost eight years, ever since I graduated from college. I work mainly with the detective division and sometimes with the K-9."

"So you're a dog person," said Sid.

"Very much so," answered Christine, "but not so much in field operations, my main focus is in the training area."

"Do you teach them to attack?" asked Jennifer.

"I'm more into the detection stuff, you know drug sniffing, bomb sniffing, cadaver dogs.

"Sounds interesting," said Sid. "Just how effective are cadaver dogs at finding bodies? That's the kind of thing that would interest a medical examiner."

"It's a constantly expanding field that still hasn't earned the respect that it deserves," answered the officer. "I've read reports where dogs have identified human remains buried at depths exceeding fifteen feet. Ten feet is pretty common. Depends on the conditions. From what I've read, their performance record is quite impressive"

"What is your personal experience?" asked Sid.

"My division hasn't approved any cadaver dogs at this point but I've got a personal pet at home, a Labrador Retriever who shows exceptional promise. I work with her every day and I have a mentor who's trained over a dozen cadaver dogs who claims she's a natural. I'd say that she's already as good, if not better than any other dog out there. I'm just looking for the chance to prove it."

The door opened and Sergeant Duffield walked in followed by the younger officer who held a small black box in his hand. "We may not be of much help on this one," said Duffield. "This looks like one of those cheap generic tracking devices that's not married to a dedicated receiving unit. Anybody with a computer or cell phone with the right application can tune in to this. No way of telling who was following it. John here is a computer geek so if he can use your garage, he'll rip into it and see if he can do any good."

"Fine with me," said Ross.

"If it's okay with you," said Duffield. "Me and my other officer would like to head on over to Bay City to interview our new subject. Anybody want to come along?"

"I can't leave the office right now," said Deputy Ross

"We'd like to come if we can stop by my office for a few minutes. It's right on the way," said Sid.

Duffield responded, "Not a problem, let's mount up."

Chapter 39

"I'm worried," said Lefty. "The doctor's truck hasn't moved from the sheriff's lot for two days, nobody's parking in his reserved spot outside his office, and now the secretary's car has disappeared."

"I'd say that it's safe to assume that the tracking unit has been discovered and they're taking steps to remain unseen," said Sammy. "There could be no other explanation as to the truck being held. And you say it's in a fenced enclosure with a padlock on the gate? Sounds like an impound lot to me. Are you sure they can't trace anything?"

"Not a chance," said Lefty. "The setup has no connection to Slim, me or anybody else we know. The bigger problem is keeping tabs on the doctor. I know you don't like it but I'd say that we have to do it the old fashioned way. I've got to just follow him but don't worry, I'll be careful."

Sammy shook his head. "I don't like it one bit but I suppose it's necessary. I'll have to trust your judgment. I assume you have a plan."

Lefty shifted in his chair. ""It looks like I'll need to start at his house. I've driven by there plenty of times and have checked out the whole area. There are only a handful of full time residents, it's mostly vacation homes and weekend cottages. During the week a lot of the places are vacant, especially across the road from the lake. There's a row of about seven places over there where nobody stays there during the week. One of those places sits back into the woods a little bit and has a shed that I can hide my car behind. There's a straight line of sight to his garage door from there so I could easily watch from a pretty concealed location. At least I'd get an idea of what he's using for transportation. After that it should be easy."

Lefty decided to wait until it was almost dark outside so that he'd stand less chance of being seen sneaking into the back yard of the little yellow cottage. He spent the daylight hours getting things prepared. He stopped by his apartment in Bay City; picked up his night vision binoculars and installed fresh batteries, A couple of changes of clothes including shorts and deck shoes, then headed to Bad Axe. He cruised past the sheriff's headquarters just as they were pulling Sid's truck inside the county garage. He slowed down until the truck had disappeared inside the building and he could see a man in a mechanic's uniform jump out of the driver's side door. He continued on to the health department building where he saw a State Police cruiser parked in Doctor Benson's reserved spot. Lefty pulled into the lot and parked away from the door but in a crowded area of the lot. He didn't have to wait long. Soon Doctor Benson exited the building followed by his secretary and two State Police officers, one a very big man, the other a young woman who, in spite of all of the accessories hung on her belt displayed an attractive and athletic looking figure.

Lefty sat there until the police car had left the parking lot and was out of sight on a southbound highway. He tried to speculate on their destination. It was early in the day and from the direction they were going it looked like their intended landing place could be either the regional hospital in Lapeer or State Police headquarters in Lansing. Lansing would be the most likely target. That would put them out of the area for a minimum of five hours, plenty of time for Lefty to do a little reconnoitering. He headed north to the neighborhood where Sid made his home, stopping at a gas station along the way to change into shorts and deck shoes. A grey polo shirt completed the effect.

Lefty pulled into a deserted roadside park along the lakefront and parked the Toyota. He locked the car and strolled down to the beach. People dressed in shorts and polo shirts walked the beach all the time. He would be inconspicuous and invisible. Doctor Benson's home was a little less than half a mile up the beach. A nice leisurely walk.

As he approached the doctor's house he pulled the small digital camera from his pocket and snapped a couple of photos of the boat and jet ski that rested in the hoist that sat in slightly deeper than knee deep water. A narrow but sturdy looking dock stretched from the beach out to the boat. Turning his attention toward the house he studied the massive limestone patio that sat just above a stone fire pit that showed remnants of a recent beach bonfire. Beyond the patio stood a wooden deck with a round umbrella table at one end and a gazebo at the other. A deck box stood against the railing next to the table. The house was practically all glass in the front like many of the other lakefront homes. It wasn't as expensive and rich looking as some of the other waterfront homes but it was certainly above average, fitting for a doctor on a municipal salary.

Lefty didn't want to linger too long but he made sure that he recorded every inch of the frontage. He continued to walk in the same direction for another three hundred yards and then, after removing his shoes and wading out just past ankle deep water, he returned to shore, sat down on the trunk of a tree that had washed up on shore and put his shoes back on. On the way back to his car, he didn't stop or even look at the house. He was just a tourist on the beach.

Looking at his watch, he estimated that it was about two hours until sundown, enough time for a run into town and a quick burger and beer at one of the bars.

Caseville was quiet this afternoon. A few women dragging their children behind them wandered in and out of the gift shops carrying colorful souvenir pennants and bags stuffed with even more gaudy beach towels. The bars were bustling though. Most of the charter boats were back in the harbor after a day of chasing fish around the bay and the sunburned fishermen were in the taverns lying about the ones that got away and embellishing their stories with Budweiser.

Lefty blended in effortlessly, smiling and tipping his beer bottle as he waited for his sandwich. He paid his bar tab with cash and wandered out the side door to the parking lot that the bar shared with the harbor. It was the same lot that was used by many of the commercial boats including the Charity Island Dinner Cruise ferry.

Twenty minutes later Lefty sat in his car directly behind a low wall that hid his headlights and nestled between the trees and a storage shed, fighting sleep as he stared at Doctor Benson's garage door.

It was almost ten o'clock when Lefty was jarred awake by the light across the road. He opened his eyes in time to see the garage door closing but couldn't tell what kind of vehicle was inside. He caught a glimpse of grey but that was all. He watched as Sid and Jennifer walked to the house and were suddenly bathed in the blaze of the motion sensor activated rear porch light. Sid opened the door and Jennifer went inside. Soon it seemed like every light inside the house was on. Lefty couldn't follow their movement from room to room but it appeared that one of them went upstairs and turned on more lights. It finally settled down to just one light on upstairs and another ground level toward the front of the house. He considered waiting for all the lights to go out and then sneak across the road and peek in the garage windows and then he remembered the motion sensors, they might be all around the perimeter. Too risky, he thought. He waited another hour until the house was dark and then set his travel alarm clock for five thirty and put it on the dashboard. He unrolled the air mattress and tried to make his six foot frame comfortable under the old army blanket. He'd pick up where he left off in the morning.

Chapter 40

Sergeant Duffield didn't waste any time getting down to Bay City. He wheeled into a parking spot at McLaren Bay Region Hospital and led the group inside. The information desk directed them to Bill Brown's room. He was sitting up in bed watching a cooking show when they walked in. The other bed was vacant. "Hello," said the sergeant. "I understand that you have something you'd like to discuss with us."

"I thought that the prosecutor's office and my attorney would do all of the negotiating," said Brown.

"We're not here to negotiate," said the sergeant. "We just wanna see what you've got and if we like it we'll call in the lawyers. We won't be Mirandizing you at this point."

Jennifer moved to a chair in the corner of the room and set up her little recorder on the bedside table.

Brown shut off the television. "I really don't know if I have anything or not but a guy that I know said he needed to use my hunting cabin for a day or so. He didn't say why he needed it and said I shouldn't ask. But he said that I should keep quiet about it. I don't know the guy real well but I've always been under the impression that he's some sort of mob hit man. Guy's name is Greg Smith but everybody just calls him Lefty. Scary guy."

"So where does this Sammy come in?" asked Duffield.

"Well," said Brown. "I'm not sure what his role is but Lefty mentioned him twice. Said that it would make Sammy happy if he helped me out and then later, when he returned the key he told me that Sammy says thanks. I just figured that Sammy must be his boss. I don't question this stuff I just nod and say you're welcome."

"Where is this place? This hunting cabin?" asked Duffield.

"About a hundred and twenty miles almost straight north, a couple hours drive," answered Brown. "Kalkaska County. It's a Christmas tree farm. Two hundred and forty acres."

Christine spoke up for the first time. "How long ago was this?"

"About a week," said Brown.

"It's been dry for about two weeks," said Christine. "What does the land look like? Any trails through it?"

"Oh yeah," said Brown. "There's a trail, four rows of trees, another trail, four more rows of trees and it repeats like that across the whole place."

"What about the soil?" asked Christine.

"It's a soft, mostly sand. No clay," said Brown. "Crummy stuff. About the only things you can grow there are Christmas trees and potatoes and potatoes are too much work. The trees are good though, they help out with the deer hunting.

"Mind if we take a look?" asked Duffield. "Can you get the key to us some how?"

"It's right in that closet," said Brown. "I put it on my key ring right after Lefty gave it back to me. There's a plastic bag with all my stuff in it. It'll be in there."

Sid went to the closet and dragged out the bag. He handed the key ring to Brown and let him sort them until he found the one he was looking for. Duffield opened his folder and filled out a receipt form for Brown acknowledging that he had surrendered the key and that it would be returned.

"I advise you to get your attorney in here and go over everything that we said. We'll leave a transcript of the tape. It looks to me like you could be innocent of any complicity but I'm no lawyer. All I need now is directions."

"It's easy," said Brown. "It's a mile southwest of the intersection of two State Highways on the southwest corner, one half mile by three quarters. Driveway will be on your right in the first quarter mile. It's a log place just a couple years old. I built it with my wife's life insurance money."

The ride back to Bad Axe was punctuated with lively conversation. Hey Christine," said Duffield. "I know what you were thinking but I wouldn't bet on getting clearance from headquarters to bring that fleabag of yours along on this investigation." Duffield had a broad grin on his face and hunched his shoulders against Christine's response.

"Vicky has a great pedigree," shouted Christine. "As a matter of fact, if she could talk, she wouldn't even speak to the likes of you. Her table manners are even better than yours. At least she doesn't talk with her mouth full."

Duffield was folded over with laughter. "Take it easy young lady, I was only teasing."

Christine spent the rest of the trip home pleading her case to run home and pick up her prized cadaver dog. She said it was a perfect opportunity because of the soil composition, the fact that it hadn't recently rained and if there was a body there, it would have been a recent burial."

Sergeant Duffield couldn't refute any of her arguments and finally conceded that if there was a canine car available tomorrow they would stop and pick it up and she and her dog Vickie could put on their show for everybody. Christine looked thrilled.

At County Headquarters the entire team reviewed the day's events and added the results to what they already had. The GPS tracking device had proved useless but the trip to

Bay City might bear some fruit. Deputy Ross summed things up. "When this thing first started we were told to treat it as a hate crime. It sure doesn't seem that way now and there may be a second murder as well. When a guy with a shady reputation wants to quietly use a secluded cabin for one day and it isn't even hunting season, it's usually bad news. The owner of that cabin cruiser in the marina across the bay has yet to show up and everything points to him being the one who dumped the body and probably even killed her. As bad as the wind was blowing the night she was left there suggests that he probably had help and that's where this Greg Smith or Lefty comes in. But we still don't know who Sammy is.

Sid and Jennifer were late getting back to Sid's house, made a couple of Bloody Marys and went out to sit on the deck listening to the night birds and the ripple of the tiny waves that broke on the shore. "So it looks like we're on the road again tomorrow," said Jennifer. "If we're not on duty this weekend, I'd like the chance to play in the lake all day. I hear it's supposed to be sunny and hot.

"Right," answered Sid. "Can't see a thing wrong with your logic. Until then, I vote that we get up early and go into town for breakfast. That way we won't need to do dishes in the morning."

Chapter 41

Sammy leaned back in his chair with his eyes closed. The word had been out for a couple of days that Sammy was looking for information on Doctor Sidney Benson, the Huron County Medical Examiner.

Now he listened to a trusted street dealer as he told his story. One of his customers actually knew this doctor. He was a hospital orderly at Huron Medical Center and the doctor had approached him one day at lunch in the cafeteria about getting to know some people in the gay community. Apparently their conversations finally settled on Trish.

Hearing that there could be some money in it if he came up with any good information, the orderly had begun discreetly asking questions among members of the hospital staff to see if he could get a feel for the doctor's routine and habits. One of the nurses aides claimed that she sees him having breakfast regularly at a sports grill in Caseville and she's pretty sure he goes there frequently for dinner in the evenings as well. The orderly said he'd stay on it and see what he could come up with.

"Tell him to be careful," said Sammy, "and make sure he doesn't ever tell anyone what he's doing or why. We already have one dead person to deal with. I don't want any more. I'm not crazy about amateurs who think they can be detectives or spies. Since he's already acquainted with the doctor, I would think he'd be the most help to us if he just stayed close to him, you know have lunch with him as often as possible and show some enthusiasm for the doctor's investigation. That's when information usually comes out, during small talk."

"I've already warned him about getting too aggressive," said the dealer. "He knows we don't want him connected to us in any way. And he knows that he can't let the doctor catch on to what he's up to. He's smart enough to keep his mouth shut and I slipped him a fifty for a little insurance."

"I'll see that you get your money back plus a nice bonus if anything he gets us actually pans out," said Sammy. "The important thing is that he stays close and keeps his eyes and ears open."

Chapter 42

"Man, you're up early," said Nick

"So are you," answered Sid. "Jennifer, allow me to introduce you to Nick my favorite nighttime bartender. I never expected him to be here this early."

"Summer season is just beginning," said Nick. "The boss needs a little help training all of the tourist season help. Says there's a promotion in it if I help things flow easier. I'm just giving him a hand."

"I hear you've got killer omelets here," said Sid. "Any truth to that?"

"If you heard it here, you know it's true," said Nick with a wink. "I'll send you a waitress."

The Wooded Island Sports Grill is one of the few bars in the county that serves breakfast because they want to snag the fishing crowd before they head out onto the big lake and hope that they'll return for dinner. It's a spacious upscale place with a couple of seventy inch televisions on each wall and various sports banners hanging everywhere. There's even a shark mounted over the office doorway.

The cook peeked out of the kitchen door and waved to Sid.

"Is this your hangout?" asked Jennifer. "Everybody seems to know you here."

"I don't really have a hangout," said Sid. "When I was new with the county, I had an embarrassing experience because I had a couple of drinks on my own time and so I don't want to be labeled as a barfly. Nobody in here knows what I do for a living. Well, nobody except Nick."

"How's the food?" asked Jennifer.

"It's the best," said Sid. "I'm gonna recommend the farmer's omelet. It's on special today."

"Sounds good," added Jennifer.

After they had finished eating Nick found his way to the table. "A guy's been asking around about you," he said. "It's a local guy who was in my high school, a year ahead or a year behind me. I don't recall but I do remember him being a little strange, kind of a loner. Some of the guys said he was queer. Name's Jack. I don't know his last name. I think he works in a doctor's office or maybe the hospital. He wants to know what you're doing for the Sheriff's Department. Says that he's heard that you're on a real interesting case. I told him I don't know anything but he doesn't believe me because he thinks that bartenders know everybody's business."

Sid trusted Nick. He had known him for a long time and Nick had been in the bar business forever. He had always been a serious entrepreneur, and was the senior investor in a growing business but a few years back a partner had embezzled all of the cash, left Nick broke, foreclosed, hundreds of thousands of dollars in debt and was still on the run somewhere on this earth. Nick didn't quit. He began to rebuild his life slowly without whining. Working his way up from nothing, he was well on his way to credibility these days and was looking toward the future, alone. No more partners.

"I'd just as soon you kept everything quiet. But I'd sure like to know why he's interested," said Sid.

Nick nodded and said, "I've got your number saved in my phone."

Sid and Jennifer went out the door.

The ride to Kalkaska included Sergeant Duffield, his rookie patrolman, Sid and Jennifer. Christine would meet them for an early lunch in West Branch where she was picking up a Michigan State Police K-9 car, an SUV outfitted with a dog cage in the rear seat. She insisted they meet where they could eat outside so that the dog wouldn't be locked in a car. Everybody agreed. It was obvious that Christine was suffering some anxiety. It was to be the first test that would not only tell if her dog has what it takes but it would speak to the competency of Christine's training talents and go a long way toward selling the State on the value of cadaver dogs.

Vickie didn't seem to have a care in the world. She crunched down the dry dog food that Christine had put out for her, lapped up the water from the stainless steel bowl that sat in the shade of a pine tree and laid down to take a nap. The rookie patrolman rode with Christine for the rest of the trip.

In the other car Duffield said, "My buddy opted to ride in the car with a dog. I guess I'm a little intimidating." Sid and Jennifer laughed.

They had no problem locating the cabin. It was exactly where Bill Brown told them it would be. It was right around noon when Sid opened the door and went inside followed by Christine and her dog. Vickie had her nose on the floor immediately, tail wagging and sniffing every inch of the room.

Sergeant Duffield appeared in the doorway. He held a plastic bag in his hand that contained the bloody t-shirt that was found on the cabin cruiser. "Would this help you any?"

Christine's face brightened. "I read that you have a blood soaked shirt in the evidence room. Thanks for bringing it along." She grabbed the dog's collar and held the shirt up to her nose. Vickie sniffed and wagged her tail. "Okay, let's go hunting," said Corporal Christine.

Sid stood outside the cabin and studied the access roads that scattered in a half dozen directions among the neat rows of Christmas trees. "Only one of them shows signs of recent use," he said.

Vickie bounded off the low porch dragging Christine behind her. The dog stopped next to Sid and Christine surveyed the scene. "I think you're right," she said.

The dog followed by five humans trotted off down the trail. As they traveled it became obvious that the tracks they were following were not made by a car or truck, the tread pattern was definitely that of tractor tires. They had gone about a quarter mile when the path took a hard right turn between a couple of trees and came to a small clearing covered with traces of movement. Sergeant Duffield pointed to two perfectly flat square patches in the sand about twelve feet apart. "Looks like this is where outriggers were put down. I'd say there's been a backhoe in here."

Vickie was barking and straining at her collar. Finally Christine released her. The dog ran to one spot and began sniffing furiously at the ground, kicking up clouds of sand with her frequent snorting. She circled a wide area always coming back to the same spot next to a couple of small trees and barking relentlessly as she sniffed.

Duffield pulled his cell phone and punched in a number. "We're going to want some equipment and a crew out here," he said.

It was another hour before a truck arrived towing a trailer with a backhoe followed by a State Police Suburban with four patrolmen in it.

The operator jumped out of the truck followed by two laborers with shovels. "I figure we've got almost six hours of daylight left. In this soft soil, I can dig a pretty big hole in that amount of time. Show me where you want me to dig and let's get started."

Duffield pointed out the depressions that were left by the previous piece of excavation equipment and the dog did the rest.

"I'd trust the one with the nose," commented the operator. Using the bucket, he gently lifted three trees out of the way and began swinging the boom back and forth moving large quantities of loam with each pass when he reached a depth of five feet his moves became slower with observers on each side of the bucket. If there was a body down here, he didn't want to damage it. Finally, just past the seven foot mark, one of the teeth on the bucket snagged something. It turned out to be a man's belt and it lifted the body almost completely out of the ground before the belt snapped and dropped him back on the sand. The two laborers put on face masks and gloves and climbed into the hole and lifted the body onto a makeshift platform rigged to the backhoe bucket so that he could be lifted out of the hole.

Jennifer, claiming the stench was too much for her, started walking back to the cabin. Sid said, "I'd love to go with you but this is where I have to go to work."

"Am I done here?" asked the operator.

Not if Vickie has anything to say about it," said Christine pointing at the Labrador who was in the bottom of the hole, frantically digging. Finally an arm was exposed and the crew went back to work to recover a second body.

How many damned bodies are down there?" asked Sergeant Duffield.

Before sundown, both bodies had been processed and were on their way to a stopover at Huron Medical Center before being transferred to the Lapeer Regional Hospital for autopsies. The excavation had been backfilled and everybody was on their way home. Sid and Jennifer hitched a ride with Sergeant Duffield while the other two officers and the dog headed back to West Branch to drop off the K-9 vehicle and pick up Christine's car. Sid called Deputy Ross and filled him in on the day's activities.

"It's getting curiouser and curiouser," said Ross.

Chapter 43

"Blood type from one of the victims is a match with the bloody tee shirt," said Ross. "For now, let's assume he's Henry Mason. No family. We'll have to identify him forensically. The other one is a John Doe."

"The guy from the marina where Henry kept the cabin cruiser, knew him real well," said Sid, "maybe he could identify the body for us."

"I've already requested that he come down here this afternoon," said Ross. "The bodies are scheduled to go to Lapeer tomorrow for autopsies."

"Gonna be mostly a formality," said Sid. "Both of them had bullet holes in the back of the head."

"Got a bunch of Greg Smiths in the system but none with the alias of Lefty so far," said the deputy. "Common name. Unless we get awful lucky, it's going to take some time to put together an interview list."

"Oh yeah," said Ross. "Another thing. The people who run the dinner cruise business to Charity Island have a high definition surveillance camera in the marina where they keep the ferry boat. It runs all the time in case of vandalism. Anyway, it records every single person that boards that boat and I'm thinking that the cell phone that made that mysterious call from the island had to have been in someone's pocket on the last dinner cruise. I've requested those tapes and we're going to interview everybody connected with the dinner cruises. We're gonna be busy."

"Any more activity on those cell phones?" asked Sid

"Nothing," replied the deputy. "I'm assuming they've

both been destroyed by now and they're working with new ones."

Sid and Jennifer checked Sid's pickup truck out of the impound lot and drove over to the Health Department office complex. "Well, half of my fantasy luxury lifestyle is gone," said Jennifer. "The air conditioning in this truck doesn't even work. I liked that car so much more."

It's only nine o'clock in the morning," said Sid. "The temperature is only in the seventies. I didn't even turn the air conditioning on."

"Do I complain too much?" asked Jennifer.

Sid was silent.

There was plenty of work to keep them both busy until two o'clock in the afternoon and Sid knew that he'd be tied up a good part of tomorrow with autopsies. He called the sheriff's office to see if they'd be needed and was informed that one of the bodies had been positively identified as Henry Mason but the other was still unknown. No other team business was planned for the day. He suggested that Jennifer could get in some water skiing this afternoon if they could find another person to ride along as an observer. Jennifer loved the idea.

When they got to Sid's place, he noticed a neighbor's car parked in a driveway and announced that it looked like they had found their observer.

Sandy, a young widow who lived year round just a couple of doors away from Sid said she'd be happy to join them for a boat ride as long as they supplied Mai Tai's for a beach party later.

While Jennifer was cutting back and forth across the wake of the boat, Sandy mentioned to Sid that a strange car had pulled into the yard of one of their neighbors across the road last night and stayed there all night. She didn't think much of it at the time because the houses along this strip were the kind that people frequently loaned to friends or family for getaway weekends. But this was different. The car arrived at dusk and was gone right after dawn. Because it was unusual, Sandy paid special attention to it and had noted that it was a fairly new Toyota Camry and she had a partial license number.

Eventually Jennifer became tired and as they passed the front of Sid's house, she cut hard to the right and let go of the tow rope handle. Her momentum carried her like a surfer to within a few feet of the beach where she stepped off the ski and walked ashore. By the time Sid got the boat turned around and nosing its way into the hoist, Jennifer was standing on the beach running a brush through her long auburn hair.

Sid had pulled a slab of baby back ribs out of the freezer last night and as soon as the boat was secured and covered in its hoist he headed up to the deck to get the barbecue started. He invited Sandy to stay for dinner and she readily accepted. Jennifer ran in the house to change into her beach party clothes.

Jennifer and Sandy prepared a salad and some black eyed peas while Sid handled the ribs and mixed the sauce. They dined outdoors on the deck and just as the sun began to descend in the western sky, Sid went into the house and emerged carrying a bottle of Bardolino in an ice bucket and three wine goblets. The three sat sipping wine and gossiping about nothing as the sun disappeared into the bay in a blaze of color. Eventually Sandy brought up the subject of the car that she saw last night and this morning. Jennifer sat straight up when she heard the word, Toyota. She immediately wanted to know more. When Sandy read off the two license plate numbers that she was able to read in the dim morning light, Jennifer jumped up and ran inside. She came back out with her purse in her hand and talking a mile a minute. "I haven't said anything because I didn't want you to think I was paranoid or stupid or something," she said to Sid. "But my first day here I saw a car cruise by out there on the road and it seemed to be going kind of slow. After that tracking thing you found on your truck, I guess I was being a little extra cautious and alert. Anyway it was a Toyota Camry. And then yesterday I could have sworn I saw the same car driving slowly again past the sheriff's office. We pulled out behind it and followed it about a half of a block before you turned off. We were right behind it so I wrote down the license number." She pulled a notebook out of her purse and asked Sandy what numbers she had seen this morning.

Sandy said without hesitation, "Five and six."

Jennifer held her notebook up so that Sid could see. The number she had written was CDD 7256.

Sandy sat there looking back and forth between Sid and Jennifer and then just shook her head. "You guys have sure left me in the weeds," she said.

Sid spent the next hour explaining as much as he could about the case without revealing any privileged information. Sandy said that she was both amazed and impressed. "I'll have to start following the newspapers a little more closely," said Sandy, "but that doesn't let you off the hook on those Mai Tai's."

"Ya know," said Sid. "I just happen to have all the ingredients in the house. I was wondering how I was going to use those limes." Sid made three generous drinks using Bacardi Light as well as Mount Gay Amber Rum. "These will help us all sleep tonight but I suggest that everybody lock their doors.

Chapter 44

Sid knew that Deputy Ross was one of those early freaks who always arrived at work about three quarters of an hour before his shift started so he stopped at the Sheriffs office on his way to the Health Department. Jennifer had driven her own car this morning because Sid would be gone most of the day doing autopsies about seventy miles away in Lapeer.

Ross looked up when Sid walked in. "I'm guessing you've got something pretty good this morning," said Ross. "Am I right?"

"I think so," said Sid. "It looks like somebody's still interested in my daily routine. I'm pretty sure I'm being followed and I've got some evidence to back it up. Got a car description and a license number for you."

Ross's eyebrows went up. He grabbed a pencil and said, "Let's have it."

Sid read information out of the notebook that Jennifer had given him and said. "I never noticed any of this. Everything I've given you came from either my secretary or one of my neighbors."

"This should give us something good," said the deputy. "That license number isn't from a rental car. I'll have an answer for you before lunchtime."

"I'm hoping that it belongs to someone named Sammy," said Sid. "I'll be doing autopsies until sometime this afternoon but I'll leave my cell phone turned on in case you get lucky."

"Just to be on the safe side, I'd like to send you off to do your job in one of our marked cruisers and an armed deputy today," said Ross. "Until we get this thing figured out, I don't want to take any chances."

Jennifer was pulling into the parking space at the health center when she noticed a Toyota Camry moving toward the parking lot exit. She jumped out of her car just as the driver of the Toyota reached the highway. He turned his head and they made brief eye contact but Jennifer continued to stare until the car was out of sight. She could tell that the driver kept checking his rear view mirrors to keep her in sight. He had to know that his cover had been blown. She hurried into the office, locked the door behind her and called Sid. "It's him, the guy in the Toyota. He was in our parking lot when I got to work. He took off when I got here but I'm scared out of my mind," she shouted into the phone. "I'm in the office with all the doors locked and the shades drawn. I don't know what to do."

Sid tried to sound calm. "I'm riding in a sheriff's department cruiser right now, the deputy will radio the dispatcher and have them send someone to keep you company. You'll be all right."

It was probably less than five minutes when Jennifer, peeking through the blinds saw the deputy pull into the lot and park in Sid's reserved spot.

Trying to look unruffled, she unlocked the door and invited the middle aged, pot bellied sheriff's deputy into the building. "Make yourself comfortable," she said. "I was just putting on a pot of coffee."

"As soon as you're ready," said the officer. "I need you to tell me exactly what happened. We don't take these things lightly."

Jennifer was impressed with just how thoroughly the deputy questioned her. He dug out enough details of the thirty second encounter to fill three pages of a report. The officer's cell phone rang and he went outside to take the call. When he came back in, he informed Jennifer that Deputy Ross had sent a message to Doctor Benson that he was to immediately return to the sheriff's headquarters and he wants me to bring you there to meet them in forty five minutes or so. You can drive your own car and I'll follow you.

Sid was already sitting across from Deputy Ross and waiting when Jennifer got to the sheriff's office.

"You must not have been too far along when they caught up with you," said Jennifer.

"No more than a mile or two out of town when we got the return to base order," said Sid. "Things must be beginning to pop."

"We've got lots of popping to do," said Ross. "So we'd better get to it. First of all, we've got good news and bad news on the owner of that Toyota. The name is Greg Smith all right but the address is phony. Bay City police said they'd do their best to track him down for us. In the meantime you guys will be getting a couple of guardian angels. Nobody can figure out why he's so interested but we can't take any stupid chances.

Have both of you received your CPL or better known as CCW training?"

"I have," said Sid.

"I have no idea what you're talking about," said Jennifer.

"It stands for Concealed Pistol License or Carry Concealed Weapon," said Ross.

"Why would I need that?" asked Jennifer.

"Well," said Ross. "I asked the Sheriff about it this morning and he said that I should deputize both of you so that you're authorized to carry a weapon. If there's even a remote chance that someone would want to harm you, the Sheriff feels that you should have the means to defend yourself."

"Does any money come with this promotion?" asked Jennifer.

"I'm told that you'll be getting the standard contractors rate for any hours that you put in," said Ross. "And that it will be retroactive."

"Where do I have to go to take this training that you're talking about?" asked Jennifer.

"We can do it right here," said Ross. "We've got some NRA certified trainers on the force. I'll get it scheduled."

"Sounds like fun," said Jennifer. "Let me know when I can start."

Ross reached into the bottom drawer of his desk and pulled out a large wooden "Whamo" slingshot. "One of our guys found this on a school playground after we responded to a report of a fight. In the meantime you don't need a permit for this but it can be pretty deadly at close range." He handed it to Jennifer and all of the men laughed. Jennifer silently slid it into her purse, her face beet red.

Chapter 45

Lefty sat in Sammy's office and told him what had happened this morning.

"So now they not only know that you're following them, they know what you look like and what kind of car you drive," said Sammy.

"I'm afraid it's that bad," said Lefty. "I was expecting the doctor to show up in his pick up truck. It caught me off guard when his secretary came rolling in driving her car."

"You'll need a different car," said Sammy. "Let's get rid of the one you've been driving before the sun goes down. Park it in a crack neighborhood somewhere down in Detroit and abandon it. Pull the license plate and destroy it. You say that it's registered to a nonexistent address?"

"That's right," said Lefty

"Take Slim with you and get it done right away," said Sammy. "I'll have a new vehicle with an untraceable registration waiting here for you in the morning."

As soon as Lefty was gone, Sammy called his contact at the county hospital and told him to stop by later this afternoon.

"I'm going to have to ask you to stay real close to that doctor," said Sammy. "He knows you so you can only keep tabs on him while he's in the hospital. You won't be able to follow him in public but didn't you say that you ran across a bartender friend of his who you figured could be bought?"

"Bartenders are not known for making high wages," said the orderly. "So I figured he'd be happy to make a few extra bucks. Want me to feel him out? I'll be careful."

"If you can get real close," said Sammy. "You won't have to pay another dime for weed for the rest of your life and we can fix you up with some much better stuff as well."

The orderly's eyes lit up. "I'm on it."

Jack headed straight for the Wooded Island Sports Grill and as he walked through the door, he smiled to see Nick working behind the bar and one lone customer sitting all the way at one end. Jack made a beeline for opposite end of the bar. He jumped on a barstool and studied the array of beer taps.

Nick stopped in front of him. "Pretty sure we have your brand here, got a little bit of everything."

"Yeah," said Jack. "Just gimme a Bud Light. I'm not feeling too adventurous this afternoon."

When Nick set the glass down in front of him Jack said. "Hey, I've got this buddy who's a freelance news reporter and one of the major Detroit papers said they'd give him a full time job if he could get some kind of exclusive story about that murder over on Charity Island last week. The word is that one of your regulars in here is right in the middle of the investigation but he's not supposed to talk about it."

"I'm guessing that you're going to ask about that guy you mentioned to me a day or so ago, right?" asked Nick.

"Yeah, that's right," said Jack. "My friend is willing to pay generously for information and everybody knows that people confide in their favorite bartenders. He probably tells you stuff that he wouldn't tell his own mother. There could be some big money available for inside information on that investigation."

"Why so much interest?" asked Nick.

"It's about the victim," said Jack. "I understand that she was a transsexual, you know, a guy who had a sex change operation. That makes it a hot story. Might even be able to sell it nationally if it's juicy enough."

Nick drummed his fingers on the bar and stared at the ceiling for a long minute then said, "I'll see if I can come up with anything for you."

Jack smiled. "I'd love to know what he's got so far. Any suspects? Any solid leads? Witnesses? Those kinds of things.

Nick nodded. "Sure. Why don't you stop back in day after tomorrow, I'll be working the same shift then."

Nick stood in a spot where he could see the parking lot and watched until he saw Jack pull out onto the highway and then he dialed Sid's number.

"Hello, Doctor Benson here." Sid didn't recognize the number that showed up on his cell phone.

"Hey, it's Nick. Would you have time to stop by the bar today? My shift ends at nine o'clock. I've got some information for you."

"I can probably fit it in," said Sid.

Sid followed Jennifer back to his house and after she parked her car, she jumped in with Sid and they left for Sid's appointment with his bartender friend.

"There's just something kinda creepy about the guy," said Nick. "He comes in here looking for information about that murder case. Says that you're working on it. I suppose you're involved because you're the medical examiner but he seems to think you're a lot more than that. Like a detective or something."

"What's his story?" asked Sid.

"Well," said Nick, "he claims that he has a friend who's in line to get this great newspaper job if he can get a good story on this murder. It actually sounds kind of phony to me, if you know what I mean."

"I think we need to know who his friend is," said Sid. "You any good at harvesting information? When is he supposed to stop in again?"

"Day after tomorrow," said Nick. "I'll keep you up to date."

Chapter 46

"This thing is really fun," said Jennifer as she sat on the patio in front of Sid's house picking small stones out of the pea gravel that surrounded the limestone. She was playing with her new slingshot and shooting the stones out over the lake. The distance that the shots would travel was quite impressive.

"I don't think that Whamo still makes slingshots," said Sid. "A liability thing. They were originally sold as hunting slingshots capable of killing things like squirrels and rabbits. Their advertising said that they had the impact of a twenty two caliber rifle and they're absolutely silent."

"You seem to know a lot about them," said Jennifer.

"I always wanted one when I was a kid but my parents would never allow it. The closest I ever got to one is the one in your hand right now."

"Well don't get any big ideas," said Jennifer. "You're not getting mine."

"We'll get some better ammo tomorrow," said Sid. "Steel ball bearings. There's a sporting goods shop in town that sells them. If you want to do any serious hunting you'll need something better than rocks."

"Maybe to help with the accuracy," said Jennifer. "Although I'm actually quite pleased with how well I can do with stones." Jennifer demonstrated her point by snipping the bud off of a dandelion that was at least fifteen yards away.

"Wow," said Sid. "You're a natural with that thing."

"But I won't be harming any bunnies or squirrels with it," said Jennifer. "Strictly a sport, no malice intended."

Sid went into the house and came out with two giant glasses of iced tea. "Best thing in the world on a hot day like today," he said

"And maybe a refreshing swim afterwards," added Jennifer.

Sid and Jennifer enjoyed the clear waters of Lake Huron for nearly a half hour before returning to the house and changing into casual summer clothes.

"Feel like dining out today?" asked Sid.

"Well, yes," said Jennifer. "But I'm not in the mood for anything fancy,"

"I've got just the place then," said Sid. "We'll slide over to the center of the universe and have a Heckleburger."

"A what?"

"There's a little old country bar not far from here that calls itself the center of the universe and their specialty is called the Heckleburger. They're famous for it. Seems like everybody in the county knows about Heckleburgers."

At Heck's Bar it seemed as if everybody in the friendly crowd knew each other and they all seemed to be ordering Heckleburgers. Country music exploded from the jukebox and beer flowed abundantly from the taps. It was a totally stress free experience that gave Sid and Jennifer a brief chance to forget the fact that they were being watched by murderers, even though the two men sitting at a nearby table drinking Coca-Cola were plain clothes sheriff's deputies.

The following morning at the strategy meeting, Deputy Ross brought everybody up to date on the progress. Although they had a name to connect with the mysterious shadow that was following them, the name didn't match up with anything helpful in police files. There were plenty of

Greg Smiths on the books but none of them appeared to be the one they wanted.

Sid relayed the information that Nick the bartender had given him yesterday. "I think I know who the guy is that's pumping Nick for information on me," he said. "Remember that hospital orderly that I told you about? The one who introduced me to the flower lady?"

"Yeah," said Ross. "But I thought you said he was helping you."

"I'm not so sure," said Sid. "I'm thinking that he's probably more concerned with helping himself. I figure somebody's paying him. All of his questions are about the investigation. It's not like he's trying to find out if I'm a trustworthy guy or anything."

"Can you get me some information on the guy?" asked Ross. "I'd like to check him out and see if we've got anything on him. Maybe a picture too, if you can."

"I should be able to get all of that for you today," said Sid. "He eats lunch in the hospital cafeteria every day."

On the ride to the hospital, Sid laid out his plan to Jennifer. "I'll occupy his attention and you can get a half dozen or so cell phone photos of him. Can you take pictures and not be obvious?"

"Are you kidding?" asked Jennifer. "I was a teenager not that many years ago and all teenage girls learn the art of stealth with their cell phone cameras. I mean, there were a lot of hot looking guys in my high school."

Sid looked at her but didn't comment.

Jennifer and Sid walked into the cafeteria separately. Jennifer stood in front of the pastry display acting like she was having trouble making up her mind while Sid ordered a chicken salad sandwich and slice of peach pie and took his tray over to a corner table where there was one lone man wearing scrubs who seemed to be absorbed in a bowl of chowder. Jennifer bought a coffee and positioned herself at a nearby table where she had a clear view of the orderly but he would have to turn his body to have a good look at her. She put the cell phone in camera mode and raised it up to her ear. Casually turning her head from side to side as she pretended to carry on a conversation she was able to get about ten pictures before two nurses sat down at a table between her and her subject, blocking the view.

Sid sat across from Jack and asked, "Okay if I sit here?"

Jack looked a bit nervous but just shrugged and asked, "How's things going with you? Still working on Trish's murder?"

"Well, the sheriff's department is," said Sid. "I'm just helping them out a little."

"I hope you get it figured out soon," said Jack. "That was a horrible tragedy. It will help if you can bring closure to her family."

"I'm not sure if there ever is closure," said Sid. "But we're trying to reach a solution to the case."

"Any progress?" asked Jack.

"Some," said Sid. "Little clues here and there. Eventually, they'll all add up to something. It's intriguing how these investigations work. Some of the stuff is mind boggling."

"Those kinds of things have always interested me," said Jack. "I'd love to hear all about it."

"Maybe when it's all over," said Sid. "But at this point I'm not allowed to talk about it. It's kind of a legally sanctioned Omerta thing. It's fun playing cop."

Without another word, Sid picked up his tray and headed to the exit.

Chapter 47

As soon as Jack's shift ended, he jumped in his car and headed toward Bay City. An hour later he was sitting in Sammy's office.

The doctor hinted that they had plenty of clues to work with and that they were studying them," said Jack. "He seems to think that they aren't too far off. But I don't believe they have any names so far."

"So you don't have anything specific yet," said Sammy.

"I'm close," said Jack. "I'm sure that I'll be of great value to you very soon. You'll be glad we got together."

"Time will tell," said Sammy. "What about your bartender contact? Has he given you anything worth mentioning?"

"He's working on it," said Jack. "I'll be seeing him tomorrow and hopefully he'll have something. He sounded like he was going to do his best and he's one of those kind of guys who can get people talking."

"Bartenders," Sammy smiled. "Everybody's best friend.

Jack left the office with a bag of marijuana and the possibility that he was on his way to a life of luxury.

Sid had walked into the hospital personnel office with a sheaf of papers in his hand and hurried past the secretary's desk waving the papers saying, "I just want to use your copying machine in the back room, I'll only be a minute."

The secretary, engrossed in her computer screen barely looked up.

Alone in the file room, Sid quickly went to the drawer containing Jack Dell's file, pulled out the folder and hurried over to the copier. Within three minutes he had everything he needed, walked out of the office still waving all the papers and saying, "Thanks."

The secretary mumbled, "No problem."

Sid drove back to his office and finished up some monthly reports for the health department and then informed Jennifer that they were done for the day and he was heading over to the sheriff's office. She was welcome to join him or since she had his spare garage door opener and key to his house, she might want to go straight to the beach.

"What do you think?" she smiled.

Sid stopped by Deputy Ross's office and dropped off the information on the hospital personnel records that he had copied earlier today. Ross said he'd run it through the system and see what he could find.

"Nobody's seen that Toyota around either," he said. "My guess is that he ditched it right away after your secretary made him. These guys operate like pros and it sounds like their organization isn't willing to risk their future on a hot car, especially a Toyota.

Sid left town and took the scenic route home, following the coast line for a little over nine miles. When he got to his house he found Jennifer lying on the beach on a towel listening to a CD of a steel drum band. "I can't help it," she said. "This lake front living is far more exotic than I ever expected. It's like being on a Caribbean Island, absolute paradise.

"You haven't seen it all yet," said Sid. "If you look real close, you can see that I have those rope lights installed in recesses all along the timbers and railings on the deck. They come in handy for finding my way back home if I happen to be out on the lake after dark. I turn them on for beach parties too. They outline the deck and railings in several different colors. Nice effect."

"What are you in the mood for as far as dinner tonight?" asked Jennifer. "I was thinking something light so I stopped at the store and picked up some stuff for a salad and a couple of orange roughy filets. Sound okay?"

"Sounds delicious," said Sid. "You trying to soften me up for something?"

They had barely made their way up to the deck when a man walked around the corner of the house.

Jennifer let out a startled shriek.

The man stopped dead, threw up his hands and said, "Hey, I'm just the bartender."

"Hey Nick," said Sid. "What brings you out this way? Got your lady with you?"

"Naw," said Nick. "If I'd have known you were having a party, I would have though. Actually, I've got some serious business, but if it's a bad time…"

"No problem," said Sid. "You can speak freely. Jennifer is on the sheriff's payroll and is our irreplaceable record keeper."

"Then she knows all about this guy who's asking questions then?" Asked Nick.

"I know everything," said Jennifer.

"Okay," said Nick. "I just want to know how you want me to handle him. Should I feed him some crap or pump him to see what he's really after?"

"When are you supposed to hook up with him again?" asked Sid.

"My shift starts at four tomorrow afternoon," said Nick. He said he'd be stopping by sometime after that."

"Do you think you could scoot over to Bad Axe and meet with the deputy in charge of this investigation before you go into work tomorrow?" asked Sid.

"One o'clock okay?" asked Nick

"Great," said Sid. "I want Deputy Ross involved. He's the guy who has to take the heat so he should make the decisions."

Nick sat across the desk from the sheriff's deputy as Ross brought him up to date on things that he needed to know. Then Ross turned to Sid and Jennifer. "Some of the possibilities that I'm considering could put you at risk so I want your input."

"As far as I'm concerned," said Jennifer, "we're already at risk. The guy who's following us looked me straight in the eye in our parking lot. He knows that I can identify him. That's enough for me. How could you make it even worse?"

"How about you?" the deputy asked Sid.

"I'm in. Been there from the beginning."

"What I'm considering," said Ross, "is having Nick here drop a few vague hints that we're making rapid progress and that we've found some extremely incriminating clues, specifically through the Medical Examiner's research. It's my guess that they're aware that we have one of their cell phones and that's enough to make them nervous. I doubt that they know about us finding the bodies up north, we haven't even notified all of the local county authorities yet. I've talked to the local sheriff and asked him to keep it under his hat so technically, we haven't broken any rules. But my thinking is that we should be able to get this hospital orderly excited enough to make him want to run to whoever is paying him. They already seem to have an unusual interest in you, Sid. Hopefully, the big man will make sure that sensitive information be delivered in person. We've got some excellent surveillance people on our staff and we can hopefully follow him right to the boss. Still willing to work with us?" he asked Nick.

"Are you kidding?" asked Nick. "I've dreamed bout doing stuff like this ever since I saw my first James Bond movie."

"Okay," said Ross, looking at Sid. "Got anything we can use for bait?"

"I've been thinking about that all morning," said Sid. "Forensic medicine is something that the general public knows very little about so I think it would be easy to come up with a convincing scenario. Ready?"

"Go ahead," said the deputy.

"Okay, here's my story," began Sid. "Everybody knows that DNA evidence is iron clad and so that's what might scare them. I'm going to say that science can now capture DNA samples through the same technology that led them to develop the transdermal patches that they use for smoking cessation only in reverse. Instead of introducing a substance into a body, they can extract it, specifically DNA. It takes a great deal of pressure to strangle a person, therefore a lot of trace DNA has been recovered from the body and I'm currently leading the testing team that will eventually identify it. Think that'll bring them running?"

Chapter 48

The supper crowd usually starts drifting into the Wooded Island Grill at somewhere around five thirty in the afternoon. At four o'clock Nick was behind the bar taking advantage of the lull to set up all of the liquor bottles in the proper order so that he could mix the dinner cocktails as efficiently as possible. The components for the most popular drinks were waiting in the most accessible wells. As if on cue, the hospital orderly came through the door at four fifteen. Every stool at the bar was empty.

"Anything new?" asked Jack as he swung his leg over the barstool.

Nick smiled. "Yeah, as a matter of fact there is. Are you prepared to pay?"

The response appeared to catch the orderly by surprise. "I can't give you anything now but if you can provide useful information, I'm sure I can have something for you by tomorrow."

"The doctor was in here for breakfast this morning and I played dumb with him. I said that I thought his only role in the investigation was to determine the cause of death. He said that there was a lot more and I asked him what it was."

"This could get interesting," said the orderly.

"I don't understand all that stuff," said Nick. "But the doctor claims that the killer left some kind of evidence on the body. Something he was trying to identify."

"What kind of evidence?" asked the orderly.

"Can't remember what he called it," said Nick. "But the victim was strangled and whatever the doctor was working with was something that the killer left on her neck."

"DNA?" asked the orderly.

"Yeah," said Nick. "That was it. He said he had some great samples and he was doing some kind of tests on it to identify who it came from. Said he was getting really close. Should have a positive ID within the next week or so."

"Sounds like you've got some money coming," said the orderly. "You working tomorrow?"

"Early shift," said Nick. "I'm outta here at five."

The orderly left the grill and headed straight toward Bay City. Thirty minutes later he was sitting in Sammy's office telling him everything that Nick had relayed to him. The plain looking Ford Taurus stayed three cars behind him all the way to his destination. The sign over the door that Jack disappeared through read, "Import and Export – Fine Clothing."

Sammy listened intently and then opened a desk drawer and counted out six one hundred dollar bills. He put five of them in an envelope and handed one to Jack saying, "One of those is yours and the other five are for that bartender. I want him to be interested enough to keep digging. Tell him I want more." Sammy walked over to a filing cabinet and took out a bag of high quality Columbian Marijuana and handed it to Jack. "We just may be very good for one another," he said.

After Jack left, Sammy spent some time pondering his options. He always liked and trusted Lefty and there was never a question about Lefty's loyalty. But his mistakes were beginning to make him a liability and Sammy knew he couldn't afford that. Something needed to be done and it wasn't going to be pleasant. He worried about it late into the night. If it was just a matter of visual identification, that could be fixed but you can't outrun your DNA signature. A decision would need to be made very soon and it had better be the right one.

Sid's cell phone rang. It was Nick. "Brace yourself," said Nick.

"He bought it?" asked Sid.

"Like an old man with a young hooker," answered Nick. "Anything else you need me to do? I could get to like this stuff really quick. The only things missing are the mysterious guys with foreign accents and the gorgeous babes with the high slits in their tight skirts."

"Oh, I'm sure there will be more," said Sid. "But we don't make any moves on our own. Everything has to go through the sheriff's office. You understand that, right?"

"You know me better than that," said Nick. "But I do have a question. What if they offer to pay me for spying on you?"

"You'd better run that one past Deputy Ross," said Sid. "But I'd bet that he'd want you to turn over the money to be held as evidence."

"Or I could just put it in my pocket and keep my mouth shut," said Nick.

"I wouldn't recommend that," said Sid. "It's always best to stay on the right side of the law. There's always a chance that any money they paid you could be legally yours after all the trials and appeals are over"

"You sure know how to ruin a guy's fun," said Nick.

"That's my job," answered Sid.

Chapter 49

Lefty and Slim had just left the Toyota in Detroit near the border of Highland Park and were headed north on I-75 on their way to Bay City. Lefty sat in the passenger seat of Slim's Buick LaCrosse. "I wonder if Sammy's going to set me up with something like this," he said as he swept his arm around the car's interior. "I never really liked that rice burner to begin with. Some salesman talked me into it."

"So Sammy's going to supply the car?" asked Slim.

"I'm sure that I'll wind up paying the bill," said Lefty. "But the car will be completely unconnected to me. It'll have some bogus registration that's good enough to get me past a traffic stop but won't really identify the owner."

"I hear that Sammy's using that weird guy from the hospital to try and dig up more stuff on the doctor," said Slim.

"Yeah," said Lefty. "That makes me nervous. Makes me think that Sammy is losing confidence in me."

"Well, that secretary can probably identify you now," said Slim. "Sammy most likely is just playing it safe."

"Yeah," said Lefty. "But the hospital guy's an amateur and they'll get you into trouble."

Slim dropped Lefty off at his apartment and said he'd pick him up in the morning in time for breakfast before they went to their meeting with Sammy.

Sammy stayed up much later than usual wrestling with the problem of what to do about Lefty. He was unsuccessful in his searches on latest developments in DNA collection methods but that didn't mean that major advances hadn't been made. Much of his research told him that there were dozens of studies being conducted on DNA collection by forensic teams but there was nothing specific. Given the rapid advances that occurred almost daily in that field, Sammy felt that it was best to assume that the doctor was employing the latest technology. He had to surmise that they were on to something. Something that tied Lefty to the murder. He decided that keeping Lefty around would jeopardize his entire operation. He considered sending Lefty out west to work with his former boss but there was still the DNA thing. The Computer database on that sort of stuff was virtually worldwide so distance didn't mean a thing. Lefty would have to be eliminated, a decision that would have Sammy tossing and turning most of the night.

Lefty and Slim showed up at Sammy's office at ten o'clock in the morning. Sammy led them out to the parking lot and presented Lefty with the keys to a dark blue Chevrolet Impala. "I figured a big guy like you would need a full size car," said Sammy. "Not sure if there's any fuel in it so you'd better make your first stop a gas station. Now get outta here."

Lefty gave him a blank look and climbed into the shiny new car. He shoved the key into the ignition, smiled, closed the door, and drove away.

"C'mon in the office," said Sammy. "We've got a lot to talk about."

Slim followed him into the building.

"How do you get along with Lefty?" asked Sammy.

"We've got each other's backs," said Slim.

"I want to know your deepest feelings about him, likes, dislikes, pet peeves, and so on," said Sammy.

Slim stared at Sammy for a few seconds before answering. "I dunno, I guess we get along okay. Everybody gets on someone's nerves sometimes. I suppose I get on his nerves too. But all in all we're cool. I wouldn't have recommended him to you if I didn't trust him"

Sammy said. "Tell me more."

"What is it that you're looking for?" asked Slim. "Are you thinking that he's gone sour or something?"

"There's the possibility of trouble in the near future and I'm just trying to figure out how to head it off," said Sammy.

"What kind of trouble?" asked Slim.

"Well," Sammy began. "I don't believe that Lefty would ever double cross us but it seems he has become a little too careless. Of course you know about the secretary getting a good look at his face but it gets worse. Much worse. It looks like he may have left his DNA on Trish's body."

"How could that be?" asked Slim. "He only used his hands on her neck, never touched her clothes or anything. And he never touched her after she was on the ground. Those two other guys took it from there. And they were wearing latex gloves."

"I told you in the beginning that I was uncomfortable with the fact that there was a doctor working with the investigating team," said Sammy. "The reason just became obvious. This Doctor Benson is involved in some sort of research on new ways to extract DNA and my source tells me that he found something significant on Trish's neck. Even though none of us could have foreseen it, that puts Lefty in a very bad position."

"I see what you mean," said Slim. "You thinking of cutting him loose?"

"I wish it were that simple," said Sammy. "If the cops have his DNA signature and he's wanted for murder, that information will go into a nationwide data base, the FBI gets involved and he would automatically become a time bomb. Couple that with the description that the secretary will undoubtedly give to a sketch artist and it makes it even worse. I'd love to find a way to just send Lefty away somewhere but it's way too risky. He's a liability and the problem has to be dealt with."

"And you want me to do it," said Slim.

"Do you see another way?" asked Sammy.

"It is what it is," said Slim. "Life isn't always fair. I'm not nuts about it but your point makes perfect sense."

"I don't like it any better than you do," said Sammy. "But I'm afraid it has to be done."

"How much time do I have?" asked Slim.

"Take whatever you need to make sure that it's done right and doesn't leave a trace," said Sammy. "We can't afford any special attention."

"You want me to call you when I'm ready?" asked Slim.

"That'd be good," answered Sammy.

Chapter 50

"Y'know, these drug guys mean business," said Jennifer. "Those bodies we dug out of the sand up north kinda proves that, dontcha think?"

"They're dangerous," said Sid. "That's why we've got to stay on our toes. By the way, has the sheriff's department scheduled your handgun training class yet? The fact that you looked that character in the eye could put you in a bad position."

"Yup," said Jennifer. "Tomorrow's the big day. I don't own a gun though so they said they'd provide one. I guess I'll have to do some shopping once I figure out what kind of gun I want."

"The guys in the department can help you with that," said Sid. "I have a forty caliber that I like just fine and I can actually hit the target with it. You could probably handle one."

Jennifer closed the filing cabinet drawer and checked her watch. "You about caught up? We've got a meeting with your favorite deputy in a half hour."

"I'll be ready," said Sid. "It makes me feel sorta guilty that we are only putting in a couple of hours a day in this office and aren't falling behind in our work. Maybe we should only be part time help?"

"Shut your mouth," said Jennifer. "I'm not a rich doctor, I need a full time job."

Deputy Ross opened the meeting by asking Sid how well he knew Nick the bartender.

"We go back to when he and another guy opened their first bar. It was Nick who did most of the work. The other guy was mostly an investment partner who came across some big life insurance money when his dad died. The partner said he'd take care of the books and stay out of Nick's way. Nick always ran the joint like it was in Vegas. Everything in the place was classy and spotlessly clean and tasteful. Lots of people predicted that he'd never make it because his place was too fancy for this rural area, too much overhead but Nick bit the bullet and kept his prices competitive even though his operating costs were higher. He's one of those kind of guys who makes friends easily and is just generally likable. He brought a little class to his customer's lives and they appreciated it. It was a very prosperous business. When his partner got into trouble with some big time gamblers, the guy cleaned out the bank account and skipped town leaving Nick with a bunch of unpaid bills and no money. Nick had to declare insolvency, sell everything and start over from scratch. He didn't leave the creditors high and dry though. It took a while but he eventually settled every last account. I'd say that says something about his character."

"Good endorsement," said Deputy Ross. "It's not like I didn't trust him, I just don't know him. Sounds like he's got this hospital orderly drooling for more information. You willing to keep pushing?"

"We've got to get to the bottom of this," said Sid. "None of us will be safe until it's over. Keep it moving."

"Okay," said Ross. "We're going to let it leak that we've got a name linked to the victim and that we're gathering evidence to make sure we have enough for an arrest. That could very easily bring someone out of their hole."

"And right to our door," said Jennifer. "I wish this was over, it's scaring the daylights out of me."

"You'll have twenty four hour protection until we can put this thing to bed," said Ross. "We're taking this situation very seriously. Sergeant Duffield from the State Police called this morning and said that they've assigned extra people to try to get a handle on this Greg Smith slash Lefty guy. He says they've got plenty of Lefty's to work with and they're on it in a big way. So far nobody's got a Sammy on their radar, although we believe that he's the guy in the office building that your orderly visited yesterday. We have a mess of surveillance photos of everyone who entered and exited the place and we've set up a post in an unoccupied gas station directly across the road so we're still collecting information. We've contacted the owner of the office building and we'll be meeting with him later today. He's been instructed not to talk to anybody about our conversation and told to bring copies of the lease agreement with him. We want to know who his lessee is. Got a full day ahead."

Sid called his friend Nick and told him the plan. Nick seemed eager to get it going. "That Jack guy said he'd be back today," said Nick. "I'll be ready for him. Hey, I got this idea. I have one of those mini voice recorders that I used to use during meetings when I had my own place. I can stick it in my shirt pocket and nobody knows its there. It picks up voices really good. I wouldn't worry about him catching on. It's not like he was trained by the CIA or anything."

"Sure, why not?" said Sid. "Any information we can get will help."

Sid told Deputy Ross that he would gladly supply temporary living quarters to any officers that were assigned to his protection. They could park their vehicle in his garage and keep it out of sight if they wished. Ross thanked him and said they'd take him up on his offer and the County would cover expenses in accordance with surveillance policy.

Sid and Jennifer drove to his house with an undercover car behind them. After both vehicles were locked safely in the garage, they made their way inside followed by two plainclothes deputies carrying overnight bags. Once inside, Sid showed them to the two unused guest rooms, threw each of them a set of sheets and pillow cases and told them that they were responsible for making their own beds. "I hope you guys brought bathing suits," said Sid. "We have daily beach parties in this neck of the woods followed by a cookout on the deck and then a bonfire on the beach. Burgers, dogs, and beer provided" Both deputies smiled, nodded and began putting their stuff away.

Chapter 51

It was only six thirty in the morning when Sammy answered the phone, it was Slim. "Good morning boss, Okay if I stop by for a chat?"

"I've been waiting for your call," said Sammy. "I'll be here all day."

"See you soon," said Slim.

Sammy made a quick call to Lefty. "I'd like you to run over to Grand Rapids today and see if you can get a feel for who comes and goes from that Winston guy's store. I'm not sure I believe his story."

"I know what you mean," said Lefty. "I'll take care of it."

"There's fresh coffee in the pot," said Sammy. "I've sent Lefty over to the other side of the state so that he won't pop in here unexpectedly."

Slim poured himself a cup and both men sat down to talk.

"What about the car?" asked Slim. "The one Lefty is driving now?"

"There is absolutely no way it can be traced to us," said Sammy. "It was purchased by a third party and through a proxy and registered to a non-existent person at a phony address. It can also be triggered to be reported stolen if you need to use it."

"Sounds like you've got that covered," said Slim.

"I factored in the possibility of needing to make owner-ship invisible when I bought it. I'm not worried about losing it, that's the price of doing business," said Sammy.

"In that case, I'm ready to go as early as tomorrow night if you still want to move ahead," said Slim.

"I do," said Sammy. "Regrettably, but we must."

Lefty's phone jingled. "Hello," he said, "this is Lefty."

"Hey, it's Slim. We got a little job for late tomorrow afternoon and then we've got the night off. We can let our hair down and enjoy the party for a change. Can you meet me at Hooter's at seven o'clock sharp?"

"You got it," said Lefty.

Slim was waiting in the parking lot when Lefty arrived. "What's the deal?" asked Lefty.

"You know what a stickler Sammy can be when it comes to details, right?" asked Slim.

"Yeah," said Lefty. "It can be a real pain sometimes."

"Well, I've got to make a delivery in a few minutes and Sammy wants you to witness it," said Slim.

"Why? What's the big deal about making a delivery?" asked Lefty.

"I didn't ask. Maybe he doesn't quite trust me. You'll have to take that up with Sammy next time you see him," said Slim.

Within a few minutes a dark colored Volkswagen CC pulled into the lot. The driver stepped out and opened the rear door. Slim walked over and shoved a box into the back seat and the driver got back in and drove away. No words were exchanged between the two.

Slim walked over to Lefty's car and said. "That's it. I did it, you saw it, we're done. Why don't you park this thing right down there by the river and we'll take my car. I can be your designated driver." Slim pointed to a spot in the corner of the lot where the overhead light was burned out. After sunset it would be the only dark place in the whole lot.

Lefty pulled to the end of the parking lot, his headlights shining out over the Saginaw River. He put his new car in park and pulled out the keys, stuffing them in his pocket. He joined Slim in the other car.

"Where are we headed?" asked Lefty as he slid into the passenger seat.

"Nowhere in particular," said Slim. "I thought we'd just cruise around like we did in the old days."

Yeah," said Lefty. "But back then we were drinking beer and trying to pick up girls."

"I can't help with the girls," said Slim. "But I can bump up the beer thing up a notch." He reached into the console and pulled out a fifth of Jim Beam Kentucky Bourbon and handed it to Lefty. "Crack it open, it's all yours. I got my own." He held up a bottle of clear liquid with a Smirnoff label. "I know that you love bourbon but I'm more of a vodka type."

Lefty unscrewed the cap and held up the bottle. He smiled and said, "Salute."

They drove around downtown Bay City for almost two hours and then headed to Saginaw. They spent another couple of hours ogling the topless dancers at a bar near downtown. When they had their fill of the incessant noise they wandered back to the parking lot. Lefty was beginning to show the effects of the alcohol and looked to be near the point of no return. Slim made sure that Lefty had the liquor bottle back in his hand as soon as they got back in the car and immediately proposed a toast. Lefty was too far gone to realize what was happening. He took a giant tug on the bottle. By the time they rolled back into Bay City, Lefty was clearly over the hill. His words were horribly slurred and his sentences made no sense.

It was well after three o'clock when they finally returned to the Hooter's parking lot. The building was totally dark except for nighttime security lighting and Slim was pleased to see that Lefty's car was almost invisible in the dark corner of the lot. He put on a pair of latex gloves. Lefty was passed out in the front seat of Slim's car and had no idea where he was. Slim pulled up across the back of Lefty's car blocking the line of sight from the road. There was a cyclone fence along the seawall supposedly to prevent cars from accidentally rolling into the water but it was only residential quality and most likely had been installed as an insurance requirement. Slim took the fencing pliers from his back pocket pulled all of the tie wires that secured the fence fabric to the posts. Once they looked as if they'd been stretched to their limit, he used the pliers to break the wires. He left some of them hanging on the fence and some wrapped around the posts. The next thing he did was run back to his car and dig through Lefty's pockets until he found the car keys. He opened up Lefty's car and stuck the key in the ignition turned it to the accessory position and lowered the rear windows. He then returned to his car and pulled Lefty out, attempting to stand him up. Lefty groaned and rolled his head, not even remotely aware of his surroundings. Slim was able to get Lefty into the Impala, slumped over the center console with his feet safely inside the passenger compartment. He returned to his car and retrieved two twelve pound barbell weights. He threw one of them on the floor on the passenger side and positioned the other just above the accelerator pedal. The car was about fifteen feet from the water's edge. Slim started the engine and made sure that the front wheels were pointed straight ahead and then stuck his leg inside and stepped on the brake pedal. He moved the shift lever to the 'drive' position and then raised the barbell weight directly over the accelerator. He quickly dropped the weight pulled his foot off the brake, stepped back and slammed the door.

The car lurched forward and had built up enough momentum to slide under the cyclone fence and launch over the low curb and off the seawall. It floated for a few seconds but when it began to sink, the water rapidly poured in through the open windows. In a matter of minutes, it was gone with only occasional bubbles rising to the surface. Slim stood waiting on the seawall for a full five minutes before returning to his car.

"So Long old Buddy," he murmured as he drove away.

Chapter 52

It had been almost two weeks and things were returning to normal on Charity Island. Rick Todd, the caretaker had resumed his regular sunrise walks along the shoreline. Ever since finding that body, he was hesitant to wander in the westerly direction from the lightkeeper's house but today he was covering the same territory where he had made the grisly discovery. A few of the guests who had visited the Island recently wanted to see just where the victim had been found. Rick usually led these groups and took them to a spot almost fifty yards from the actual site. The original location had been virtually untouched. Rick didn't want people stomping around where that pretty young lady had died. Today as he walked along the shore, the sunlight caught something fluttering in the breeze. There were a few scrub plants that grew right at the water's edge and right next to the spot where the boat had been pulled up on the beach there was something tangled in the branches of the little shrub. He walked up to it and leaned over without touching anything. It was a latex glove. About the same color as the sand, it would be very easy to overlook, especially since everybody had been looking at the ground and not a foot above it. That Medical Examiner had given Rick his cell phone number and told him to call if anything new showed up.

Sid and Jennifer were on their way to town to attend their regularly scheduled meeting with Deputy Ross and then Jennifer would report to her concealed pistol license class. It was another one of those beautiful cloudless mornings that the farmers hate. The music from the radio was interrupted by the sound of a cell phone ringing. "Hello," said Sid.

"Hi, this is Rick, the caretaker from Charity Island. You said to call you if I found anything else that might be important. Well, I might have something for you. I found a glove like the ones you doctors always wear."

"Oh yeah?" said Sid. Did you touch it?"

"Nope," said Rick. "It's still tangled up in the weeds right where we found that girl."

"Can you tell if it's inside out?" asked Sid.

"Y'know, I don't know why I paid attention to that but I did. It's right side out. That might be what caught my attention. Every time I see someone take those gloves off they wind up inside out. Maybe that's why it looked weird to me."

"Good," said Sid. "I'm more interested in what I might find on the inside of the glove. If you can carefully remove it from where it is without touching the inside, I want you to do that. Put it in one of those evidence bags that I left with you and seal it up. We'll be out to pick it up as soon as we can get there."

"It looks pretty well twisted around the weeds," said Rick. "It was pretty windy that night and it looks like it's tied in a knot. I'm sure it won't be going anywhere if I just leave it alone. I'd rather not touch it. I'm afraid I'd tear it."

"If you're sure it's secure where it is, just leave it alone and I'll be out to get it," said Sid. Does it look like it will still be there in a couple of days?"

"There's nothing showing on the weather radar," said Rick. "It will be okay."

"What was that all about?" asked Jennifer.

"Looks like you'll have at least one more chance to visit your island paradise. The guy over there on Charity Island just said that he found a surgical glove at the crime scene. I don't know how we could have overlooked it but we'd better get ahold of it and check it for trace evidence."

"So we get to go back out there?" asked Jennifer. "How cool, I'll have to get a new outfit for the occasion."

When they got to the sheriff's headquarters, Jennifer was told to report to the pistol range and Sid headed upstairs to Deputy Ross's office.

Ross was impressed with the latest news. "What do you think you can get out of it?" he asked.

Whoever wore it had to leave their DNA on the inside and from the way that the caretaker described it, it's undisturbed. Looks like a good chance of getting something useful."

"I hope so," said Ross. "What do you think of combining it with the story that your bartender buddy is going to pass along to his contact this afternoon?"

Sid was quiet for a moment and then said, "You know, that just might make them even more nervous and knock them a little out of balance. It's probably a good idea to keep hitting them with more than they can handle. Might force them into a big mistake. We need some bold moves to get them into a panic mode. I'll call Nick.

Nick had just walked into the Wooded Island Sports Grill but had not started his shift yet when his phone rang. "Talk to me," he answered.

"Hey Nick, this is your buddy Sid. Got more stuff for you. How about you tell this hospital orderly that something of great significance has been discovered out on Charity Island and it looks like only a matter of days until they have a positive ID on the killer. Tell him that a team of forensic investigators will be sent to the island very soon."

"Love it," said Nick. "Can I go with you guys?"

"It's just cover," said Sid. "We're trying to flush them out."

"I'll let you know how it goes," said Nick.

At five o'clock in the afternoon Jack Dell came through the doorway at Wooded Island. A few diners were scattered among the tables, mostly families with young children. Nobody was at the bar, the drinking crowd wouldn't show up for another hour or two. Nick activated his voice recorder and made sure that the microphone was oriented properly. "What's up, Jack?" he said.

Jack made his way to the end of the bar, hopped up on a stool and ordered a Bud Light Draft and said he wanted to run a tab. When Nick set the glass in front of him, Jack slid an envelope across the bar and said. "Sammy says thank you."

Nick said thanks and stuffed the envelope in his pocket.

"Got anything new?" whispered Jack.

"You don't have to worry about anyone eavesdropping," said Nick.

"They're all too far away to hear."

Jack looked around, checking each customer and satisfying himself that it was safe to talk. "Just wondered if you've heard any more from your doctor friend."

"Yeah," said Nick. "Him and his secretary were in for breakfast this morning and since I'm being groomed for general manager of this place, I'm on long hours so I'm here from open to close all week. Anyway, they were in a real chatty mood. I sat down with them and he told me a lot about what's going on."

"Really," said Jack. "Can't wait to hear it." He leaned in closer to Nick.

"Of course he couldn't tell me everything," said Nick. "After all, it's an ongoing investigation."

Jack was becoming impatient. "Yeah, I understand, so what did he tell you?"

Nick smiled. "Looks like they've discovered something new out there on Charity Island. He says it's blockbuster, something they never expected. He wouldn't say exactly what it was but he said that he was going to take some doctors or scientists out there in the next few days to evaluate it. He was just getting ready to put his team together."

"I wonder what it could be," said Jack. I work around doctors all day long so I know a little bit about forensic medicine and I can't imagine anything being that important."

Nick, improvising now said. "I guess it's something that's still in the research stage. That's why the doctor needs certain experts to check it out. He's trying to get this one particular guy to go with him. Some guy who works for the government. Department of Health or something."

"I suppose we'll just have to wait and see," said Jack.

"There's more," said Nick. "Remember what I told you about that new method of recovering DNA from a victim's skin? Well according to the doc, they've been able to connect a name to whoever it was that strangled her."

"Wow," said Jack. "My friend will be very interested to know that. Of course the doctor didn't tell you the name, right?"

Nick gave him an exasperated look and said. "Are you nuts? Do I look like a cop or something? Nobody's gonna give me that kind of information."

Another customer sat down at the bar a few stools away from Jack and so Jack paid his tab and left.

When he finally had a chance for a break, Nick wandered outside to the patio area and pulled the envelope out of his pocket. He opened it up and looked inside without touching anything. He counted five one hundred dollar bills. He shut his eyes and slammed the envelope shut. "I wish I hadn't looked. Why do I have to be so damned honest? I sure hope the Sheriff appreciates people like me." He went back inside and called Sid. "Hey tell your cop buddies that I've got some evidence money for them half a K worth. I'll drop it off in the morning and don't worry, I won't fondle it and wipe any evidence off of it."

Chapter 53

The big wrecker was parked in the Hooters parking lot and surrounded by four Bay City police cruisers. The entire end of the lot was cordoned off with police barrier tape. There were three divers in the water and a team of four detectives were examining the cyclone fence that had been stretched and distorted by the car that passed through it. "I'm not entirely convinced that I'm seeing everything," said one of the detectives. He held up one of the broken tie wires that had held the fence to the post. "Usually they stretch a lot farther before they break."

"Made in China," said his partner.

"Be just a few minutes more," said one of the divers who had just surfaced. "The Lieutenant wants the body out first. I'll let you know when we're ready."

The harbormaster boat cruised slowly back and forth on the river warning gawkers away.

As soon as the body was out of the water it was covered, loaded on a gurney and slid into the back of an ambulance. A wallet, retrieved from the victim's back pocket was being dissected by detectives on the hood of one of the cruisers. "Gregory Smith," said one of the cops as he held up the driver's license. "Why does that name sound familiar?"

One of the other detectives chimed in. "Yeah, seems like we've been hearing that name a lot lately. I think it's come up within the last few days."

"It did," said the first detective. "I just remembered. That deputy sheriff up in Huron County said they wanted to talk to him about a murder. Can't remember the deputy's name but I've got his card in my desk drawer. I'll call him when we get back to the precinct."

"That's right," said another detective. "It had something to do with that guy who got run over by that stolen car. Seems he was dirty too and getting almost killed made him want to clear his conscience. I think he ran over someone too, a while back."

The diver's team leader hollered up to the wrecker driver. "The hookup is all set, we can start dragging it out any time. The vehicle is pretty much in a straight line with your winch cable. Should be an easy pull."

The diver climbed out of the water and stood on the seawall. His two partners disappeared below the water, one on either side of the car to observe the progress and prepared to shoot to the surface if any problems should pop up. The leader gave the signal to begin.

The tow truck was lashed down by four large steel stakes driven deep into the asphalt and connected to all four corners of the truck with three quarter inch steel cables. The driver stood to the side where the hydraulic control console was mounted. The rig seemed to pull effortlessly at first but when the rear end of the water filled car broke the surface, the winch began to creak and groan. The operator slowed everything down to a crawl, allowing the water to pour out of the open rear windows. As soon as they were clear of the water, the two divers reached up and pulled open the rear doors, creating a minor deluge and the big car rocked back and forth on the hook.

The detectives, who had been watching commented that the retrieval was moving along painfully slow. The tow truck operator and the divers all agreed that progress was absolutely perfect. The operator smiled and told the cops, "It's all our show for now. We'll let you know when we're done."

One of the detectives had donned a motorcycle rider's rain suit so that he could climb into the car and sit in the seats without getting his clothes drenched. As soon as the car was on solid ground and the rigging removed from the frame, the cop climbed into the driver's seat with a notebook in his hand.

"Everything in here looks new," he said. He rummaged through the glove compartment. "Owner's manual still sealed in a plastic bag."

Another detective added a thought. "Lots of new cars are involved in accidents because the driver's are unfamiliar with them. Happens all the time."

"It bothers me that the back windows were rolled down," said the first detective. "Nobody runs their windows down anymore unless they have a dog. The windows in the front doors were all the way up."

The tow truck operator had a flatbed car hauler waiting out in the street. "Wanna get this thing back to your pound so you can give it a good going over?"

"As soon as we get all of the pictures of the scene," said the detective.

Slim pulled into the parking lot at Sammy's office around ten o'clock in the morning. "Didn't get to bed until almost five," he said. "But it's all done. It was clean and painless and, with a little bit of luck it will be written off as an accident."

Sammy folded his hands in his lap and stared down at his desk. "I truly liked Lefty. You don't know how tormented I was while making this decision. If only there could have been another way. I will mourn and grieve properly but I will never be able to forgive myself."

"You have a business to run," said Slim. "You can't allow it to suffer or all of this will have been for nothing."

"How are you?" asked Sammy. "If you need some time for yourself, I'll understand."

"I think it's best if I stay busy," said Slim. "There's plenty for me to do. Somebody's got to keep an eye on that doctor and right now, I'm all you've got."

Sammy had not moved since Slim walked in the door but now he came to life. He stood up and walked around the desk perching on a corner. He leaned toward Slim and said. "I don't know how much longer I want to screw around with this medical examiner. I've had a bad feeling about him from the beginning. We might have to make a move on him very soon."

"What about his secretary? He doesn't seem to go anywhere without her," asked Slim.

"Collateral damage," said Sammy. "You can't make an omelet without breaking a few eggs."

"Do you want me to figure out how to pull it off or do you have a plan? I'm okay either way," said Slim.

"Give me a day or two to think about it," said Sammy. "As it stands right now, the cops are only worried about one dead body. This would wake up a lot of sleeping cops. We've got to be very careful. We'll talk some more about this and I'll tell you when to move."

Chapter 54

"Something big is going to happen," said Jack. "So far I haven't been able to find out exactly what it is but it's going to involve a trip out to Charity Island. My source tells me that Doctor Benson will be taking a team of scientists out there to look at something that's extremely important, something that he says will answer all of his questions."

"Interesting," said Sammy. "And that's all the information you have? Did he give you any clues at all? This is from your bartender friend, right?

"Yeah my bartender friend said that the doctor was in there for breakfast this morning and told him that they'd be calling in experts from as far away as Georgia," said Jack. "They plan on going out there as soon as their expert is available, probably within the next two or three days."

"Hmm, Georgia," said Sammy. "The only research facility that comes to mind down there is the Center for Disease Control. They do some real cutting edge stuff at that place. But they're too big to bother with some little homicide in a small town in Michigan."

"Unless it had something to do with one of their current research projects," said Jack.

"I suppose we can't discount that," said Sammy. "Do you think there's any chance that you can find out when this exploratory trip will take place? I'll need all the details you can get. I mainly want to know if there will be any cops going along. I know it's sensitive trying to tiptoe around digging out that kind of information. Do you think you can you do it?"

"I've been pretty successful so far," said Jack. "All I can do is try. Oh, and I almost forgot, I have more information."

"I'm listening," said Sammy.

"The doctor also said that they knew who strangled Trish," said Jack.

"Now that would be interesting," said Sammy. "I wonder how they figured that one out."

"It has something to do with recovering DNA samples," said Jack. "When a person strangles someone, their fingers exert lots of pressure and it's kind of a transdermal infusion thing. I hear it's developing technology."

Sammy went back to his filing cabinet and drew out another six one hundred dollar bills, putting five of them in an envelope. Then he turned to Jack. "How are you doing on grass, got enough for the next week or so?"

"I'm fine for now," said Jack. He left by the back door and drove back to his mobile home in Bad Axe.

Sammy called Slim and asked him to stop by as soon as possible. Slim said he was up north tracking Doctor Benson but it looked like he was in for the night. "I'm about an hour away," said Slim. "I'll get there as quick as I can."

The sun was setting as Slim pulled in behind Sammy's office.

"Something new has come up and I don't know what to make of it," said Sammy. "Do you have the means to get over to Charity Island without getting on that ferryboat?"

"Been there dozens of times," said Slim. "It's tricky unless you go in through the main channel but I've landed a twenty footer on the beach with no problems lots of times when the water level was down. It's almost a foot higher now. I can handle it. What have you got in mind?"

"My little spy buddy was just here and said that he's been told that the doctor has found some sort of amazing discoveries that will lay their investigation wide open," said

Sammy. "It's something scientific in nature and he's bringing in outside help to try to figure it out. Whatever it is, they have to go to Charity Island to work on it. They're planning their trip to be within a few days."

"Fascinating," said Slim. "So you want me to be there waiting for them? How many will there be? And what do you want me to do?"

"At this point, there are still a lot of things I've got to find out," said Sammy. "If it turns out to be something extremely damaging to us, we can't afford to let it happen. I wish I had someone like Lefty to send with you."

"I'm used to working alone, actually prefer it," said Slim. "I've got access to a boat that's perfect for a job like this. I can pick it up in the morning and run it up to one of the marinas near Point Lookout along the west side of the bay and tie up in a transient slip. I can be within a thirty minute ride of the island and ready to go. Is that okay with you?"

"I like the idea of being ready to move at a moment's notice," said Sammy. "As far as I can estimate, it will be the doctor, his secretary, the island caretaker, and one or two scientists. I don't know about any law enforcement people."

Slim nodded his head. "I don't think any of them should be armed unless they have a cop with them. Even if they do, I should be able to handle it with no problem."

"I have absolute faith in you," said Sammy. "It's all I can do to hold the street operations together with all this turmoil going on around me. It's a good thing that I've got competent and reliable people working for me. Stop by here in the morning so that we can work out some sort of code. We'll have to communicate by cell phone and the cops have no problem intercepting those conversations."

"Got it," said Slim. "See you in the morning"

As soon as he left Sammy's office, Slim called the manager of one of the Bay City marinas that he dealt with on special occasions. "Hey, this is Slim, I'm gone need a boat for a few days, something around eighteen, twenty feet or thereabouts. Gotta have a shallow draft and a cuddy cabin."

"I got a couple like that to choose from," said the voice on the other end. "When do you need it?"

"Around noon tomorrow," answered Slim.

Slim got back to his apartment and turned in for the night, trying to make up for the three hours of sleep that he had the night before, At seven o'clock the next morning, he had a shower and was packing a duffel bag. He packed a couple of pairs of jeans along with the summer clothes that would help him blend in with the other boaters at the marina. In the bottom of the bag was a nine millimeter Ingram Machine Pistol with a suppressor and two spare thirty two round magazines just in case extra firepower was needed and his forty caliber Glock rested in his inside the waistband concealment holster. He threw the bag in the trunk of his car and set off to meet with Sammy.

There was a fresh pot of coffee on top of a filing cabinet and a box of donuts sitting on the credenza when Slim walked in. He sat down across from Sammy and they went over the key words that would allow them to talk over unsecured cell phone signals.

Chapter 55

Sid walked out of the sporting goods store with a plastic bag in his hand. He opened the pickup truck door, jumped into the drivers seat and handed the bag to Jennifer. He fastened his seat belt and fired up the engine. Jennifer looked inside the bag and asked, "What's this all about? Looks like a package of shiny marbles."

"It's slingshot ammo," said Sid. Usually they recommend one quarter inch balls but they were out of them so those are three eighths of an inch, half again as big. Now you can hunt big game. Ever shoot a moose?"

Jennifer rolled her eyes, "You guys just never quit, do you."

"Well, you were doing so good with rocks, I figured I'd get you something more balanced and symmetrical. They're bound to be better.

Jennifer scowled and jammed them in her purse.

Sid pulled into his driveway followed by the unmarked patrol car and closed the door behind both cars once they were in the garage. As soon as they got in the house, his cell phone began ringing. It was Deputy Ross.

"The Bay City Police called and said that they recovered a body from the Saginaw River this morning and it's been tentatively identified as a Greg Smith. They're thinking he might be our Lefty. They'll be shooting some facial pictures of him as soon as they can and they'll be emailing them to me. I'll forward them to your email address and you can ask your secretary to look at them. I hope she can make a positive ID. Also, there's been an extra high level of activity at that office building that we've got staked out just outside of Bay City. That makes me nervous and it should get your attention as well. Keep your guard up. I'll be briefing your two babysitters next.

One of the heavy's that we've seen around visited there this morning and stayed inside for quite a while. Then, a bit later that hospital orderly showed up. Was inside for over an hour. After he left, the heavy returned and stayed there for a long time again. That place has got to be headquarters. I'm sure of it. So far, there's no name for the tenant. It's leased to a clothing import company but the actual lease was signed by somebody out on the west coast. It's intentionally foggy.

"We fed them a lot of crazy information through our bartender buddy so it might be causing some panic," said Sid. "If that guy that they fished out of the river turns out to be the one that Jennifer spotted, it would prove that they're desperate. Remember, Trish was one of their own and they didn't hesitate to kill her when they thought she was turning on them. If they viewed Lefty as a threat to expose them, it would follow the same pattern."

"You're beginning to think like a cop," said Ross. "You guys will be here early tomorrow, right? Your secretary has that concealed carry class at nine o'clock and so we should try to get together around eight."

"That should work," answered Sid. "The sports grill is open at six for breakfast and I'll tell Nick I want him to meet me there. He probably closed the bar last night so he'll be groggy and crabby, but he'll show up. I want to know everything that was said during the time that Jack Dell was there. Anything you want me to pass along?"

"Naw," said Ross, "he's doing a great job. Stopped by here this morning and dropped off an envelope with five one hundred dollar bills in it. Said that it came from a guy named

Sammy. He asked if he could have it back after all the legal proceedings were done. I told him I'd do whatever I could. The prosecutor will probably release it when we're all done.

"When are we going to run out to Charity Island?" asked Sid. "I'd like to get to work on that glove, especially since we've got a new body to compare it to."

"Day after tomorrow," said Ross. "It's all set up. I'll have a deputy go with you and that Sergeant Duffield from the State Police wants to go along too, gonna meet us at the dock at nine in the morning. So with your secretary, that'll make four altogether. I'll contact that caretaker kid tomorrow and let him know you're coming. Oh, and another thing. A judge in Kalkaska County where you dug up those two bodies has issued an order that the information be made public within seventy two hours. The decision came down at three o'clock this afternoon, so we've got just under three days before Sammy and his gang explode."

Sid and Jennifer walked into the Wooded Island Sports grill at six o'clock on the dot. There were already customers seated and going over their menus. Two waitresses scurried from table to table filling coffee cups and promising to return in a few minutes to take the breakfast orders. Five minutes later Nick walked in the door looking like he just rolled out of bed. "This is becoming not fun anymore," he said. "I'm already short on sleep, the Sheriff has all the money that I worked for, and now you're dragging me out of the sack in the middle of the night. Where do I go to sign up to quit?"

"Have a coffee," said Sid, "it'll change your whole viewpoint on the world."

"Yeah, right," said Nick. He winked at Jennifer, sat down across from Sid and asked, "What do you need?"

"It looks like the information you gave that orderly yesterday has stirred the pot in somebody's world. Just how far did you go?"

"I did just like you told me," said Nick. "I said that you were on to something big. Bigger than you could handle and that you asked for outside help. Told him you'd have to go back to the island the day after tomorrow to figure it out, whatever it was. And then I told him that you had ID'd the strangler."

"I want to warn you," said Sid. "These guys are killers. We might be able to connect them to four murders so far and we have no idea how far they'll go or what they're thinking. Don't get in too deep."

Chapter 56

Slim was delighted to see an eighteen and a half foot Sea Ray Cuddy Cabin waiting for him. It was plain enough looking and a couple of years old. It was powered by a potent five liter Mercruiser engine with a hydraulic outdrive. The fuel gauge rested on full and it had all the accessories including a GPS, ship to shore radio, and binnacle compass. There was even an AM-FM radio and CD player with plenty of speakers.

Slim had checked the NOAA website this morning and the nearest low pressure cell was still west of the Rockies. The weather looked calm and stable for at least the next week. Slim had brought along a couple of folding lawn chairs, an air mattress and a sleeping bag. He stowed his gear bag and the rest of his things in the cuddy cabin and sat his cooler on the deck next to the captain's seat. He paid cash for four days rental and took the key from the marina manager. Ten minutes later the Bay City skyline was disappearing behind him.

The northward trip was as uneventful as it could be. Slim found an empty transient slip at his favorite marina. It included wi-fi, dockside power, and water plus a key to the bathrooms and showers. There was a barbecue grill mounted on a post next to the slip as well as a small picnic table. There was even a pay phone in an old style phone booth. The place was only one block off the main drag where there were two bars, a pizzeria, and a party store with a deli counter. He had everything he needed.

Slim secured the boat and locked the cuddy and then strolled into town. The bars were both full of sunburned fishermen fresh off the lake and they all seemed to be inhaling the beer by the gallon. Slim decided that he wouldn't hang around very long because that much beer was bound to cause trouble. The crowd was happy and laughing right now but they were only a few more drafts away from a waterfront donnybrook. He wandered into the pizzeria and ordered a small one with pepperoni. While he was waiting, he swung around the corner to the party store and grabbed a six pack and a couple of newspapers.

Fifteen minutes later Slim was sitting at his picnic table devouring a slice of pizza and reading the local news, a cold Budweiser sitting on the table. The newspapers were pretty dull reading, full of local stories that meant nothing to Slim. He found himself reading the letters to the editor section. One letter in particular caused him to sit up straight. It was from a woman in Kalkaska County demanding to know why the State Police were digging holes on her neighbor's property. She had called the Sheriff's office as well as the State Police Post and they all refused to answer her questions. She had seen a total of three State Police vehicles enter the property and then a truck pulling one of those tractor like digging machines. Later in the day a county fire department ambulance pulled in. She was convinced that they had found Jimmy Hoffa and were keeping it hushed up. Slim read the article twice more before getting up and calling Sammy, telling him to get near a secure land line and wait for his call. Sammy said he was in his office.

Sammy picked up the phone. "It can't be good news if we've got to talk on this line. What happened?"

"I'm not a hundred percent sure," said Slim. "But it's possible that our two ex employees have been found."

"How is that possible?" asked Sammy. "You told me that they were gone for good."

"The only way anyone could have found those two is if somebody told them," said Slim. "That place is seriously in the middle of nowhere. Nobody would stumble on them by accident. They were deep."

"Can you read the article to me?" asked Sammy.

Slim read the letter word for word. Sammy listened and then said, "We can't go check it out in person. That would be way too risky. I wouldn't panic just yet. This might be something totally unrelated to our thing. I'll get on the internet and monitor the area newspapers for that county and see if anything shows up. If I hear anything I'll let you know right away."

Slim went back to the picnic table and scoured every inch of the newspaper. There wasn't one word about clandestine police operations. He put the paper down and popped open another beer. It couldn't have been Lefty who leaked the information, wouldn't make any sense. After all, he had pulled the trigger. Nobody else knew. There was the guy who owned the cabin but he didn't really know anything other than Lefty borrowing the place for a couple of days. Slim didn't even know who the guy was. He was Lefty's friend. Slim had never laid eyes on him.

Slim tried to put it out of his mind. The lady who wrote that letter could be anywhere in that county and a lot of her story could have come from her imagination. For now, there was nothing he could do about it so he tried to simply relax.

Sammy is not a man without resources. Some of his dealers work the Kalkaska area and so he made some calls from his secure line. He told his contact to dig for any information that he could round up on that newspaper article. His man in Kalkaska was well known for his tenacity and thoroughness. He assured Sammy that he'd have something for him within twenty-four hours. Sammy had confidence in this man and was sure that whatever the guy came up with would be reliable.

And then there was that hospital orderly. He was probably closer to the doctor than anyone else. Maybe he could do a little more snooping. At this point, Sammy didn't want to leave any possibilities uncovered. He made a quick call. Within an hour, Jack Dell was sitting in Sammy's office, leaning forward like a kid at his first job interview. "It's my understanding that the doctor and two other people are going to Charity Island tomorrow. I guess they've found the scientist that they needed."

Sammy studied the man in front of him, wondering just how far he could be trusted. "That's valuable information. Thank you, By the way, have you ever been arrested?" asked Sammy.

"No," said Jack. "I've always been too careful for that."

Sammy smiled. It was the kind of answer a man like Sammy wanted to hear. Jack didn't say he had never done anything wrong, just that he was careful.

"I'm not suggesting that you quit your job," said Sammy. "Quite the contrary. I'm hoping you'll stay right where you are but I might have room for you in my organization as well, sort of on a part time basis, no paperwork, no taxes, cash payments and a little lagniappe."

Jack cocked his head.

"It's an old Creole term. Means a little something extra."

Jack nodded. "I'm your man."

"If you can get close to this doctor friend of yours," began Sammy. "I'd like to know if he's heard about any strange goings on up north. Up Kalkaska way."

"Like what?" asked Jack.

"Anything at all. I'm just curious. I need to know right away."

"I'll do my best. If he knows anything at all, I'll get it for you."

Sammy produced a cell phone and a slip of paper from a desk drawer. "This is an untraceable trac phone. I want you to memorize the number on that piece of paper and then destroy the paper. You can either arrange for the day off or call in sick tomorrow but I want you out of sight somewhere down at Caseville harbor in the morning. When the doctor and his group get there, I want you to call me and let me know exactly how many people get on the boat and if any of them are cops. Got it?"

Jack nodded.

"Here's your first payment," said Sammy. He handed Jack four one hundred dollar bills and an extra large bag of weed. It looked like a half pound. "You're going to really like this stuff, said Sammy. "It's premium stuff and soaked in hash oil."

Chapter 57

Jennifer said that she felt very good about herself after completing the concealed weapons class, claiming that she learned a lot of things that made her feel less intimidated around guns. She fired almost a hundred rounds at the range and surprised both herself and the instructor with her consistency. The classroom work was informative as well, giving her a full understanding of her responsibility when she chooses to discharge a weapon. All in all she gave the class high marks and had spent extra time with both instructors discussing her choices in handguns. At this point she was leaning toward the Ruger LC9 model because that was the gun she had used in class and it seemed to fit her hand well, as was attested to by her targets which showed impressive accuracy including a handful of bull's eyes. She found the recoil quite manageable and you could buy it in an array of pretty colors. Deputy Ross suggested that she try the sporting goods store just down the road because the sheriff's department had a discount agreement with them.

Jennifer and Sid visited the sporting goods store with its wide selection of handguns and Jennifer was awed by the choices. The clerk told her that they didn't have the model that she specified in the color that she wanted but he could have it in two days. Jennifer said that she wouldn't need it any sooner because they'd be spending tomorrow on Charity Island and she'd have a couple of armed law enforcement officers with her. She placed her order and left a deposit.

"Why do you need that particular color?" asked Sid

Jennifer gave him a perplexed look and said, "My favorite pair of shoes is exactly that color."

They stopped back at the Sheriff's office to see if there were any last minute changes in the plan and Deputy Ross told them that the Sheriff's office would provide the skipper and the boat for tomorrow's journey and Sergeant Duffield would be meeting them at the launch ramp in Caseville. The island caretaker had been informed and he would be expecting them around eleven in the morning. Things were all set.

Sid and Jennifer drove back to his lakefront house followed by the two deputies in their vehicle. Sid was glad that the same two officers had been there every night. They knew the routines and had developed their own schedule that allowed them to take advantage of the lake activities as much as possible while remaining vigilant. It worked out well for all concerned.

It was another blistering hot day so Sid and Jennifer spent most of the afternoon in the lake, swimming and tossing a frisbee back and forth. It was nearly six o'clock when they decided to dry off and do something about dinner. Jennifer disappeared into the house to change while Sid poured a little charcoal in the grill. Both of the deputies jumped in to help get things ready. Soon there was a table cloth draped over the picnic table and a patio umbrella adjusted to provide a little shade. Pork chops and asparagus sizzled over the fire and Sid provided a couple of beers for himself and Jennifer and some iced tea for the deputies. "Sorry about the drinks. You guys will have an all out beach party on my dime as soon as this thing is wrapped up," said Sid to the officers. They both smiled.

"Are you joining us on our trip to the island tomorrow?" asked Jennifer.

"Not tomorrow," said one of the deputies. "You'll have the search and rescue deputy who always runs the boat and that State Police sergeant. You won't be needing us. But we'll be around in case the situation calls for the cavalry."

Sid's cell phone rang, it was Deputy Ross. "Remember me telling you that the Kalkaska people would be going public with the information regarding the bodies we found?"

"Yes I remember," said Sid.

"Well, a neighbor saw some of what was going on that day and is highly upset that the information is being suppressed. She wrote a letter to the editor of the local newspaper and it was published in today's edition. I understand that the local State Police post is being besieged by reporters. It's very possible that our killer has been alerted by now and we've lost the element of surprise."

"Won't make things any easier," said Sid. "Just make sure that we've got someone stationed in the Caseville harbor tomorrow to alert us if anyone tries to follow us to the island tomorrow."

"We'll have it covered," said Ross. "I plan to be there myself. I can't let anything happen to you guys, I've already got my neck stuck way out by deputizing civilians. But now that you're officially part of the department, I want you to go to your computer and log on to our secure site. There are some pictures there that I want your secretary to look at. We think it may be that guy in the Toyota."

Sid and Jennifer went in to Sid's den and powered up his computer. He dug out the paper with all of the log on codes and was soon staring at a close up facial picture of a man with his eyes closed. Jennifer strained to see, enlarging the photo as she studied the features. "That's him," she said. "That's the face that looked out the car window at me. But why does he have his eyes closed?"

"Because he's dead," said Sid.

Chapter 58

Jack Dell couldn't wait until he got home. He was only a short distance north of Bay City when he found a little store that sold cigarette papers. He bought a couple of packages and a disposable lighter and jumped back in his car and headed north. His next stop was a busy little strip mall at the very edge of town and he found a parking spot out near the road, next to the driveway that was isolated from the other cars. He carefully rolled a joint using his new stash. After looking around to make sure that nobody was paying attention to him, he started the engine and innocently pulled out of the driveway, merging with traffic unnoticed and anonymous. After he was three or four blocks away and nearing the last of the commercial district, he lit his delightful creation and accelerated onto the state highway. It was much safer being out of city traffic where some upstanding citizen might get a whiff of his smoke and check out his license plate number and report him. Now he had the road all to himself. It was an amazing drive back to Huron County, avoiding all the small towns and getting higher with every mile. Sammy was right about the new product. Jack had never smoked anything nearly as potent. He could hardly tell if he was on the road at times and had to force himself to keep his car between the lines. In his euphoria he decided to pass up the turn that would lead him home and head straight into Caseville. He had work to do for Sammy and he planned to get right to it.

Twenty minutes later he was in the parking lot of the Wooded Island Sports Grill. He had driven the last fifteen miles with all the windows down to help get the marijuana smell out of the car and off of his clothes. Just to be on the safe side, he sprayed the car with a room deodorizer and spritzed a generous amount of men's cologne on himself. He felt as if he was pretty clean when he walked into the building.

Nick was behind the bar and the few customers seemed to be clustered at one end. Jack headed to the other end.

Jack's attempts to cover up the odor fell a bit short of the goal but it wouldn't have mattered because his glassed over eyes easily betrayed his condition.

Nick stood across from him, both hands on the bar and a smile on his face. "Just why in the hell did you come in here? You know damn well I can't serve you when you're in this shape."

Jack looked around and didn't say a word for an uncomfortably long minute. Finally he half whispered. "I'm not here for a drink. I'm here because I need your help. All I can get."

Nick laughed at him. "You need help, all right. And you didn't need to tell me."

"I'm serious," pleaded Jack. "If I can't get some information soon, Sammy's gonna toss me out. I have to find out what's going on in that investigation. My whole future depends on it."

Nick looked around and saw that the dining room was mostly quiet, a few couples finishing their dinner and no new customers. He gestured for one of the servers, one who sometimes substituted as a bartender, to come over to the bar. He steered her away from where Jack was sitting

"What's up?" she asked.

"You real busy?" asked Nick.

"My last table just left," she answered. "I was just bussing the dishes."

"How about watching the bar for a few minutes?" asked Nick. "I got a problem customer that I need to get outside. It won't be anything obvious. He's just a guy who needs help."

"I smelled him when he walked in," said the server. "You do what you gotta do and I'll watch the store."

Nick reached under the bar and retrieved his tiny voice recorder. He clicked the on button and slipped it into his shirt pocket. Jack never even looked in his direction. Nick followed Jack out the door and into the parking lot, jumped up and sat on the trunk lid of Jack's car and said, "Let's hear it. What is so urgent?"

"I need to know what you've heard," said Jack. "Is there anything happening up north that might be connected?"

"Up north? Where up north?" asked Nick.

"I don't know," said Jack. "Kalkaska maybe?"

Nick shook his head. "I have no idea what you're talking about. The only thing I've heard is that they've found something new over on Charity Island and that they're headed over there sometime tomorrow."

"Yeah, well they might just get a surprise when they get over there," Jack shot back. Realizing that he'd said something out of line, he immediately began back pedaling. "I mean it could turn out to be nothing at all." The look on his face told a different story. He tried to get off the subject by rambling on about rumors from up north.

As his buzz began wearing off, Jack was becoming more aware of the fact that his stupor had loosened his tongue and he needed to try to undo some of the damage. But his logic was still skewed by the effect of the drug. "After all, if whatever is out there is so important, you'd think they'd have already checked it out."

Nick studied Jack's face and answered. "Yeah, you're probably right."

Jack was getting more nervous by the minute and had visibly begun to shake. He appeared frustrated and out of control, unable to stop the tremors. He abruptly said. "Hey I have to leave right now. I just remembered that I've got an appointment."

Nick slid off the back of Jack's car just as Jack was climbing behind the wheel. The car roared out of the parking lot spraying gravel everywhere and covering Nick with dust. As soon as he was out of sight he called Sammy to tell him that the Charity Island trip would take place tomorrow. Sammy thanked him and hung up.

When Nick's relief showed up at six o'clock, he made a quick call to Doctor Sidney Benson and then hopped in his car and headed east along the lake shore. He arrived at Sid's house just about the time everybody was finishing dinner and enjoying the first cold beer of the evening.

Sid introduced the two deputies to Nick and then handed him a beer. Nick proceeded to describe his strange encounter with the highly impaired hospital orderly. Then he produced the recorder, placed it on the table and turned it on. Everyone listened intently and one of the deputies took notes. When the tape finished, Sid said. "It sure sounded like a threat about tomorrow's trip to the island, if you asked me."

"It was even more obvious in person," said Nick. "You should have seen his eyes light up when he realized what he'd blurted out."

Sid looked at the deputies and then back at Nick and said. "I'd like to take that with me tomorrow and have Sergeant Duffield and Deputy Ross listen to it. Ross will be staying behind to keep an eye out for anyone who tries to follow us but he'll be interested in the Kalkaska reference.

"Neither of us is assigned to Deputy Ross's detail tomorrow," said one of the deputies.

Nick slid the recorder across the table. "You've already got my money and mastering the art of not allowing me to sleep, you might as well take this too."

Chapter 59

Sammy stood looking out the window of his office. He'd been leasing this place for close to a year now and for that entire time, the gas station across the road had stood vacant. In the past few days there had been lively activity around the place with people coming and going. Sammy's first thought was that a new tenant must be moving in but there were things going on over there that just didn't seem right. All of the vehicles that frequented the place were cars, no trucks carrying supplies or tools. And the people didn't look like gas station workers either. None of them were wearing clothes suitable for manual labor. Maybe it was just his imagination but he decided that he'd pay attention to their movements until he figured them out.

Sammy didn't sleep well last night. He had horrible dreams about being charged with murder and was very concerned about the progress that this Medical Examiner was making in the investigation. If it hadn't have been for that doctor, this whole thing would have begun and ended with the death of Trish. Whether or not she had planned to betray Sammy was irrelevant.

As for Winston, the guy from Grand Rapids turned out to be nothing more than a support system for derelicts. Sammy dismissed him as no threat. Winston would mourn the death of his friend but carry it no farther.

It was definitely the doctor that needed to be neutralized. He and his secretary were the ones who had identified Lefty and started closing in on everyone else. And he was with those state cops when they all disappeared for a full day and then a few days later some nosey old lady up north spots State Police cars, an excavator, and an EMT unit going in and out of the woods near Kalkaska.

And today he was taking a trip out to Charity Island. The word was that some kind of major discovery had taken place over there and that some sort of scientific expert had been added to the team and was going out there today to have a closer look.

Sammy had always been a decisive man but not so much lately, at least since he began to doubt his judgment about ordering the death of Trish, he had been hesitant to take emphatic action. He had thought that calling for the murder of Lefty would help him get back to his resolute temperament but doubts still lingered when it was decision time. He pounded his fist on the desk and told himself that action was necessary right now, without delay.

He called a friend who had a fast boat in a marina not far from his office. He made arrangements to borrow the boat for a couple of days. Now he hurried through his office, changing into a pair of jeans and sneakers then pulled the CZ 75 D nine millimeter semi-auto pistol from the safe along with two extra magazines and several handfuls of hundred dollar bills. He grabbed a couple of untraceable trac phones from his desk, stuck the money in his pocket, threw the pistol and spare ammo into a bag and ran out the back door to his car. He watched the rear view mirror for quite a distance to see if any vehicles pulled out of the old gas station parking lot behind him. Satisfied that he wasn't being followed, Sammy decided to let Slim know what he was doing. On his way to the marina he used one of the phones to contact Slim.

"Go ahead," said Slim

"I've been doing a lot of thinking," said Sammy. "We've got to eliminate our main problem right away. We can't let this guy do any more damage."

"Tell me what you need and I'll have it covered," answered Slim.

"It's become personal and I want to be there and help take care of it myself."

"Are you planning to come to the island?" asked Slim.

"I'm on my way right now," said Sammy. "I've got a boat and will be headed up there right away. I figure it will be about two and a half hours before I get there."

"Can you navigate the waters?" asked Slim. "It can be pretty tricky."

"I've been there before and as long as I stay on the safe course, I should be fine," said Sammy. "I just hope I don't run into the doctor and his crew in the open water."

"That shouldn't be a problem," said Slim. "I'm guessing that they won't be leaving Caseville harbor until nine-thirty or so. They usually leave about that time."

"I'm just coming up to the marina," said Sammy. "I'll be underway in a few minutes."

Sammy stopped at a small store across the road from the marina and picked up a box of donuts, a six pack of Coke, a couple of deli sandwiches, a small cooler and a bag of ice. Ten minutes later, he was on board the twenty foot Bertram Moppie and casting off the lines. He fired up the two hundred-ten horsepower motor and pointed the bow north. Sammy had been to Charity Island a couple of times a few years back, once actually driving the boat and remembered that the entrance channel was protected by a limestone man-made breakwall. He planned to stay in deep water until he located the channel entrance and then guide the boat straight in so that he could avoid the legendary reefs.

Dozens of scenarios flowed through his mind as the big boat knifed through the calm water. The long trip would give him plenty of time to sort through the possibilities. He leaned back in the helm chair, popped open a Coke, placed it in the cup holder and munched on a chocolate covered donut. His heart was beating rapidly with rage and he needed to calm down, compose himself and try to envision as many versions of the scene that he was likely to encounter when he got to the island. He needed to be prepared and should have the advantage of surprise because nobody was expecting him to be there. Sammy prided himself in his marksmanship and was extremely confident that he could take out all of the law enforcement officers before anyone could draw his weapon. Years of competitive shooting in his younger days had taught him how to handle stress in a firefight. And then there was Slim who could be a pretty cool adversary in his own right. Between the two of them, they'd handle it. There was going to be considerable carnage left behind but the remote location would prevent its discovery for close to a full day and by then Sammy and Slim would be far away.

Being forced to take drastic action was going to have some serious repercussion but Sammy was prepared for that as well. His connection out west, the man who got Sammy started in the business had agreed to provide sanctuary for both Sammy and Slim complete with new identities and a new territory, possibly somewhere on the east cost or maybe even the Pacific northwest. They would be starting over, but with an invisible past.

Chapter 60

The group, except for the deputy in charge of the boat met for breakfast at a small restaurant in a nearby town and discussed the plans for the day. Sid claimed that he wanted to see exactly where the glove was found to see how it correlated with the rest of the scene. After covering that area three times, it was hard to believe that they'd missed anything. Sergeant Duffield said that he'd seen some of the most experienced investigators miss obvious clues regularly. He said that is why they like to work in teams.

Nobody knew how much time they'd be spending on the island so Jennifer and Sid played it safe by packing a dozen sandwiches, assorted snacks, and a variety of soft drinks in a cooler. They picked up a bag of ice on their way to the dock and met the rest of the gang in the harbor parking lot.

Sergeant Duffield jumped right in helping the deputy prepare the boat for the trip. The deputy already made his visit to the fuel dock and was now running through the maintenance and safety check list. Deputy Ross was chatting with some of the local boaters who were preparing to venture out into the Bay. Sid rolled the cooler down to the pier and the deputy helped him hoist it aboard the boat.

"We'll be tying up at the main dock when we get there. Orders," said the deputy. "The boss doesn't like it when I land on the beach. Says that all the rocks make it way too risky."

"Fine with us," said Sid. "Me and Jennifer and I enjoy the walk to the lighthouse it's only a few minutes."

"How long before we leave?" asked Duffield.

"About ten minutes," said the deputy. "I've just got to run the sniffer and bilge blower for a few minutes and then start the motor and wait for it to come up to operating temperature."

"Sounds good," said Duffield. He had just turned to walk away when his cell phone chirped. "Duffield," he answered. It was Lieutenant Elam.

"I'm afraid I've got some bad news for you Sergeant," he began. "A Fred Sanders, a biologist with the United States Fish and Wildlife Service has filed an official complaint with the Federal Government that you personally interfered with a survey of a rare species of waterfowl and the State Commander has ordered you to an immediate administrative leave status until this thing gets sorted out and you are to be informed that it begins at this moment. There shall be no more discussion on the subject."

"Wait a minute, lieutenant," protested Duffield. "I'm in the middle of an investigation and we're getting ready to head out on the water, the boat is warming up right now."

"I wish I could help you," said the lieutenant. "But I've got my orders. They'll just have to get along without you."

No cop wants to be held out of the action for petty and stupid reasons but during Duffield's twenty five years on the force plenty of these situations had arisen and like all good cops, he had just learned to live with them. "Returning to the station," he replied.

Duffield stood in front of the sheriff's deputies and ranted. "Every time the federal government gets involved, this is what happens. They screw up everything they touch, create problems where none exist, solve nothing, blame everybody else and then walk away patting themselves on the back. Remember that screwball wildlife biologist that we ran into on the island, you know, the guy who was looking for pelicans? Well he decided to flex his muscles and persuaded some idiot politician, who's probably never even seen a pelican to file a formal complaint against me personally. I've been removed from active duty while his charges are being investigated. You guys will have to get along without me."

Deputy Ross looked at the ground and shook his head. "Our tax dollars at work. Don't it make you proud?"

"It shouldn't compromise the mission, should it?" asked Sid.

"Naw," said Ross. You're only going to the island and the only other person there should be the caretaker. You'll be fine with one deputy."

"And you'll have one less mouth to feed," added Duffield.

Jack Dell was following Sammy's wishes this morning and had called in sick to his boss at the hospital. It wasn't a problem because Jack had a half dozen sick days in the bank. He got to the harbor just as the early fishermen were arriving, some towing trailers with small runabouts and others who had trustworthy craft moored to pilings at the docks. Jack followed three vehicles through the access road and found a vacant spot that put him in a position that was inconspicuous, yet had a broad view of the parking lot. His attention was focused on one county owned pickup truck that was attached to a trailer holding a good size Sheriff's Department boat. There was nobody in the truck and no activity going on in the area. He settled back to see who was going to show up.

In small towns, it's not uncommon for people to recognize your vehicle and Nick, on his way to work this morning thought that the maroon Buick a couple of cars ahead of him looked very familiar. It reminded him of the one that he had perched on the trunk lid to talk with Jack Dell when jack was flying high on drugs. It was definitely the same car. Jack didn't work or live in Caseville so it was strange to see him driving through town, especially this early in the morning. When Nick saw Jack turn into the harbor lane, it set off alarms about Jack's impulsive statement regarding a surprise waiting for Doctor Benson and his party when they get to Charity Island. Nick instinctively turned in behind him and navigated to an empty spot where he could see what Jack was up to. He pulled out his cell phone and called the grill where he worked. The lady who answered was the woman he had been training to become the daytime kitchen manager and her progress had been outstanding. Nick informed her that he was going to turn her loose effective immediately and let her try her wings. He said that she could call him if she had any pressing problems. He hung up and slouched down in his seat. Nobody paid any attention.

Within a few minutes a deputy sheriff walked up to the waiting boat with a tall coffee in a travel mug. He had come from the direction of the restaurant across the road. He immediately went to work getting the boat ready to launch. Soon a State Police cruiser entered the lot followed by a county Sheriff car. A huge man stepped out of the state car and slightly smaller deputy who Nick recognized as the lead investigator got out of the other. They walked over to the boat. Between the three of them the boat was in the water and floating in a matter of minutes.

Doctor Benson and his secretary emerged from a third vehicle dragging a cooler behind them. The cooler was loaded on the boat and it looked like everyone was about to climb on board.

Then the State Cop started talking on his cell phone. The conversation, too far away to hear seemed very animated and it was obvious that the cop was extremely upset about something. He finally slammed the phone back in its case, went back to the boat and waved his arms around while talking to the group and then abruptly turned, stalked over to his car and roared out of the parking lot.

The doctor, his secretary and one deputy boarded the boat and cast off the lines. The other deputy returned to his car and sat there, not moving. An obvious back up.

Nick watched as Jack Dell punched a number into his cell phone and held it up to his ear. He had to be calling somebody with a report.

Jack finished his call and a hand reached through his open window and snatched the phone out of his hand. The next thing that happened was that his door was pulled open and Nick was dragging him out of the driver's seat.

"What's going on?" demanded Jack. "What's the matter with you? I'm not bothering anyone."

Nick had him by the throat on the ground when he heard a voice behind him saying, "That you, Nick? You'd better let me handle this." He looked up and saw Deputy Ross.

It was another quiet trip across the dark blue waters of Saginaw Bay. Jennifer was becoming familiar with the view and spent most of her time reading a book about the history of Big Charity and Little Charity Islands. She found one report that said the island had been named by Jean Cavalier de La Salle when his ship the Griffin encountered violent weather and he had anchored in the lee of the island to ride out the storm. The vast history of the area never ceased to impress her. Soon the sheriff's boat was making the big swing around the seawall and entering the calm waters of the channel. The fenders hanging over the side of the boat gently bumped the dock as they reached the landing. Sid took care of throwing the stern line over the piling while the deputy handled the bow line. They were soon nestled comfortably up against the wooden pier and the trio stepped off the boat. Rick, the caretaker was there to meet them with his little motorized four seater cart. Sid and the deputy loaded the cooler into the back seat of the cart. The deputy hopped into the front seat next to the caretaker while Sid and Jennifer opted for a pleasant walk.

They chatted about the serenity and beauty if the island as they walked. Sid commented that walking was therapeutic. Jennifer said it was an opportunity for bonding. They both smiled as they walked.

With the cooler safely stowed in the picnic pavilion, Sid and the Deputy followed the caretaker down to the area where the body had been found. Jennifer tagged along out of curiosity and to take notes. Once Rick pointed out the glove, it was easy to understand how everyone had missed it. Just above the high water mark there were dozens of spindly little shrub like plants with sparse leaves and scores of angling twigs that seemed to sprout in random directions. About halfway up the trunk on one of these bushes, a surgical glove was wrapped around one of the branches. Rick said that he had scoured the area every day for more than a week before he finally noticed it. After taking several pictures, Sid put on a pair of his own latex gloves and began to gently unwind the ragged glove from the tentacles that gripped it.

Jennifer said that she had left her sunglasses in her purse aboard the boat and that shewas going to run back to the dock and get them. Said she'd be back in a minute. She disappeared down the path.

Chapter 61

Slim was buttoning up the boat to get underway when his cell phone rang. "Hello," said Slim. It was Sammy.

"Did you tell me that there was a telephone booth by your slip at that marina?" asked Sammy.

"Right next to my boat," answered Slim.

"Does it have a door?" asked Sammy. "Can you have a private conversation?"

"Affirmative," said Slim.

"Okay," said Sammy. "Go over there and call me at this number."

Slim climbed off the boat and looked around, The marina looked fairly deserted. All the fishermen were already out in the lake and the closest human being he could see was an old man working on a boat that was tied up at least two hundred feet away. He stepped over to the payphone, swiped an anonymous gift card through the reader and dialed Sammy's number.

"Here's the deal," said Sammy. "My source in Caseville harbor just notified me that the State Police Sergeant who's been working with that doctor didn't get on the boat with the group this morning. My guy says that the state cop didn't seem any too happy about it but he couldn't get close enough to hear what was going on. I don't know what it means but it sure looks like our job is going to be easier, we've only got one cop to deal with. Oh, and there's no other people going along. That means that the story about that expert scientist is nothing more than smoke screen. That's another reason I want to be there."

Slim listened and answered. "This is going to change a lot of things for you and me, right?"

"It will be nothing we can't handle," said Sammy. "I've already forwarded enough money to last us a full year from a ghost account to a new untraceable account out west and I'm carrying a lot of cash. I've got a solid connection who will be setting us up in a new territory. Sammy and Slim will be gone and we'll have entirely new identities."

"So I should head over to the island right now and make a quiet landing somewhere up the beach where they'll be working. After I get there I'll take out the deputy and maybe the caretaker then leave the doctor for you. Is that what you want?"

"You'll probably arrive there first so I'll have to contact you when I get there," said Sammy. "I assume you're appropriately armed."

"Don't worry about a thing," said Slim.

Slim stopped by the marina office, checked out of his slip and headed east into Saginaw Bay. In a short time the island was in full view showing its beaches as well as the foreboding features of its rocky coastline. As a kid, Slim and some of his buddies had made numerous trips to the island in search of adventure. With the rise and fall of lake levels the approaches to the beach seemed to be ever changing. But Slim knew of one safe channel that sat in a perfect place for the landing that he planned for today. He could swing to the south and approach the island unseen from the area where the investigators would be working. It was perfect.

In the parking lot at Caseville harbor, Deputy Ross had Jack Dell in handcuffs and sitting in the back seat of the police cruiser. The air conditioning was turned off and Jack seemed to be in a state of panic. He had never been handcuffed before and his anxiety was showing. Deputy Ross told Nick to go wait in his car and they'd talk later.

"Who were you calling?" asked Ross.

"I don't have to talk," said Jack. "I know my rights and I want my attorney."

"I haven't arrested or Mirandized you yet and you're not guaranteed that right until I do," said Ross. "Would you like me to place you under arrest?"

"If I haven't been arrested, why am I in handcuffs?" asked Jack.

"You're being detained while I investigate suspicious behavior and the cuffs are for your own protection," said Ross. "When I was standing next to your car, I was sure that I could smell marijuana. There will be another deputy here soon with a warrant and we'll have a closer look. I called it in when I was walking Nick back to his car. He told me that you were the guy who's been pumping him for information about the doctor and the investigation. Let me warn you, if we find anything over an ounce in that car, you will be arrested for sure and you could be in for a rough time in court. If you want to bargain, it would be much better if you do it before you are arrested."

"What if you find something? Then what?" asked Jack.

"I'd rather talk about that phone call you just made," said Ross. "It might be important and it might be timely to our mission. If your actions put any of my officers in harm's way, the charges will quickly escalate."

Jack began to shake uncontrollably in spite of the elevated temperature in the car. "My only intent was to try to help someone stay out of trouble," he said. "I'm not a violent person. I hate violence. I don't want to see anybody hurt. Ever."

"Then you'd better tell me exactly what's going on," said Ross.

Jack turned his head from side to side and then began. "He calls himself Sammy. I think he was originally from Bay City. He's pretty smooth, sharp dresser, very articulate and polite. Always has a lot of cash and he likes to pay with drugs, nothing hard, just grass. From what I've seen I'd guess that he's got a pretty good size organization going and he hinted that it might be getting bigger. Anyway, after Trish died I guess he was worried that the cops would be coming after him. It turns out that the guy I've been buying my stuff from, the guy who Trish set me up with, is one of his dealers. That's how I know so much about him."

"Did he have Trish killed?" asked Ross.

"As far as I know he never admitted it," said Jack. "His guys say that he liked her. All I knew was that he wanted to keep an eye on the murder investigation so that he could protect himself and his business if things started heating up around him. That's all."

"So what did you call him for just now?" asked Ross. "What kind of information did you pass along?"

"Nothing real important," said Jack. "He just wanted to know who got on the boat to the island this morning. You know, how many people, how many cops. What time they left. That kind of thing."

"He wanted to know how many cops?" asked Ross

"Yeah," said Jack. "That was one of his questions."

A County Sheriff car pulled into the parking lot and slid up next to Deputy Ross. Ross stepped out of his car and spoke with the other deputy for a few minutes and then returned to his car. Opening the rear door he grabbed Jack by the arm and helped him stand up, dripping with sweat outside the car. "I'm going to put you in this other car while the deputy executes the search warrant on your vehicle. If he finds any contraband he will transport you to the county jail and we'll talk later."

"Are you going to give me a break?" asked Jack. "I told you everything I know. I didn't hold anything back."

"I said we'd talk later," answered Ross. "If you've been on the level with me, I'll see what I can do. That's the best I can offer."

Ross walked over to Nick's car and knocked on the window. Nick had the air conditioning running and seemed to be snoozing.

"What's up?" asked Nick.

"I'm going to have to borrow a boat and head over to the island," said Ross. "I might have just uncovered that surprise that your friend Jack mentioned. Looks like our people might have company over there and, as far as I know only one of our men is armed."

"I know a couple guys with boats in this harbor," said Nick. "Want me to call someone?"

"Normally, I'd go through channels," said Ross. "But time is critical. See what you can do."

Nick stepped away and began making calls. He got lucky on the second number. "I got us a boat," said Nick.

"Technically I shouldn't even allow you to come along but since you're providing the boat I probably can't argue," said Ross.

He followed Nick down one of the piers until Nick stopped at one of the deck boxes, looked at the slip of paper in his hand and began turning the dial on the combination lock. He opened the deck box and reached all the way to the back then stood up smiling with an ignition key in his hand. "It's the blue and white Sundancer right there," said Nick pointing at the sleek looking Sea Ray.

The two men jumped aboard and Nick inserted the key and turned on the bilge blowers. He began to laugh. "You ain't gonna like the way that this is starting out," he said pointing at the fuel gauge.

Deputy Ross looked over his shoulder. "Not to worry, I have a Huron County credit card. Let's get over to the gas dock."

Chapter 62

"They've got more than a half hour head start on us," said Deputy Ross.

"Want me to try to catch them?" asked Nick.

"We'll never make up that distance," said Ross. "Just keep going and pull into the main dock."

They were about three quarters of the way to the island when Nick spotted another boat coming from the south. He pointed it out to Ross and they both watched it. The new boat rounded the breakwall and disappeared up the entry channel.

"I don't think he saw us," said Nick. "His head was turned toward the island the whole time. He never looked in our direction at all."

*   *   *

Slim had given himself plenty of time to get to the island well ahead of anyone else. The spot he chose to land was sort of a mini-cove surrounded by cattails that made a perfect cover to hide the boat. He slowly approached the shore and then turned the boat around and shifted into reverse. He backed in toward shore until he could see the water off the stern changing from blue to the color of sand. He stopped the boat and made sure that it was still fully floating and then securely anchored it and waded ashore carrying a small backpack.

He worked his way down the shoreline until he could see the lighthouse and keeper's quarters. It didn't take long to find a clump of shrubs growing next to a small sand bluff where he could sit comfortably out of sight and still have a clear view of everything on the beach. He figured that he was only about twenty yards from the area where they first found Trish's body. He settled in to wait.

*   *   *

Jennifer started rooting through her purse looking for her sunglasses and realized that her ipod, sun block and lip balm were also in her bag so she decided to just bring the whole thing along with her. She clipped the ipod onto her shorts, stuck the earbuds in her ears, threw the purse strap over her shoulder, and climbed out of the boat. As she walked back to the path she didn't hear the boat that quietly wound its way up the channel and nosed into the dock about ten feet from the Sheriff's boat. Jennifer had already rounded the first turn and was out of sight before Sammy looked up. He secured his boat to the pilings and then dialed Slim's number.

Slim felt the cell phone vibrate in his pocket and quickly whispered into it. "Yeah. I'm here and in position."

"I've landed," said Sammy. "I'm on my way up the trail. Only a minute or so away. You're green to go whenever you're ready."

Slim moved to his right a few steps to get in a better firing position and raised his gun.

*   *   *

Jennifer was digging in her purse as she exited the access road and had pulled her pesky slingshot out to get it out of her way. As it came out, it snagged the bag of ball bearings scattering them all over the path. She dropped to her knees and was gathering them up when she glimpsed some unnatural movement out of the corner of her eye. There was a man crouching in the weeds out of sight of Sid and the Sheriff's Deputy. He had something in his hand that looked like a gun. Then he stood up and raised his weapon. Jennifer had the slingshot in one hand and three ball bearings in the other and she instinctively jumped to her feet, dropped one of the ball bearings into the slingshot, stretched the surgical rubber to its limit and released the pouch.

* * *

A loud popping sound broke the silence as Sid labored to free the tangled latex glove from the bush. The deputy who had stood watching him collapsed suddenly and Sid rushed to his aid. As Sid examined him, it was obvious that it was a gunshot wound. It had entered the deputy's back near the shoulder blade and exited through the muscle on the back of the shoulder. Sid spoke to the deputy. "It's not life threatening but it's going to hurt like hell. There's a pretty good first aid kit on your boat. I'll patch you up and we'll get you back to town."

Rick Todd, the island caretaker had been standing there the whole time and was too shaken to speak. He grabbed Sid's arm and was pointing to a clump of brush a short distance away. "There, there."

Sid saw a man lying motionless on the sand. He sprinted over to his side and could see no bleeding or other immediate signs of injury. The man had a pulse but was clearly unconscious. A handgun rested in the sand not far from the man's right hand. Sid kicked the gun away and yelled to Rick. "Get the deputy's handcuffs and bring them here."

Rick did as he was told and it was when Sid was placing the cuffs on the man's wrists that he noticed the ball bearing in the grass. He picked it up and instantly knew where it came from. Sid took a closer look at the man on the ground and could see some swelling around his right temple. "Nice shot," he mumbled.

Sid stood up and looked back toward the harbor trail. There was no sign of Jennifer. He yelled for her several times and got no response.

*   *   *

Sammy walked carefully up the trail to the lighthouse and suddenly saw a woman on her knees picking things up off of the ground. She abruptly stopped and stood up, pulling back the pouch of a slingshot as she rose. Sammy lunged at her but she had released her shot a fraction of a second before he reached her. He wrapped one arm around her waist pinning both of her arms down at her sides and clamped a hand over her mouth to silence her. As Sammy tackled her, he could see two men fall almost simultaneously in the scene before him. One of them was a man in a police uniform and the other was Slim. Two men were left standing, the island caretaker and the doctor. Sammy clamped his hand over the woman's mouth and dragged her backwards toward the dock. She would die for what she did to Slim. Sammy was enraged. They would both die, first her and then the doctor. He was so mad that he almost missed seeing the two men, one in a uniform coming up the trail behind him. He quickly spun into the wall of tall ferns and choke-cherry bushes that bordered the trail, dragging Jennifer behind him. It soon became clear that the woman had no intention of submitting quietly. He began applying pressure to sensitive nerves until she settled down. Now he was able to concentrate on the two men who were approaching. They surprised him by charging into the heavy foliage just a few feet from where he stood. They stood there for a few seconds before the woman realized what was happening and then she began to squirm. Sammy threw her toward the two men with all his strength, drawing his gun at the same time. He had the advantage now.

*   *   *

Nick tied off the boat as soon as they reached the dock and Deputy Ross vaulted over the side and began running up the dock with Nick in close pursuit. They had gone less than twenty yards when Ross abruptly stopped putting out his arm to halt Nick. He grabbed Nick by the shirt and dragged him backwards into the heavy brush. "What did you see?" whispered Nick.

"I'm not sure if I really saw anything but it looked like movement up ahead on the trail," said Ross.

Suddenly the brush exploded and a woman came bursting through, half stumbling and arms flailing as she tried to maintain her balance. She crashed into Ross and Nick taking them both off of their feet with her sprawled on top of them.

A man stood in the opening that she had just come through. He had a big handgun pointed at them and a look of insanity in his eyes. Jennifer was the first to recover and popped to her feet like a jackrabbit. She stood behind the two fallen men. Nick, with Deputy Ross on top of him appeared to have had the wind knocked out of him or possibly unconscious but he wasn't moving. Deputy Ross seemed dizzy as he struggled to stand. The man across from them had his eyes on the deputy. A cop with a gun represented the biggest threat and Sammy seemed to recognize that. The enraged drug lord was clearly dangerous and the look on his face said it all. It was obvious that he intended to kill all of them. He raised the gun and carefully aimed it at a dazed Deputy Ross.

Jennifer suddenly realized that her hands had been clenched through the entire ordeal and she still held her slingshot and had a couple of ball bearings in the other hand. She quickly readied the weapon and prayed for the best shot of her life.

Sammy was violently thrown backward by the adrenaline enhanced force of the steel ball. It hit him directly between the eyes and the only shot he was able to get off rocketed toward outer space. The gun came out of his hand and sailed into a deep green maze of Charity Island sanctuary. Deputy Ross shook his head and ran to the prostate form lying in the weeds. "What happened?" he said. "I didn't hear anything. No shots, no nothing." He was looking around still trying to gather his bearings when Sid appeared on the trail with Rick Todd bringing up the rear.

"Two down?" asked Sid.

Nick held up his hand. "Just one, Doc. I'll be okay." He was on his knees and seemed to be fine.

Sid examined the man on the ground. The wound looked serious and so he asked Deputy Ross to call for a helicopter evacuation.

Ross made the call and asked, "Where's my deputy?"

"He'll be all right," said Sid. "But he's injured and it may not be a bad idea to send him back to the mainland with this guy."

Jennifer was sitting on a log sobbing. Sid went to her side and put his arm around her. "It's okay. Everything you did needed to be done and you probably saved three or four lives"

"But I've killed two men," she cried.

You haven't killed anyone," said Sid. The guy on the beach is already conscious and this guy has a good chance to make it. You're the hero."

"I don't want to be the hero," said Jennifer. "I'm a secretary. That's plenty good enough. You can be the hero."

"Well, what you did was perfect except for one small thing," said Sid.

Jennifer looked at him with a puzzled look on her face. "What?"

Sid smiled at her. "The color of that slingshot doesn't match your shoes."

59434643R00149

Made in the USA
Charleston, SC
04 August 2016